HIGH STAKES

Clark was pulled to her as her eyes became wistful and bright. His own unspoken pain responded to the indefinable emotion that traveled between them. His hand reached for her face as if by instinct. He wanted, needed to touch her.

"Sabrina, I . . .

The sudden vibrations that raced through Sabrina made her step back just in time. Before he touched her. She wanted to walk away, but her knees felt weak and she wasn't sure she could.

"You just saw what happened to the last guy who tried to do that."

Clark couldn't ignore the hunger that was swirling in his gut, in his groin. Sabrina had always been able to get him going in a second.

"But he doesn't know you like I do, Sabrina. He doesn't know that underneath that austere and composed shell is a woman full of fire."

"And ice," she said, her voice catching in her throat. "For you at least."

Suddenly they were only inches from each other. Had she stepped forward or had he? She wasn't sure and her body didn't care.

"Even your ice is hot," Clark said as his body was urging him to do what his mind told him would only bring him hell.

When his lips came down on hers, Sabrina's heart jolted and her body pulsed with excitement. The hunger his lips showed her awakened a giant within.

BOOK YOUR PLACE ON OUR WEBSITE AND MAKE THE ARABESQUE ROMANCE CONNECTION!

We've created a customized website just for our very special Arabesque readers, where you can get the inside scoop on everything that's going on with Arabesque romance novels.

When you come online, you'll have the exciting opportunity to:

- View covers of upcoming books

- Learn about our future publishing schedule (listed by publication month and author)

- Find out when your favorite authors will be visiting a city near you

- Search for and order backlist books

- Check out author bios and background information

- Send e-mail to your favorite authors

- Join us in weekly chats with authors, readers and other guests

- Get writing guidelines

- AND MUCH MORE!

Visit our website at
http://www.arabesquebooks.com

ANGELA WINTERS

HIGH STAKES

ARABESQUE

BET BOOKS

BET Publications, LLC
http://www.bet.com
http://www.arabesquebooks.com

ARABESQUE BOOKS are published by

BET Publications, LLC
c/o BET BOOKS
One BET Plaza
1900 W Place NE
Washington, DC 20018-1211

All Kensington Titles, Imprints, and Distributed Lines are available at special quantity discounts for bulk purchases for sales promotions, premiums, fund-raising, and educational or institutional use. Special book excerpts or customized printings can also be created to fit specific needs. For details, write or phone the office of the Kensington special sales manager: Kensington Publishing Corp., 850 Third Avenue, New York, NY 10022, attn: Special Sales Department, Phone: 1-800-221-2647.

First Printing: January 2004
10 9 8 7 6 5 4 3 2 1

Printed in the United States of America

HIGH STAKES is dedicated to all those who are brave enough to bet on the biggest gamble of all, real love.

ONE

"Look at me, Sabrina. Please, just look at me!"

Sabrina Scott heard Clark's plea, but she couldn't do as he said. It was too painful. When she thought her heart couldn't break anymore, she would look at him and it would. Her misery was like a lead weight and every time she saw him, it pulled her down further. This man that she once loved, still loved, and would probably, regretfully always love.

"You shouldn't have come here." She placed the last suitcase in the trunk of her car and slammed it shut. Her bones were shivering. It was so cold in Chicago in February. Cold and cloudy.

Clark Hunter's spirits sank as the trunk slammed shut. The loud engines of rush-hour traffic pounded in his ears.

With his right hand firmly in his coat pocket, he squeezed the black satin ring box he kept there with the engagement ring inside. He'd carried it with him everywhere since the day Sabrina had thrown it back at him. The day his life began to fall apart. He rubbed the box for faith. Faith that he would some day soon put it back on her finger. There was no other way this could end.

This ring was not helping. Here he was, holding on to it tighter than he ever had, but as he watched Sabrina wrap her wool coat tighter around her, the realization of her leaving brought him to despair.

How could this have happened? How could he have let it get this far?

"Sabrina, if you ever loved me, you'll . . ."

This got her attention. Sabrina's head swung around to him, her piercing brown eyes on fire. She tried hard to ignore the desolate look in his eyes. "If I ever loved you? Is that what you just said?"

"Sabrina, please." Clark ached to reach out to her, touch her, but he knew better. That would only get him another slap in the face and end the conversation like the last three times. It was hard, so hard not to touch her. Her ginger-brown skin, so soft to the touch, her deep cocoa-brown eyes, that tiny defiant nose, and those full lips all expressing her sorrow, her anger. It was like instinct for him to see her in such pain and wrap his arms around her to make it go away. Now, he was the source of her pain. Or so she believed.

"I just want you to listen to me. To look at me."

"Do you actually think what you want means anything?" she asked, her voice cracking under the pressure of her emotions. What was so pitiful was the fact that this was the best she could muster so far.

"Yes, I do." Clark was defiant. His love for Sabrina made him that way. He boldly met her angry gaze.

"I love you, Sabrina, and you love me. At least you used to."

"'Used to' being the operative phrase."

She couldn't stand looking at him. All of her reserve threatened to melt. His caramel skin was flawless and his green eyes were like magnets. He looked so rugged, so untamed. All of the things a girl wanted. Everything Sabrina had been certain she needed. If only she had known the whole story. When she had met him, he was only twenty-five, she was twenty-eight. He was a party boy, a player, and Sabrina was certain she could make him change his ways. Man, had she been a fool!

And still she loved him. After all that he had done to her. The ultimate betrayal, coupled with countless lies, and yet there was a voice deep inside her that begged her to reach out to him. *Just forgive him,* it said. *Forgive him and everything can go back to how magical it was.*

Sabrina was many things, but she would be a fool for no one. Not even for the man whom, just one month ago, she was certain she would give her life for. The man she was certain she could always trust.

"I thought you agreed to leave me alone," she pleaded. "This is bordering on stalking, Clark."

"I wasn't stalking you," he said, hoping to God that wasn't what it had come to. He couldn't tell anymore, so caught up in his desperation. "All I've been trying to do is talk to you, but you won't let me. I refuse to let you go over something that isn't true. Over a lie."

Sabrina sighed, the pain of her heart throbbing through her entire body. This had to stop. "Let's not go through that again, Clark. Not for the millionth time. I know you slept with that woman, Cara. I showed you the photographs."

She held up her hand to stop him just as he began to protest. "I heard your voice. I heard you tell her you were only marrying me for my money. Or my father's money for that matter."

Clark gritted his teeth. "Damn it, Sabrina. For almost three years we have loved each other. I know what you saw, but you can't believe it. Not for a second. You know me."

"I know what I saw." Sabrina felt mad with this argument. She wouldn't allow him to argue with evidence in front of her face. It was insane.

"I don't know how or why," Clark said, enraged, "but I'm going to find out what—"

"I have to get out of here." Sabrina walked past him, praying that he wouldn't touch her. She didn't know how much longer she could resist his pleadings. Whenever Clark put his hands on her, her knees went weak, her stomach tingled, and she gave in. She always did. There could be no touching.

"You can't leave, Sabrina."

"You obviously can't leave me alone like you promised you would."

"I tried to." Clark wanted to grab her, take her back to his place, and keep her there until he could force the truth into that hard head of hers. She had so much pride and was so stubborn, but he had to convince her. He had to convince the most sensible woman in the world to believe something that made no sense. He would do whatever he had to. Anything to keep her from going to Las Vegas.

"I tried to," he repeated. "I wanted to give you

some space, some time to calm down so you would listen to what I had to say. No, not listen. Hear what I had to say. But then I found out you were leaving for good and I couldn't stay away. Don't leave, Sabrina. Don't leave Chicago. Your family is here. Your career is here. Your friends are here."

She opened the car door, taking a deep breath as she looked at him with sharp, intent eyes. "You're here, Clark, and the sight of you makes me sick to my stomach."

Clark swallowed hard. There weren't words to describe the effect her words had on him. The one person in the world he lived to please.

"The anticipation of you coming around the corner," she continued, "calling me, running into you within our circle of friends is too much. I need a new start."

He took a step forward, but stopped as Sabrina's posture tightened. "At least give me your number. We need to . . . We can't leave things like this."

"No!" Sabrina didn't know how much more of this she could take. Nonstop for the last month. "We will leave things like this. You're out of my life forever, Clark. The sooner you except that, the better off we'll both be."

Clark bit back the pain. "I'm giving you one last chance, Sabrina. One last time before you get in that car and make the biggest mistake of your life."

Sabrina stared at him, her dark eyes as large as teacups. She let out an incredulous laugh, laced with her bitterness. "Are you crazy? Did I just hear you right? Maybe I'm crazy, because it sounded like you're giving me one last chance, for what exactly? To take back a cheating, lying fool?"

"I've never cheated on you!" He slammed his fist on the top of her Mercedes. He had to control himself. His emotions were just taking him over and he always lost when he let that happen.

"I never lied to you," he exclaimed. "I'm giving you one last chance to believe that. No matter what you saw. No matter what you heard. I'm giving you one last chance to go with your heart and your soul. You know who I am. We were together for almost three years. We were going to get married!"

"And *you* destroyed it all!" She felt the tears streaming halfway down her cheeks, already sore from wiping tears away earlier. She didn't think she had any tears left. Surprise. "I'm going to go with my heart, my soul, and my mind. And you can go to hell, Clark!"

She leaped into the car, locking the doors as if that were the final word. As if it could keep her from feeling him on the other side.

But he was there and Sabrina could still feel him standing there, without even looking. She could always feel this man. She had thought this was why they were connected, meant for each other. She had thought so much that turned out to be a lie, a fantasy.

The truth was it had been a fantasy, but she had convinced herself it was real. Now reality had come crashing down on her and it was more than she was certain she could bear.

Sabrina started her car. Every movement seemed a labor. Her body felt weak and her energy drained. She had barely eaten as far back as she could remember. All she had to do was make it to her parents' house in Evanston. Thirty minutes from her

Lake Shore Drive condo to the suburbs and she could break down again in her mother's arms and hopefully never see Clark Hunter again.

Clark watched in disbelief as she drove away. He was exhausted mentally, physically, emotionally— every way possible. This last month his entire life had fallen apart. A life that he cherished because where he had come from, he'd never thought it was possible. The woman he loved more than life itself had accused him of cheating on her with a woman he barely knew. A woman who convinced her with doctored phone tapes and photographs that he was a cheating dog who only wanted Sabrina for her money.

A woman who promptly disappeared.

Sabrina had been unwilling to listen to him and left, throwing his ring on the floor. To make matters worse, Clark knew he was one of the top sports reporters in Chicago. There were plenty of papers other than George Scott's, but he'd wanted to build a life there, a career there. George wasn't having it. His daughter's broken heart must have justice.

A job could be replaced, but Sabrina could not. Not ever. And now she was gone. He had spent the last month doing all he could, but there had to be more. There had to be. He couldn't just let her go. She was his life.

Sabrina wasn't strong enough yet to face up to all she was driving away from as she treaded the Chicago mean streets. Images of the last few years of her life flashed before her eyes as they had been doing frequently this past month. The excitement of something new, almost forbidden, because they had come from such different worlds. The passion, the laughter, the tender moments that made her heart leap with joy the second she woke up in the morning.

That was all gone now, and even though Sabrina's mind told her she was doing the only thing she could, her heart told her to hold on to those memories because they were never going to come again.

"My favorite girl!"

"Morning, Nick." Sabrina leaned back in the pliable chair at her desk.

Nick Stewart marched with confident steps into Sabrina's office. Touching forty now, Nick was an attractive brother. Too attractive for his own good, Sabrina thought. He knew he was a good-looking, Ivy-League-educated, wealthy, and single African-American man with more than the basics in social skills and connections. In Las Vegas, like too many other places, these stats put Nick at the top of the heap. Nick knew it and never passed up an opportunity to take advantage of it with the ladies.

His skin was smooth and dark with a reddish tint. He had brooding light brown eyes. Black wavy hair was the icing on the cake. Nick had "good time" written all over him. He was honest about it and Sabrina gave him credit for that. Still, she watched as woman after woman tried to tame him. They would never learn.

She had to admit, she loved the guy. They had been friends growing up in Chicago. Their families attended the same church and ran in the same middle-class social circles. Although leading separate lives, Nick and Sabrina had kept in touch. When

Nick moved to Las Vegas to manage the Acropolis Hotel and Casino, he had offered Sabrina a job. She turned him down at the time, happy at her father's paper as head of marketing and even happier with Clark. Nick understood, letting her know the offer stood forever. She had forgotten all about it until Nick called her one night having heard about her breakup with Clark only two weeks before. Nick's offer saved Sabrina and gave her another chance.

The Acropolis was an ancient-Greece-themed hotel and casino right on the strip. Like the other themed hotels it was gigantic and overindulgent. One was made to feel as if one were in ancient Greece at the height of its power and artistic grandeur, whether in rooms or at the spa, the pool, the casino, the entertainment complex, the shopping center, or the restaurants.

Fortunately for Sabrina, the executive offices, where she worked, were spared. They were hidden from view of the guests, the decision having been made to reserve some sense of modern-day civility and professionalism. It still had the motel motif, tacky by nature, but it was a pleasant work environment.

Nick was general manager of the Acropolis and Sabrina now worked there as director of event marketing. She had been there for four months and was beginning to get the hang of things, thanks mostly to Nick, who helped her get started and put total trust in her.

"Well, that didn't sound too enthusiastic." Nick made his way to Sabrina's desk, leaning against it on her right side.

"You want enthusiastic?" she asked. "You got the wrong girl."

"I never have the wrong girl when I have you." He winked at her, frowning as he realized it wasn't doing any good.

Nick and Sabrina's relationship had always been platonic, friends only, but that never stopped him from being a shameless flirt.

Sabrina smirked. "You forget, Nick. I'm not one of your groupies. Your winks and so-called charming banter won't work with me."

Nick winced. "Ouch. Is it that time of the month already?"

Sabrina formed a fist with her hand, socking him in the thigh as she allowed herself a bit of a smile.

"Gotcha!" He pointed to her smile as evidence as he rubbed his thigh. "Don't try to hide it. You think I'm hilarious."

Sabrina sighed. As great as Nick was, he couldn't turn her feelings around today. "Please leave me alone this morning, Nick. Okay? I'm just not in the mood for the buddy thing."

"Whatever." Nick didn't move. "Seriously, you're usually the morning girl, which is the one thing I hate about you. What's wrong?"

"Don't you have a big fat office upstairs? Shouldn't you be there barking orders over a speakerphone in an impersonal and authoritative tone?" Sabrina didn't want to deal with anyone today. It was the beginning of the week. That week.

Nick inclined his head, acting as if he hadn't heard her. "I was on my way to get breakfast and since you're always so delighted by my company I wanted to see if you'd like to join me."

"No, thanks." Sabrina looked at her desk calendar, zeroing in on the day, the week. She should have called in sick. When would life ever be good again? It didn't have to be good every day, just for more than one week before memories came flooding back, stealing the sun from her life.

Nick looked at the calendar. "What is it? What's today?"

"It's Monday. The first Monday in June." Sabrina looked at her schedule. How could she get through her meetings today? "Now, can I get to work please?"

Nick shrugged, saying, "Whatever you say, but you'll be missing me by lunch."

As he turned to leave, Sabrina thought she was in the clear until, halfway to the modern silk-screen double doors, he suddenly stopped. *Crap*, she thought.

Nick swung around, heading back for Sabrina's desk. He tilted the desk calendar toward him, studying it. The usual cocky expression turned suddenly somber as he looked at her.

"Sorry, Sabrina. I forgot about it."

Sabrina took a deep breath, trying to hold her head up high. "I wouldn't have expected you to remember."

"I couldn't have expected you to forget."

Sabrina leaned back in her chair, shaking her head. "If only I could. For a long time, my whole life revolved around this week. The week leading up to this Saturday. My wedding day."

Nick walked around the desk, placing his hands on her shoulders. He massaged them, trying to soothe her. "I know this hurts, but you've been doing a good job of getting your life back in order."

"I haven't really, Nick." She turned halfway, looking up at him. "When I'm at work, I'm so busy that I don't have the time to feel sorry for myself. But when I'm at home alone, I'm still a mess. It's been four months and sometimes it feels like it was yesterday."

"Time heals all wounds." He gave her shoulders one last squeeze before stepping away. "You're a strong woman, Sabrina. You're a fighter and a winner. There isn't a man alive that can break that. Not even Clark Hunter."

Sabrina knew that was true, but it didn't feel like it. "He sure as hell bent it as far as it can go."

"Sorry I'm late. I . . ."

When Dionne Wilson, a lanky five-foot-ten-inch beauty, stormed into the office, bringing her aura of glamour with her, she looked right at Nick and rolled her eyes.

"Damn," she said. "The one day I'm late and the boss is here."

Nick laughed. "If you actually expect me to believe this is the one day you're late, then you're not the girl I thought you were, Dionne."

"Woman," Dionne corrected, her brows narrowing. "Hey, did you just insult me? I can never tell with you."

"I'm clever like that," Nick said.

"If you say so." Dionne flipped her long, fire-red hair back in the flirtatious way that got her through life. She sat at her desk, which was across from Sabrina's. They shared an office with an admin right outside between them and the other office pair of PR people.

"Why do I have to be the assistant to the manager's pet?" Dionne asked. "If he didn't like you so much, Sabrina, he wouldn't be hanging around here all the time."

Sabrina smiled. "You're right, Dionne, your life is such hell."

Dionne actually lived the life many women wished they could. She was a striking woman who spent most of her time being wined and dined by every well-heeled bachelor in Las Vegas, not to mention the visiting high rollers who spotted her while gambling at the casino. They all spotted her. She was an Angie Everhart supermodel look-alike who loved attention almost as much as she loved to party.

Her other hobby was trying to get Sabrina back into the dating world.

"I'm out of here," Nick said, heading for the door. Before leaving, he turned to Sabrina with a sincere expression on his face. "Call me if you need to talk. You'll be fine, and I'm sure you know that."

"Thanks." Sabrina smiled tenderly.

She could never let him know how much she appreciated him. His head was too big already.

"What was that about?" Dionne asked after Nick left.

"Nothing." Sabrina pulled herself together. She was better than this self-pity game her heart wanted her to play. Plus, she had work to do. "We need to finalize plans for the high school career day."

Career day was Sabrina's idea. Each hotel sponsored an event for a summer program that worked with at-risk minority high school kids in the area. The program was focused on three values: hard work, discipline, and motivation. The goal was a better life than the statistics told them they were destined for. Sabrina had decided a "Why Go to College" day would be the Acropolis's contribution to the summer program, pulling members of the community in jobs that would interest teenagers and that also required a college degree. The plan was to encourage the kids to plan for college, and the project meant a lot to Sabrina.

Dionne tossed papers around, grabbing a steno pad. "We have Brittany Rivers, pediatrician; Rod Davis, lawyer; Ben Wright, teacher; and Jessica Ewing, crime scene investigator. That one will go over big. She's gonna bring some pretty gross stuff with her."

Sabrina didn't doubt it. The grosser the better. "The kids will love that. How about Brad Nagle?"

"The architect?" Dionne shrugged. "We'll see. I don't like him. He was a little rude to me."

"If he can't come," Sabrina said, "get another architect."

"What about the industry?" Dionne said. "You know, hotel or—"

"No. The schools trip when you do anything that might be seen as encouraging them to go into the gaming industry. Even hotel management. Let's go over the catering and giveaways one more time."

"Stop fretting, Sabrina. You've planned everything perfectly. Like you plan everything else."

"Just for me, please?" Sabrina asked.

Dionne rolled her eyes. "Pasta special and teriyaki chicken sandwiches with potato salad, potato chips, assorted fruits with brownies, cookies, and apple crisps. Prizes are Acropolis key chains, UNLV hats, and SAT Prep CD-ROMS. Happy?"

"Sounds good."

"Good. Now forget about it. What you need to be focusing on is this Saturday."

Sabrina stiffened, her eyes widening. How did Dionne know? "What are you talking about?"

Dionne hesitated, blinking in bewilderment. "What am I talking about? Uh, maybe the only thing everyone is talking about. Saturday. The fight, remember?"

Sabrina let out an exasperated sigh. "Oh yeah. The big freakin' Saturday night fight. The way Nick goes on about that thing. . . ."

This Saturday night, the top two middleweight boxers were set to fight in the Parthenon, the Acropolis's main theater. In a place where two roaches racing across the floor was considered worth betting on, boxing was the biggest game in town. It was all Nick had spoken of since the day Sabrina set foot in Las Vegas. Boxing was her least favorite sport. Not to mention the fact that one of the fighters had just been arrested this past weekend for slapping his wife around.

"With the new publicity," Sabrina said, "you'd think Nick would want out."

Dionne shook her head. "No way. Too much money. Too far in. Nick lives for this and he's expecting us to as well."

"That promoter, Tommy Gaxton, has pretty much pushed me out of the way," Sabrina said. "He wanted to manage everything. Even had the nerve to write the notes he wants me to use for the press conference tomorrow. Nick wants him to have his way, so I'm mostly staying out of it. We just need to make sure the prefight party on Thursday goes well. Let's go over that."

Sabrina wasn't a big fan of any sports these last five months. They all reminded her of Clark. He had been a new sports reporter at her father's newspaper when they met. Sports. Sports. Sports. Clark loved their wild nature and physical discipline. He was so brash and carefree, the total opposite of her generally conservative nature, but he managed to get her excited about sports. After leaving, all Sabrina wanted to do was escape it all.

Only there was no escaping sports in Las Vegas. The town was all about sports—betting on them at least. The fights, the college games, the pro games, and the horses. Even the dogs. So Sabrina had to deal with it.

And she did.

As soon as the elevator opened onto the sports floor of the *Chicago Sun Times,* affectionately referred to as the testosterone floor, Clark knew something was up. Dave, the college intern, scooted right by him, pushing his grocery cart of mail quicker than usual. Usually Dave was all high fives and "what's up, man?" Today his eyes hit the floor and he kept on strolling.

It didn't stop there. The layout of the floor was that of a typical newsroom. Scattered desks and low-walled gray cubicles were covered over every inch with sticky pads and pictures ripped from magazines and newspapers. Everyone, some with a little lift of their chin, could see what was going on.

As Clark walked down the aisles toward his desk, their eyes were on him, wide and curious before quickly looking away. Clark muttered a few curse words under his breath with a shrug of his shoulders. What did he care?

No one at the paper liked him, he knew that. He had entered their lives at the worst time in his own and was probably the least pleasant person on earth. There were a few sports reporters on staff who knew him for a long time from living the same nomadic life following teams from city to city. They had known a careless man, loving life and tenacious at his job. That was the old Clark. The new Clark was a stranger to them and nothing like they expected. He was distant and moody and negative. And that was on his good days.

Then there was Lauren Schuller, his research assistant. She liked him. Well, Clark couldn't even say that she really liked him. She tolerated him. She indulged him. She didn't take much crap from anyone and had told Clark to his face on his first day on the job that she would put up with him only to a point before he would lose his front teeth. Clark understood that and they had found a way to work together.

Everyone else could just eat it.

After Sabrina left him, Clark had been out of a job for a little over a month. George Scott, in addition to being an incredible businessman, was a logical man. He knew how good Clark was for his paper. But then again, Sabrina was his princess, his only child. His baby girl, as he had put it before he fired Clark. Like Sabrina, George wasn't open to explanations. His baby girl had been destroyed and Clark was the destroyer. The destroyer had to go down. After all, Sabrina couldn't possibly have been expected to face her cheating, gold-digging ex-fiancé on a daily basis.

Clark was thrown for a loop and hadn't thought about another job until after his equilibrium returned to him. This was a couple of weeks after Sabrina left for Las Vegas—after he accepted that she was not coming back and his pride had suffered its final blow.

"To hell with them all," he told himself over and over again until he had finally come to almost believe it.

The *Sun Times* had picked Clark up immediately, based on his reputation. Not merely a famous local journalist for the past three years, Clark had a weekly spot on ESPN and had also made the best-seller list twice with controversial books on the role of parents in Little League sports and issues of interracial dating in pro sports.

His articles continued to be the talk of the town, but the *Sun Times* hadn't gotten all they expected. Instead of the happy-go-lucky, rugged reporter, they got an angry, sullen man who was mad at everyone and everything. Everyone hated him, including the players who used to welcome him into the locker rooms. Now, he was the supreme jerk of the nation and they would run the other way when he came.

"To hell with them all," was the only response Clark had.

The truth be told, this state of mind and state of being was not okay with Clark. He hated what he had become. When he looked in the mirror, he saw an angry, bitter face staring back at him. He knew he was a better man than that, but it was hard dealing with life without Sabrina. For so long, he hated himself for letting her go. This woman was the love of his life and he let her walk away because of lies.

But he couldn't function hating himself, so Clark soon came to the realization that it wasn't his fault. Sabrina should have believed him. No matter what she had seen, what she had heard, the love they had should have been stronger than that. It had been for him.

His anger shifted from himself to Sabrina, but since she wasn't around, Clark transferred it to anyone else who crossed his path.

"Don't start with me this morning."

Clark looked up from his desk to see Lauren leaning over the top of his cubicle partition. Lauren was twenty-eight, the same age as he, but looked about six years older. She was a robust woman, with a round body and a full, red face. She had dark blue eyes that were shadowed by long, curly brown bangs. He wondered how she could even see with those things in her eyes.

To put it plainly, Lauren looked a mess, which was par for the course in the newspaper business. It wasn't anything like the broadcast world. Looks didn't matter here, which was a good thing because looks were also deceiving. Lauren, for the mess she was, was also the most organized, intelligent, and aggressive researcher Clark had ever known.

He was lucky to have her, but he would never tell her that. She already knew it all too well.

"Don't mess with you?" Clark lifted his head slightly. "I didn't even say anything. I just got here."

Lauren glanced down at her watch. "You're late, by the way. And what I meant was don't give me your usual morning attitude. You'll need the energy because you're in trouble."

"What now?" Clark was used to having some staffer or other complain to Lauren that he growled at them, or was rude in some way. He wasn't in the mood for saccharine apologies today.

"You messed up." She slapped that morning's *Sun Times* on his desk. "Your article has Levy in a fit."

Levy was Michael Levy, the sports editor for the paper. Clark found him to be a good man, better than most, but he was also an unforgiving, uncompromising boss. Getting on his bad side was worse than getting on Clark's.

"What did I do?" Clark flipped through the pages to his sports cover story: HIGH SCHOOL PRINCIPALS STEP OUTSIDE THE LINES.

"You ruffled a lot of feathers with this one," Lauren said. "And they've been on Levy all morning. They want your head or his. He was screaming for you an hour ago."

Clark waved the rolled-up sports section in the air with indignation. "Everything I wrote was true."

"You accused some principals of paying off parents?"

"I have three parents willing to back me up." Clark spoke with a cool tone. "Not that I would expose them for a second."

"I think the one that did you in was accusing them of encouraging young female students to . . . I don't even want to say it."

"I didn't name any names," Clark said. "And since when did you become delicate?"

Lauren tilted her head to the side, her face holding an as-if-that-was-necessary expression. "You were talking about the top-five-ranked football programs in the city. Everyone knows who they are. You practically called them pimps."

"I have the proof to back it up." Clark slid back enough to place his feet on the desk.

"That's not what it's all about." Lauren threw her hands in the air. "But you never listen and I don't get paid enough to have this conversation with you. That's why Levy gets the big bucks." She knocked his feet off the desk. "Get in there."

Clark pushed away from the desk. Of all of his faults, no one could question his reporting. He was better than good. He got the best scoops, the best interviews, and the best quotes. He was also professional and ethical above the board. Nothing went on paper without being checked ten times over.

Michael Levy's office looked like a junky attic. Sixty years old now, Michael had spent over forty years in the newspaper business and it looked as if he'd kept everything: files, folders, clippings, books, magazines, newspapers of all kinds. Everywhere, even blocking the windows overlooking the canal, a view that most people would cherish. Clark got the idea, in the few months he'd known him, that Levy wasn't even aware of the view he was missing out on.

"Sit down."

Levy didn't bother to look up when Clark entered. The man seemed to have a sixth sense about these types of things as far as Clark was concerned. He was the stereotypical white-haired, balding, big-bellied sports editor on the outside. Inside, he was one of the best men Clark had ever met and smart as a whip.

"My story is on the clean," Clark started. "There's nothing—"

"Shut up." Still looking down at the papers on his desk—copy from an article awaiting approval—Levy held up one finger to hush Clark.

It wasn't his index finger.

Clark sighed. "Is this junior high school, Levy? I feel like a kid in the principal's office who has to sit there and sweat it out while you kill me with silence. I won't confess to any wrongdoing because there is none. So, let's not play those games."

Levy looked up, none too pleased. "Are you giving me advice on how to manage my department?"

Don't push him. Clark knew better. This was about more than a racy story. "Lauren said you wanted to see me."

"You went too far with that article, Clark."

"How? It was all the truth? That's what we're after, right?"

"You're a sports reporter, Clark. Not an investigative reporter."

Clark loved this argument. He frowned, his eyes leveled. "Because I cover sports, I'm only kind of a real reporter? Am I supposed to overlook criminal behavior and just focus on slap shots, touchdowns, and team trades?"

"No." Levy removed his glasses, rubbing his nose before putting them back on. "But you don't do it right. You report this stuff, serious stuff, just like you were reporting slap shots, touchdowns, and team trades. You have to be more delicate when dealing with alleged criminal behavior."

"Delicate?" Clark shrugged. "That's not my strong point."

"Lately, nothing seems to be your strong point." His eyes bored into Clark.

Clark looked away. "I don't feel like one of our talks, Levy."

"You mean those talks when I sit you down and ask you to adjust your attitude and keep focused? I'm sick of those too. Clark, you're the best writer on this team, but . . ."

Clark looked at him. But? "What is really going on here?"

"You're disrupting my entire department," Levy said. "I can't have this going on. You're being a jackass to everyone."

"I'm not in a popularity contest."

"How about just being a decent human being?"

Clark looked down. He knew he was wrong here. To argue would be disrespectful to even himself. "I'm getting things together."

"You need to get away."

Clark felt his adrenaline kick up. Those weren't the kinds of words that always meant something else. "Are you talking about a leave of absence? You want me out?"

"No way." Levy leaned back in his chair. "I just want you out of my face and everyone else's face for a while."

"I can work from home," Clark said.

"You can work from home when you get back."

"Where am I going?" Clark envisioned some Alaskan dogsledding competition or anything in Utah. *Please, God, not Utah.*

"Las Vegas."

The words hit Clark like a brick. Time stood still as a wave of emotion ran over him, his stomach tightening and his senses coming to a blaring alert. He blinked, looking away and looking back. Levy's expression never changed.

"Las Vegas?" Clark asked, the words spilling from his mouth. "Did you say—"

"You heard me." Levy shuffled papers on his desk in a frustrated motion. "And don't tell me you can't do Vegas."

"I can't do Vegas."

Levy looked at him without even a hint of compassion on his face. "I know about the girl."

The girl. Clark laughed inside at the phrase. The girl. As if she was just one of many. "I know all the rumors going around here, but I don't think you know everything."

Levy gave an offhanded smile. "I know a lot more than you think I do. I know what she did to you because of what you did to her."

Clark refused to defend himself anymore over that. "Levy, I didn't do—"

"Did I ever tell you my wife left me for our gardener?"

"I just saw your wife here last week."

Levy laughed. "No, you saw Sharon. Sharon is my third wife. Lisa was my first. Alexa was my second. Alexa left me for the gardener. She was too young for me anyway, but the gardener?"

"Levy, I appreciate your attempt at sympathy, but—"

"I'm not trying to sympathize with you, Clark. I'm just telling you that this crap happens to everyone. Mistakes are made and hearts get broken. Get over it."

Get over Sabrina. Sure, no problem. Sabrina who? You're a man, aren't you? Las Vegas was a big city after all. It wasn't as if he had to go to the Acropolis.

"I want you to cover the Grove-Rodriguez fight at the Acropolis Hotel and Casino." Levy smiled as Clark's eyes narrowed. "Yup, that's what I said."

"This is punishment," Clark said. "You're punishing me because I'm a jerk and you want me to suffer."

"That's part of it. You need to be put in your place around here. A little humbling never hurt anyone. Besides, I need someone to cover this fight and everyone wants to get rid of you for a while."

"Rodriguez and Grove?" Clark wasn't buying it. "I know they're the talk of middleweight worlds, but is this really worth sending someone all the way from Chicago to Las Vegas?"

"Not until last Saturday night." Levy tossed a rolled-up paper across the room and Clark caught it against his chest. "It's the Sunday edition of the *Vegas Sun.* Grove was arrested for domestic abuse. Supposedly pushed his pretty wife around and gave her a shiner."

"So now that the guy turns out to be a jerk, it's national news?" Clark didn't like the ethics around this.

"Yes." Levy shrugged. "Sorry, but that's sports. The more controversy, the better. You know the game. Plus Grove is from Chicago, so there's the local connection. He grew up on the West Side. That's around your neck of the woods, isn't it?"

Clark didn't care to rehash his neck of the woods much. He'd grown up in a dysfunctional, abusive home until his father deserted them and left them in poverty. It was unfortunately not a unique story on the West Side of Chicago in his time, and still wasn't. Clark left it all behind him after leaving for college. He'd gone back to his old neighborhood in the past couple of years to help young boys growing up like he did. It was Sabrina who encouraged him to go back.

He had to stop thinking about her!

"We have a connection at the *Vegas Sun,*" Clark said. "Why don't we just have him follow up?"

"You're going, Clark, so shut it."

"Levy!"

Levy's hand went up. His final sign. "I've already got Lauren working on your ticket for first thing tomorrow. I want you to use your relationship with that girl to get some inside scoop on how Saturday is affecting Artemis Grove, his team, and the fight. An interview with the wife would be good."

"Her name is Sabrina."

"The wife's name is Sabrina, too?"

"No," Clark said. "That girl you referred to."

"I don't care what her name is. She works there, right?"

Clark nodded. "Does she know I'm coming?"

"What do I look like? The kid who passed notes from his buddy to the girl in science class? About three seconds ago, you started wasting my time, Clark."

Clark stood up, staring at Levy, who was now immersed in today's edition of the rival paper, the *Chicago Tribune,* as if Clark had never even been there. He knew he wasn't going to look up again and had nothing more to say. When Levy was done, he was done.

Back at his desk, Clark fell into his chair, looking at the crumbled-up *Vegas Sun* sports section in his hand. What was he feeling? Was it possible to feel everything at one time?

The anger, anticipation, fear, resentment, excitement, hope, pride, hurt, and pain. Sabrina always did have a way of getting him riled up. How many days and nights since finding out she worked at the Acropolis had he thought about the next time he would see her? How many times had he dreamed he could see her again only to, seconds later, wish he'd never see her again?

Looking around the floor, Clark felt confident enough nobody was spying on him, although he knew that Lauren always had a second eye on him. That was okay. Lauren knew everything. He couldn't have kept it from her if he tried. He had tried.

Clark slid his desk drawer open and reached for the little black satin box. Memories of their trip to Venice where he had proposed came rushing back. He opened up the box, and his eyes brimmed with tenderness and passion as he looked at the princess-cut two-karat diamond he had slipped on an overjoyed Sabrina's finger last November. He remembered the anxiety he'd felt over getting the ring just right. It had to be nice enough to show how he much cared about her, but not so nice that it offended Sabrina's sense of simplicity. She was so much more conservative than he. He would have bought her the gaudiest ring at Tiffany's, but Sabrina had too much class for that.

"Clark!"
Clark heard Sabrina call his name with her it's-

about-to-get-ugly tone. A smile spread across his face as he listened to her sandals slap the linoleum floor, coming his way. It was her fault he liked making her mad. She was so cute when she was mad. Well, not real mad. When she was real mad, it was time to head for the hills. Tonight's kind of mad was different, and the second Sabrina stepped onto the bedroom balcony of their Italian villa, Clark had to laugh at the way her lips pressed together and her eyes squinted.

She looked deceptively seductive in a palomino-yellow silk tank and white linen pants. Her long, brunette mane with copper highlights framed her glowing, sun-darkened face. An image to die for.

"You think this is funny?" she asked, her hands on her hips.

"I think you're funny." Clark leaned against the gate, looking over at the beautiful Venice streets and homes around them.

They had rented this villa for two weeks and it had been the best two weeks of his life. The two of them had vacationed at least twice a year both years they had been dating. The Bahamas, Grand Cayman, and a naughty weekend in Miami they kept entirely to themselves. But something about Venice was different. Although Clark had known what he was going to do before they left Chicago, the romanticism of the city took him over. The night before they were set to leave, he could honestly say he felt closer to Sabrina than he ever had. He had never been so sure of anything in his life than what he was about to do now.

"I'm glad I could entertain you." Sabrina scowled. "I told you I didn't want to be late for dinner. You know how I get when I'm hungry. What are you doing out here anyway? You said you'd be ready."

He smiled at her, squeezing the little black box in his hand hidden behind his back. "I am ready. There's just one thing I forgot."

"Quit your smiling," Sabrina said. "You're not cute. Well, you are cute, but not right now. Hurry up with it already, will you?"

Clark scratched his head, feigning confusion. "I'm not sure what it was that I forgot, but . . ." He began looking around the balcony as if searching for something.

Sabrina sighed, doing her part to search the balcony for some nonexistent object. "What are we looking for? It's not like you to be forgetful, Clark. I'm going to be very mad at you if you ruin our last night in . . ."

When she turned around, Clark was already on his knees with the box sitting open on his extended palm. He reveled in Sabrina's expression. It was confusion for just a second before she saw the ring and realized what he was doing. Then the shock as she screamed and her hands flew into the air. Her arms began to shake as her eyes welled up with tears.

"Will you get hold of yourself?" he teased.

"Shut up!" She reached over, slapping him on the arm. "Don't ruin this moment!"

"Fine," Clark said. "Go ahead and act hysterical. Just let me get a camera because I'm sure there are plenty of people back home who would pay big money to see Sabrina Scott lose her cool."

"Clark!" Sabrina motioned for him to get up. "Is this . . . Don't tease me!"

"No teasing," Clark smiled tenderly at her as he stood up. "This is the real thing. You have two choices. To hear my spiel or we can skip that and I'll just slip it on."

"Spiel," she said, wiping the tears of joy from her face. "I've been waiting a long time for this. I want the spiel."

Clark touched her cheek gently, his eyes melting into hers. "When I met you, I was the man I used to be. But you've made me the man I was meant to be. You've been side by side with me on my journey to finding true, honest, and real love where there are no lies, no games, and most of all, no substitutes."

Sabrina bit her lower lip, the tears coming faster now.

"You all right?" Clark asked, laughing.

She smacked him on the arm again. "Stop teasing me!"

Clark kissed her forehead before continuing. "Okay, I'm done teasing. I don't need to do that anymore because of you. I'm a more mature man now. Because of you, I'm a stronger man and happier than I ever thought I could be. If I could spend the rest of my life showing you my gratitude for the life that you've brought me, it wouldn't be long enough. But I'm hoping you'll give me the chance."

Clark took her hand, looking into her eyes. She was smiling, half laughing and half crying. He felt his own eyes begin to well up.

"You've got to say something now," he whispered after a short pause.

"Oh!" Her eyes widened as she suddenly realized. "Yes! Yes, I will mar . . . Wait, what did you ask me?"

"Shut up," he said, slipping the ring on her finger. "Shut up and kiss me."

* * *

Clark snapped the black box closed and shoved it into his drawer before slamming the drawer shut. About a month ago, he'd almost gotten up the nerve to sell it, but chickened out at the last minute. What was he holding on to?

Clark hadn't imagined he would see Sabrina anytime soon, but now he was going to and this was what it came down to. A middleweight fight in Sin City starring a wife beater was going to bring him face-to-face with the woman who, only six days from now, was supposed to have become his wife. Not exactly how he imagined it.

Sabrina felt a million times better as she lay in the large bathtub of her Henderson condo. She had to admit that every now and then, Dionne made a good point. A bad morning filled with memories of a lost promise had turned quickly into a hectic, crazy afternoon as they tackled all kinds of last-minute changes and obstacles to the career day and the prefight party happening later that week. Cancellations, additions, special requests, and even a firing of a thieving employee sprinkled the day. Sabrina and Dionne worked well into the evening, leaving after nine.

Dionne suggested that a hot bubble bath with a glass of the "good" wine was in order. It seemed actually out of order for Sabrina. It was so hot in Vegas in June that she thought of anything warm as the furthest thing from soothing.

Man, had she been wrong. With the air-conditioning blaring, Sabrina's body quickly softened in the practically scalding water. Her other senses responded to the candlelit room and the sweet smell of lavender. She felt her entire soul relaxing as she leaned back against the tub pillow and closed her eyes. This made any day worth it.

That was until memories slid their way into her peaceful meditation.

Instead of the pillow, Sabrina was leaning against Clark's strong, muscular body. She felt the electricity between them strong enough to be dangerous in the water. He was rubbing the gentle loofah scrub against her full breasts, her nipples hardening. Every move was so seductive, so intentional, Sabrina had to fight her body's response just to enjoy it. He made her lose her mind when he touched her like that. He knew all of her buttons, even those she didn't know she had.

His face lowered and his lips gently kissed her soft bare neck, sending a shiver down her spine. The touch was like a match lit with a burn that reached to the pit of her stomach. She felt him hardening against her as she lifted her arm and wrapped her hand around his neck. She lifted her face, tilting it backward.

His lips claimed hers with a passion that set her on fire. Their blazing bodies twisted and turned in a passionate challenge to each other, splashing water everywhere and putting out the candles. There was no order to the way they connected, but none of that mattered. Nothing mattered to Sabrina but their bodies connecting.

The way they worked together was sheer perfection. He made her feel lusty and unsated with every little bit more he gave her. He made love to her as if starving for her, and Sabrina thought nothing could be more perfect. But she was wrong. They were going to make it even better than perfect.

They were going to get married.

Sabrina opened her eyes, staring into space as a tear trailed her cheek. The familiar twinge of pain hit her and she gave in to it.

So much for hot bubble baths saving the day.

TWO

Tommy Gaxton was a Don King wanna-be. Visually, he was the exact opposite of the famous promoter. Tommy was in tip-top shape and he dressed in finely tailored Italian suits. His hair was trimmed and combed to perfection and barely a jewel could be found on him. He looked like a class act, a reputable, respectable businessman. That was just the exterior.

The interior was another story.

Tommy was known for being a ruthless promoter on his way up. He wasn't above dirty tricks to get what he wanted, and he was smart enough not to get caught for any of them. He was in the middleweight world now, but he was shooting for the big time, the lucrative world of heavyweight boxing, with multi-million-dollar paydays no matter who won or lost. Sabrina had done her research on him as soon as she started in her new job. She had heard so many rumors, she needed to find out the story for herself.

He had a reputation for building a fight by calling upon the worst in people. He gave in to the lowest common denominator, a sad trend in marketing as far as Sabrina was concerned. Tommy would race-bait if the fighters were different races. If one came from another country, his dig was pitting the American against the dirty foreigner. All tactics that Sabrina had no patience for.

"You're wearing that?"

Tommy surveyed Sabrina, shaking his head. He wasn't hiding his dissatisfaction. In his sharp black suit and shining blue oxford, he apparently felt qualified to criticize the dress of everyone around him. Sabrina was his next victim. Or so he thought.

"I beg your pardon?" Sabrina wasn't taking any crap from this man. They hadn't gotten along since meeting and she knew they never would. Still, she had been professional with him up until this point, but this week was not the one for her to take the higher ground. So if he wanted to take it there . . .

"This getup," Tommy said, waving his raisin-brown hand around her. "You can't seriously be wearing this."

Sabrina didn't bother to appease him by looking down at herself as if to check to see if he had a point. She knew she looked utterly professional in her crimson-red Calvin Klein pantsuit. "Tommy, I'm about to go out. I don't have time to—"

"There are cameras out there, baby!"

"Baby?" Sabrina's hand went to her hip as she leaned back. *Oh no, we will not be having that.* "You must have me mistaken for somebody you know much better than you know me."

Tommy cleared his throat. It was obvious he wasn't

used to women not responding to his style and his blessed advice. He didn't seem to care a bit for the women who weren't impressed with him.

"Loosen up, Sabrina."

"I will not," she said. "This is a press conference. It's a professional duty and I'm dressed professionally. Now if you'll just get out of my way, I'll—"

"Boxing is different than any other sport, Sabrina. Boxing is flash, sex, and gloss. You look like you're about to report to the board of directors."

"Tommy, I—"

"And it's not like you don't have the stuff," he said, ignoring her hand held up in protest. "You got the hot body, pretty face, and good hair to—"

"Good hair?" Sabrina had had enough of this. "Exactly what do you mean by 'good' hair?"

Tommy rolled his eyes. "Oh, you one of those."

"Yes," Sabrina said. "I am most certainly one of those, so you can take your 'good hair' somewhere else."

Tommy raised his arms in surrender. "I'm just trying to compliment a pretty lady."

"Thanks, but no thanks," Sabrina said. "Let's not waste each other's time. Now, if you'll excuse me, I have some work to do."

Tommy tugged at his tie. "Do you . . . do you have the notes I gave Nick?"

"No," she answered. "Nick very kindly shared your suggestions with me, but I made my own notes. You'll be up after me. If you want to add something, you can do it then. Are we finished?"

Sabrina stood there, staring at him, until he shrugged his shoulders and walked away. It was way past time for that man to know she was not having it.

The press room at the Acropolis was designed like an ancient Greek senate room. The room was porcelain white with rich purple and oxblood-red drapes falling along the walls and Greek statues decorating the doors. The seats were made of indented rich satin pillows set along benches in six rows, stadium style in a half circle. Everything was placed to focus on the podium with a backdrop of red drapes.

Sabrina stood behind those drapes as she listened to Nick welcome the reporters and dole out general information on the fight and prefight party before introducing her. Without a hint of caution, Sabrina smoothed out her suit, held her head high, and stepped into the fray. This was old hat.

Time slowed to a halt for Clark as the drapes seem to part for Sabrina with no help from a hand. The red of her outfit bled into them and she seemed more like a goddess awarding her crowd with a glimpse of her than a press agent. She looked like one, too. Everything perfectly in place as always.

He hadn't forgotten her face for a second. It was seared into his mind. Still, her beauty took his breath away. Clark knew every inch of this woman who walked with grace and poise to the stadium. It was just . . . seeing her again. It had only been four months, but every day had seemed like a year. They had been inseparable before she left him. Now, seeing her again was like water washing over him.

Drowning him, more likely. He couldn't breathe. Clark let out a deep breath, not realizing until then that he had been holding it in since she started through the drapes.

"Are you okay, man?" The young reporter sitting next to him was looking at Clark as if he was a little off.

"I'm fine." Clark nodded, but he wasn't fine at all.

"I mean she's hot," the reporter said, "but hold-your-breath hot?"

She was hold-your-breath hot as far as Clark was concerned.

He focused on her, recognizing that smile as she greeted the room. He hadn't seen that smile in so long. The sun seemed to shine brighter when Sabrina smiled. Her smooth brown skin was glowing from across the room. Those full lips moved so fluidly. Those large, intense eyes scanned the room. *I'm beautiful,* her image said. *I'm beautiful and smart as a whip.* A scary combination for a lesser man.

When would she see him? Clark wondered. What would he do when she did?

Clark felt the anticipation build within him, begin to overtake him. If she wasn't so gorgeous it wouldn't be so hard. It wouldn't be so hard to admit to himself how much he missed her. How much he still cared for her.

How angry he was with her for not believing him.

He had to pull himself together and stop acting like a love-struck teenage boy. He was a professional here to do a job that could have a say in his career, considering how things were going back home. Up until this point, he hadn't actually heard a word she'd said.

"Please bring your invitations to that party," she admonished the crowd. "Your press pass won't be enough to get you in. And remember, it's Thursday night, not Friday. Any more questions?"

"How much press do you expect at the fight?" This question from a short, stocky blond woman in the front row.

Sabrina smiled, leaning into the microphone. "We expect over one hundred press members at the fight, including over twenty from foreign countries."

"What are the odds in the Acropolis casino for the fight?" a young man in the back yelled out.

"Now, you know better," Sabrina said, pausing as some in the room laughed. "I can't comment on that. If you want to bet on the fight, you know what to do. Besides, I wouldn't even begin to know. I don't bet."

"You live in Vegas and don't bet?" from a middle-aged college type in the middle of the room.

"Shameful, isn't it?" Sabrina responded. More laughter.

She was a winner, Clark thought. They loved her for more than her looks. When she wanted to, she showed a charm and grace that pulled men and women in. She was so good at everything she did. Everything except trust, and what mattered more than that?

Clark pulled himself together again, feeling the anger awaken inside him. She hadn't seen him yet and that was beginning to tear at him. He wanted her to look at him. He wanted her to realize he still existed, and running across the country couldn't make him disappear.

Most of all, he wanted to see her eyes the way they were when focused on you. Eyes that made you believe you were the only person in the world. Eyes that made you feel you were worth something no matter what the rest of the world might tell you on any given day.

"How has Grove's weekend arrest affected the Acropolis's plans for promoting the fight?"

Sabrina blinked, feeling her heart catch in her throat at the sound of that voice. That voice!

Her eyes desperately searched the room. When they settled on Clark Hunter, a quiet whimper escaped her lips. The blood drained from her face and her body stiffened in shock as she blinked again, certain that the voice had thrown her and she was just imagining or hallucinating.

No, it was him!

Sabrina's hands gripped the edges of the podium as she felt her knees give out. She stared at him, speechless as her heart wouldn't accept what her eyes were confirming.

How could it . . . Why would he . . . What in the . . .

Clark stared back as he watched it all settle in. She was affected at least. He found some satisfaction in that fact.

"Well, Ms. . . . ." He looked down at his press brochure, looking back up. "Ms. Scott?"

Sabrina's eyes narrowed. "I . . . I didn't . . . What was the question?"

Clark stood up. "Maybe you couldn't hear me. I am pretty far back here."

Other reporters laughed at his playful stance, but Clark could tell that Sabrina was not the least bit amused.

"I asked you about the recent arrest of Artemis Grove. Does that change anything for you and the Acropolis?"

Sabrina swallowed, trying to remember how to finish a sentence. *Get it together, woman. You're on the podium.* She was experienced in these types of situations. Reporters always threw out trick questions, asked leading questions, and were downright rude at times. She had dealt with them fine. Of course none of them had been her cheating, lying ex-fiancé.

"Of course." Her voice caught in her throat. She cleared it, angry at herself. "Of course everyone was very disappointed to hear about the domestic situation Mr. Grove and his wife were involved in earlier this week. However, nothing changes the fight."

Clark stayed standing. He felt like a selfish kid wanting all of his mother's attention. Once he finally got it, he couldn't bear to give it up.

"Is that all the hotel has to say about it?" he asked. "If someone engages in criminal behavior and—"

"There has been no indication of criminal behavior," Sabrina said, realizing that he intended to make her uncomfortable. As if he needed to try. "No charges were filed, and the personal lives of the fighters are not what this fight is about."

Clark sensed the change in tone of her voice. She was angry now.

Sabrina ignored her stomach whirling. "I . . . I think that even if we knew exactly the situation, which we do not, the fact is that at this point it can only be a question of character. If we let someone's character determine whether or not they would be allowed to do their job, where would we be?"

She paused for effect. "Where would you be, Mr. Hunter?"

Clark felt the sting of her words like a fresh paper cut with a little lemon poured on it for good measure. He looked around, noticing that all eyes were on him. When Sabrina used his name, her tone let the room know there was something going on there. Clark was certain the electricity that had always existed between the two of them was noticeable to others. Even when it was negative.

"Thank you," he said quietly before sitting down.

"You're welcome."

Sabrina almost jumped as she felt a hand on her shoulder. She turned to Nick, who looked at her with concern, before smiling for the press.

"Now," he said in his *isn't this going great?* tone, "I would like to turn things over to promoter Tommy Gaxton, who, as you all know, represents both fighters."

As he flamboyantly appeared from the drapes, Tommy opened his arms wide to embrace the crowd. In her lifetime, Sabrina had never thought she would be happy to see Tommy.

"Come on," Nick whispered, leaning into her.

Sabrina didn't look out into the crowd before turning. She was certain she wouldn't have the strength to walk if she saw Clark again. All she wanted was to just get out of the room that seemed to be closing in on her.

Clark stared as she walked away, noticing the closeness between her and Nick Stewart. He had never been a big fan of Nick, but was okay with Sabrina's relationship with him. They had reached that point where two people have been friends too long to be anything more. Sabrina had never shown any romantic interest in him, which was all Clark needed. Nick was an obvious player for life and Clark knew those types of men stayed away from keepers like Sabrina. He had been one of the proud few who were willing to risk it.

When Clark had found out it was Nick that Sabrina had left Chicago to go work for, he'd felt a certain sense of comfort. At least it was someone that she had known all of her life and could trust.

Only there was no sense of comfort in Clark as he caught the quick glimpse of Nick's arm around Sabrina's waist. There was that squeeze, just a second before the red drapes closed behind them. It was a squeeze, wasn't it? Clark had seen something and it unsettled him. It made him face up to something his heart, his sanity, would not let him deal with.

Sabrina could very well be involved with another man.

Clark felt a chill run through him.

Sabrina leaned against the wall as soon as she was safe behind the drapes. She would have fallen to the ground if she hadn't done so. She felt the room swaying a bit and heard her heart beating like thunder.

Nick grabbed her by the arm for support. His anger was evident. "Damn, Sabrina. I had no idea he was going to be there. I checked the press passes just yesterday and he wasn't on the list. I would have remembered it. He must have slipped in. It's usually the same old folks."

Sabrina shook her head, pulling herself together. "It's okay, Nick. I just can't . . . It was really him, right? I wasn't imagining that?"

"No, kid. Sorry."

Sabrina stood upright, shaking her head. "Why? Why is he here?"

"It makes no sense," Nick said. "Do you think he's come for you? I remember how crazy he was when you left him."

Sabrina looked at Nick, unable to imagine going through that again. "You don't think that's why?"

"He was relentless in trying to get you back in Chicago. It's why you decided to take me up on my offer. So you could get away from it. From him."

"But that was four months ago." The truth was she almost gave in the last time. She didn't know what she would do this time. "Maybe he's just here for the fight."

"And asking the wrong questions."

"We expected someone to ask about it." Sabrina needed some water, some air. "It was all over the papers. He was just the first." Clark. It was Clark. "I felt like such a hypocrite."

"Why? You did great out there."

"I acted as if it didn't matter that Grove beat up his wife."

"We don't know if—"

"Yes, we do, Nick. Let's not kid each other. This fight already had slime written all over it because of Tommy, and Artemis Grove just made it worse."

They both turned as they heard the press room erupt in laughter.

"Tommy is taking care of everything," Nick said with a confident smile. "This fight is going to be great for the Acropolis. You have no idea what it's going to do."

"It's going to be the death of me," Sabrina said.

"Don't worry about Clark Hunter. I'll take care of him."

"Wait." Sabrina grabbed Nick's arm just before he took off. "Wait a second. Let's make sure we know why he's here. He could be just covering the fight. I doubt it, but let's not give him the pleasure of knowing he's riled me up more than what was obvious unless we have to. He doesn't deserve that."

Nick leaned forward, planting a quick kiss on her forehead. "That's my girl. Clark doesn't know what he's in for if he thinks he's gonna mess with you again."

Sabrina forced a tough-girl smile for Nick before letting him go. She felt a little sick to her stomach, still wondering if she had been dreaming. Wishing it was a nightmare.

Cautiously she walked back to the red drapes as if afraid that Clark would jump through them at any second. From the edge, she gently tugged at the drapes, peeking into the press room. They were all smiling, laughing out loud as Tommy did his thing. Offensive jokes and catchy sound bites. Everyone was having the best time.

Everyone except Clark. There wasn't a smile to be found on his face, a laugh to be heard from his voice. Sabrina stood frozen as she locked eyes with him. He was staring right at her as if he had been waiting for her, knowing exactly when she would look out and where she would be looking from. Those amazing green eyes were so mesmerizing and seemed to shine as they bored into hers.

She tore herself away, whipping her head from the drapes. She felt her stomach pulling, her body reacting to just the sight of him. The threat of desire was creeping through her veins. It was as if the last five months hadn't even happened.

What was she going to do?

Outside the executive offices for the Acropolis, Clark paced the white-and-sea-blue-decorated hallway. The walls were adorned with paintings of tortured, ancient images. Clark sympathized. He couldn't get out of his mind that last look on Sabrina's face before she turned away. She still hated him, and that hurt him at the same time it angered him because it wasn't fair. It wasn't justified, yet he felt to blame for it. He felt to blame for everything.

He hated how anxious he felt. How guilty he felt. There had been times when everything was so crazy in Chicago that he hated himself for causing this, even though he knew it was all lies.

When he had been lying wide-awake, alone in his bed those last nights before Sabrina left for Vegas, there was a little voice inside him that told him to just apologize. Just take the blame and apologize. At least that way there was a chance, albeit slight, that he could fix things. Only that would be a lie and there had been enough lying going on at that point.

"Stop it," he whispered to himself, alone in the hallway for the moment. "It's over. Let it go."

He reached for his ringing cell phone as the hallway began to fill up with people. He checked the caller ID first.

"Lauren, what do you want?"

"It went that bad?" she asked.

"What are you talking about?"

"Your pissy attitude."

"According to you, I always have a pissy attitude, Lauren."

"But it has an extra little bite of bitterness to it."

"What did you call me for?"

"You know what I'm calling you for. The press conference is over. What happened? Did she see you? Did you talk to her?"

Clark mockingly laughed like a teenage girl. "I'm

so glad you called. I couldn't wait to tell you everything." He paused to let the sarcasm sink in. "What are we, girlfriends? Do you actually think I'm going to share this information with you?"

"Look, you jerk. I put up with your crap every day. If there's a little juicy gossip I can get out of it, I'm getting it."

"I'm not in the mood to talk about it."

"Well, you get in the mood!"

Clark sighed, knowing he could just hang up on her if he wanted to. "I was a jerk."

"That, I expected."

"I saw her and she looked perfect, sounded perfect. The whole perfect thing. Then I asked a stupid question because I wanted her to look at me."

"How did she react when she saw you?"

"She seemed startled at first, as I expected. No smile, which I expected as well. Just a 'you're not dead yet?' look on her face. So I make the situation even better by asking about the domestic abuse thing."

"That's your job, isn't it?"

"She didn't like the question, so I pushed further because I'm an idiot who gets too much satisfaction from getting a reaction out of her. Look, Lauren, none of that matters. I'm here for the story."

"But don't you need her for the story? To get in?"

"I thought all I needed was you."

"Flattery. Hmmm, not your thing, but I've decided to help you anyway."

"What do you have?"

"Grove's wife, the abused and unwilling-to-press-charges Alicia Grove, left the hospital Sunday and is staying with her mother in Henderson. Got a pen?"

"Don't need one."

"Fine, but don't call me back. I won't give it to you again."

"Yes, you will."

Clark watched as Tommy Gaxton and his crew filled the hallway with greedy press members glossing away.

"Two-seventy-six Middle Avenue."

"Thanks." Clark spotted Sabrina at the end of the hallway with Nick right at her side. She hadn't spotted him yet, deep in discussion with a tall redhead. "I have to go, Lauren. I'll check her out today."

"Hey, Clark."

"What now?" he asked, feeling a lecture coming on.

"Advice from a lady."

"A lady?" He laughed.

"One that will slap you through this phone."

"Let's hear it."

"Next time you're with her, stop thinking about yourself so much."

"Now I'm a selfish bastard?"

"Don't act like you don't know that. You always feel sorry for yourself when it comes to this story. It's not about you."

Clark didn't like the way Lauren's words made him feel. "I have to go, Lauren."

Sabrina almost tripped over herself when she saw him standing there, closing his cell phone and sliding it into his pocket. She had just gotten herself together enough to feel confident she could walk to her office without falling down.

He looked so good, just as he always had. That boy you could bring home to Mother and Father, but he still had that dangerous streak that kept the nights warm. He was dressed well, but not too well. He had just enough of everything refined, but not so much to overtake those primal aspects of a man that every woman was chemically pulled to.

Even now, as she approached him, his eyes staring into her with purpose and determination, she was attracted to him. After everything that had happened, everything she knew, and all the time that had passed.

"What do you want?"

Clark kept his eyes on Sabrina. Her expression held nothing but contempt for him and he ignored the way that made him feel. At this point, it was Nick who was addressing him, and Clark had to remind himself that being a jerk, more of a jerk than he had already been today, wouldn't help the situation.

"I would like to speak to Sabrina." He smiled innocently, nodding to the tall redhead who was obviously impressed with him.

"I'm Dionne Wilson." Dionne held her hand out, with a flirtatious flip of her hair.

Clark shook her hand with a gracious smile, feeling Sabrina's eyes boring into him as if they were heat rays. She made him feel guilty for just being polite to another woman. *See, I told you he was a cheat. Look at how nice he is to a pretty woman.*

"What do you want, Clark?" Sabrina was doing

her best to be uninvolved, but it wouldn't hold out much longer.

All she could think of as she watched him touch Dionne's hand was that she wished it was her. What was wrong with her?

Clark looked at her, hoping to appear as unthreatening as possible. "We're adults, right? We can handle a civilized conversation, can't we?"

"Our recent history tells me probably not," Sabrina answered back.

"Sabrina." Her name whispered from his lips.

Sabrina could only stare at him, those eyes pulling her in. The way he said her name—just that way. What did he have? Just a name and a look and she felt her body temperature heat up several degrees.

"Fine," she said. "As long as it isn't long. I'm very busy."

"You don't have to, Sabrina." Nick gave Clark the evil eye. "She doesn't want any of your games."

"This isn't about that," Clark said, knowing that deep inside everything between him and Sabrina would always be about *that*.

"I'm fine." Sabrina placed a gentle hand on Nick's shoulder. "I'll talk to you later."

"Dionne and I will be in the office."

Clark ignored Nick's last angry look before he and Dionne went inside the double doors.

This wasn't new to Clark. Sabrina had a lot of male friends who felt as if it were their goal in life to protect her. She had that thing about her that made every man want to take a bullet for her even though she was more than capable of taking care of herself. During their relationship, any little fight and Sabrina's male friends automatically went into protection mode and made Clark the enemy.

Finally left alone with him, Sabrina felt her inner voice yelling for her to keep her wits about her, to pull it together and be the strong black woman she knew she was. She had to be strong for herself and all those betrayed women out there. She had to remember that whatever he was here to do, nothing would change what he'd already done.

"Did you mean that?" she asked, keeping a good distance between them.

"What?"

"When you said it wasn't about . . . that."

Clark's body responded to the vulnerable tone of her voice. She still felt the pain she believed he had caused her, and her eyes were asking, *Would you be so kind as to leave me alone?* She made him feel like a brute. "I'm not here to ask you to take me back or forgive me or any of . . . that."

"Good," she said, hoping she meant it. "Because it wouldn't do you any good. Nothing has changed, Clark. Not about that."

"Sabrina, I was sent here by my editor to cover the fight. I didn't even want to come. The last thing I want is to . . ." Clark blinked, wishing he could take his words back. "I didn't mean that . . ."

Sabrina swallowed, her body tightening as she braced for the blow of his words. "It's okay. You can say it. The last thing you'd want to do is see me again. Exactly how I feel. So we're on the same page. Still, you're here."

"My editor is pretty ruthless about getting the story. He hoped I could use our relationship to get some inside scoop and make a story out of something that everyone assumes is no story at all."

"We have no relationship, Clark."

"He was talking about the one we had," Clark said, hating the blunt tone of her voice now. "Or better, the one I thought we had."

"I beg your pardon?"

"Let's face it, Sabrina. There was no trust. If there had been, we would still be together. Without trust, there's nothing, right? Those were your words."

Sabrina's mouth opened wide, but nothing came out for a few seconds. "Are you lecturing me on trust? Why don't you lecture me on being faithful while you're at it?"

Clark sighed, feeling anger rise inside him. "I'm sorry I went there, Sabrina. Right after saying it wasn't about that. What I meant was, my editor—"

"I know what you meant." Sabrina bit her lower lip for just a second to hold back her emotions. *Don't give this hypocrite the pleasure.* "But you'll have to tell him it was all a waste of time. I'm not helping you with anything about this fight. You'll get exactly what everyone else gets. You're not even local, which might qualify you for some extra behind-the-scenes views, so forget it."

"This isn't personal?" he asked.

Sabrina placed her hand on her hip, hoping Clark didn't notice it had been shaking. "I'm a professional, Clark. I've always been."

"What about the domestic violence situation with Grove? I'm sorry to have to ask, but it is a story. I'm working that angle."

"You can work whatever angle you want. The

Acropolis isn't going to say anything about that incident. The fight on Saturday night is all we're concerned about."

"That doesn't sound like you." Clark knew a different Sabrina who never passed up a chance to speak up for women. "Violence against women is one of your biggest causes. This has got to be killing you."

Sabrina paused, shaking her head. She remembered how disgusted she'd felt when she heard the news. She remembered how much she had wanted to punch Tommy Gaxton in the face when he told her and Nick that it was no big deal and these things happen between a husband and wife all of the time. It was nobody's business. Violence, Sabrina told him, was everyone's business because every time we turn our head to it, we become a lesser society. Tommy wasn't feeling her.

"Personally," she said, "it is killing me, but I don't . . . I can't save the world every day, Clark. I have a job to do, and right now that job is marketing this fight."

"But I know there's a part of you that would love to get into that ring and take Grove on yourself."

Sabrina felt the edges of her lips curve into a reluctant smile as Clark mocked boxing gestures in her direction. "He wouldn't have a chance," she said.

"No man could against you." Clark had learned that lesson the hard way.

Sabrina looked away, hoping desire to step closer to him would pass. "Clark, the fact remains that special insight goes to special reporters. You're not one, so you're on your own."

"I've gotten used to that feeling," Clark said.

Sabrina knew exactly what he meant and the hair on the back of her neck stood up. "Am I supposed to feel sorry for you?"

Clark's jaw tightened, his eyes slightly narrowed. "I've never asked for pity from anyone for anything."

"Good, 'cause you're not getting it. You play, you pay." She leaned forward, her anger at his nerve feeding her on. "You see, Clark, there are two types of women in this world. The type that put up with a cheating man and the type that don't. If you don't want a life of loneliness, I suggest you go after the former."

"Or maybe I'll just go after the type who will love me enough to know when I'm telling the truth no matter what anyone else is telling them."

Sabrina pressed her lips together, her teeth gritting against each other. Still he expected her to believe him. Was he mad? What about the pictures and the phone conversations? He acted as if it was his word against some stranger! He really must think she was an idiot.

"With your track record?" she asked. "Good luck."

"Don't do that, Sabrina. Don't dig into the past. That was the man I used to be. When I met you, I—"

"The problem with the past, Clark, is that it's not the past if it keeps happening."

"That's why I called it the past." Clark was unrelenting. "I'll admit that I was a bit of a player in my youth, before I met you. But I wasn't a cheater. All the women I dated knew I was dating other women. And many of them were dating other men. It's totally different."

"I don't need to hear this!" Sabrina felt tears coming any second. How was it possible she was going through this again? "Clark, I don't want your explanations or excuses. I don't want to hear anything from you. I don't want to hear you or see you, period. Just leave."

Clark felt all the pain coming back to him. She was right. They couldn't go back to this. "I'm here for the fight, Sabrina. You're going to have to see me, but I can—"

"Keep your distance then. If you have to be here, fine. It's just a few days. Just stay away from me and it will all be over after Saturday."

Sabrina saw the expression on Clark's face soften as soon as she realized what she had said—Saturday. Their eyes held for what seemed like a lifetime to Sabrina. The lifetime they were supposed to spend together starting this Saturday.

"I have to go, Clark."

She didn't wait for a response or anything else before rushing into the office. With the door closed behind her, she stumbled in tears to her desk, where an angry Nick was waiting.

"What did he say to you?" he asked. "I'll beat the crap out of him."

"Don't," Sabrina said, knowing that as strong as Nick was, he wasn't a match for Clark. The last thing she needed was a friend in the hospital over her unmendable heart.

"Are you okay?" Dionne rushed to her desk as Sabrina sank into her chair.

"I'm . . ." Sabrina tried to speak through choked tears. "He makes me so weak."

"Stop it, Sabrina," Nick said. "Don't let him make you feel like this."

"It's okay," Sabrina said. "He's going to stay away from me from now on. I'm sure of it."

"You don't look sure of it," he said.

"Maybe you're not sure you'll stay away from him?" Dionne asked, handing her a tissue.

Sabrina looked up at her, knowing that was exactly what upset her the most. "I hate him, Dionne."

"I can see that," she said. "But that doesn't mean you're over him. The right guy can make a girl do things with her better judgment screaming at her from the rooftops not to. I have the remedy for you."

"Anything." Sabrina wiped away her tears, feeling embarrassed for losing her cool at work like this. This was not the professional image she wanted to build.

"The best way to get over a guy is to jump into a new one." Dionne smiled mischievously. "Or jump on top of a new one. Underneath. In front of. Whatever your taste is."

"I get the picture." Sabrina had to laugh despite herself. "Thanks for the laugh, but the last thing I need is another man in my life."

"Who said anything about him being in your life?" Dionne asked. "We're talking about a distraction here. Not a boyfriend."

"It's not my game, Dionne." Sabrina wondered if she should loosen up a little bit. Being a good girl and looking for relationships instead of casual sex hadn't gotten her anywhere so far. "No, I just need to stay away from Clark for the next five days. How hard could that be?"

"With that one man that can push your buttons," Dionne said, "five hours can be impossible."

"I'll be fine." Sabrina didn't believe that for a second. Clark didn't just know how to push her buttons. He put them there in the first place. "I've got so much work to do, these next few days will go by like nothing."

Nick squeezed her shoulder. "Just in case, I'll keep an eye out for him."

Sabrina smiled at him appreciatively, inside knowing that what she really needed was someone to keep an eye out for her.

THREE

Middle Avenue was in one of the many planned communities of Henderson, a suburb of Las Vegas made up of so many new developments it was beginning to look like a house farm. Two-seventy-six Middle Avenue was one of the more colorfully decorated houses on its block, and as Clark approached the front door, it appeared to be one of the loudest.

"Who are you?" In the doorway, a little face with fat cheeks and ketchup smeared over the lips stared up at Clark.

"Aren't you a cute one." Clark bent down, coming face-to-face with the little girl. She was red Indian brown with large eyes as black as coal, like her ponytailed hair. She was so tiny, her body practically hung like a doll from the doorknob she clung to.

"I know," she responded quickly. "You're not so bad yourself."

"How old are you?" Clark asked, knowing she couldn't be more than five.

"You don't 'sposed to ask a girl that." She pressed her lips together in a scolding gesture. "Mommy told me that."

"Is your mommy home?"

She nodded, seeming already bored with Clark and his conversation.

"Can I talk to—"

A tall, thin woman in her late twenties appeared at the door, opening it wider at the same time she shooed the little girl away. She was wearing Jackie O sunglasses and was a mile away from a smile.

"Alicia Grove?" Clark asked. Sunglasses indoors gave her away.

"What do you want?" she asked, looking him up and down.

Alicia Grove was the textbook fighter's wife. She was glossed out in a tight, black, low-cut silk blouse and red leather pants. She was a fair-skinned woman with wild, curly, light brown hair that had sandy blond streaks running wild through it.

"My name is Clark Hunter and I'm—"

"You're a reporter." She spoke with a slight Jersey accent. "I told you guys I'm not talking to anyone."

"I understand how you feel."

She let out a deep, grainy laugh. "Oh, please. Give me a break."

"I'm not trying to kiss up to you, Mrs. Grove." Clark had his own painful memories of abuse to fight. "My father . . . Let's just say that my parents' marriage wasn't a good one and I lived every aching moment with them."

He couldn't tell if he had any effect on her behind the sunglasses, but her face seemed to soften.

"I'm not talking to any of you," she said. "Besides, there is no way for me to know if you're lying. Even if you are, your business has nothing to do with my business."

"I wouldn't lie about that," Clark said. "Those memories are too painful. I can accept that you don't want to talk to me, but I do think the public has a right to know who they are rooting for."

"My husband is a good man."

"Good men don't beat their wives," Clark said. "You are going to get help, aren't you? My mother never got help and she paid for it for the rest of her life. Even after he left."

Alicia waved her hand in the air. "Oh no, this is nothing like that. I'm sorry about what happened to your mother, but this wasn't like that."

"Maybe it's just beginning."

Alicia looked behind her as she stepped farther out onto the porch. She closed the door, sighing heavily before removing her sunglasses. The bruise around her left eye had raised and was loudly purple, blue, and black. She looked intently at Clark, who tried not to wince.

"You're not lying to me, are you? About your parents, I mean. Because that would be low. Even for a reporter."

Clark shook his head. "I told you. Besides, I would never lie about my mother. Will you tell me your story?"

"No, I won't." She replaced the sunglasses. "But I will tell you something."

"I'm listening."

Alicia ran her long, manicured fingers through her hair, looking around as if to catch a spy or hidden camera. "My husband has never, ever laid his hands on me before. He's made a lot of changes in his life. Where he grew up—"

"Is where I grew up," Clark said. "The West Side of Chicago. I know all about that."

"So you do," she said, her voice calming, seeming more comfortable. "Well then, you probably knew a lot of boys like Artie growing up. All the odds were against him, but he overcame them. He's made something of his life. He's not that person anymore, but if I go to the press and let this out, it will be like he never left that neighborhood and that life."

"He did abuse you, Alicia."

"We've been together for seven years, married for five." Alicia began to slightly sway from side to side as if to calm herself. "We have two children together. Never has that man hit me. Laid even one finger on me. Yes, he has a temper, but he always took it out in the ring. What happened four days ago does not define our marriage."

"Then why did it happen?" Clark knew it was none of his business, but he wanted to know. He always took this kind of thing so personally.

"Things have been very hard on Artie."

Clark had heard this before. "From my bedroom I could hear my father telling her it was his hard day at work, his boss getting on his back, the bills that made him do it."

"But it was that man!" Alicia slammed her fist against the doorpost, her tone biting and angry.

"What man?"

"Tommy," she said. "Tommy Gaxton. He's like a vacuum, sucking the energy and happiness out of my home. He's been putting pressure on my husband."

"What kind of pressure?" Clark's journalistic instinct kicked back in.

Alicia paused as if wondering if she had already said too much. "I don't know. He won't tell me. All I know is that he goes out to meet that man and comes back angry. Whenever Tommy comes over to the house, like he did that night—"

"The night Artemis hit you?"

She nodded. "That night, I heard Artie yelling at that man. 'I can't do it! I can't do it!' He kept saying it over and over."

"Can't do what?" Clark's mind was already racing around the possibilities. This was boxing after all.

"That's what I asked." Alicia brought her hand to her head, frowning as if she had a sudden headache. "He didn't want to talk about it after Tommy left. I kept pushing. I shouldn't have pushed."

"You have a right to know what's upsetting your husband and what's going on in your own home."

Clark had an idea of what this was about, but didn't want to mention anything to Alicia. The last thing she needed right now was more strife between her and her husband.

"I thought he was saying he couldn't win," Alicia said, "but that wasn't it. Artie could beat this guy ten ways without trying. So what was it that had made my husband an angry, moody stranger for the past three weeks?"

Clark saw a tear begin to trail her cheek. He wanted a story, but he really wanted her to be okay.

"I've asked you more than I have a right to. I respect what you're going through, but I have to tell you, I'm going to write about this story. I won't write anything you've told me unless you tell me I can."

"No," she said bluntly.

"Well, if you need to talk to me or . . . anything, I'll be at the Acropolis until Sunday morning. Clark Hunter."

"I won't need you," she said, opening her door behind her. "I'm fine. My marriage is fine."

"There are people who are trained," he said. "Educated to help you."

"I got that whole lecture at the hospital."

"It's not a lecture. It's sound advice and it's anonymous."

"Nothing I do is anonymous anymore." Her voice held resignation.

"You may be right," Clark said, "but they'll do everything they can. Maybe you could take advantage of that."

"Are you married, Mr. Hunter?"

Clark looked down at his ring finger just as Alicia did. Its bareness seemed glaring at the moment. What a thing to ask.

"No." Clark was still staring down at his nakedness. "I was . . . No, I'm not married."

When he looked up, the door to 276 Middle Avenue shut closed and the lock turned.

"Are you drunk yet?"

Sabrina turned to Dionne. "Who, me? No way."

She was completely wasted. After a night of crying herself to sleep, Sabrina woke up late, got to work late, and was a step behind all day. Unable to get her mind off of Clark, she was back to being a mess as she had been when they'd first broken up. Only now it was more critical because Daddy didn't run the Acropolis. Her broken heart wouldn't be taken into account this time.

To salvage some part of the day, Dionne offered to buy her a round at the Agora, the main bar and lounge at the Acropolis. Although she wasn't a drinker, Sabrina agreed, wishing for anything that could take her away from her sad state of being.

As always in Las Vegas, the bars and lounges were on and hopping at all hours. The Agora, named after the Greek word for meeting place, was no exception when Dionne and Sabrina showed up. They garnered more than a few stares from the men who were already half in the can, but their warning stares made it clear that this was a girls' night out and men were not in the picture. Any approachers were thoroughly dismissed, discouraging any others from taking a try.

The lights were dim, the drinks were flowing, and a woman dressed in an obscene shade of yellow was belting out jazz tunes. The perfect atmosphere for a girl wanting to drown her sorrows.

Dionne was an expert on getting the party started. Especially a drinking party. One shot of tequila for both of them to begin with, followed by a shot of Jaeger, and then the gin. This night was about the real stuff. None of those fruity drinks like amaretto sours that Sabrina liked to nurse all night. Bourbon, rum, and Scotch. Dionne ordered doubles down and Sabrina cringed at the sound of it all, but kept on drinking.

She wasn't sure exactly which one she was on when Dionne asked the question.

"You're totally drunk," Dionne said, laughing. "I love this. You're always so prim, proper, and well behaved. I've never seen you . . ." She seemed to be at a loss for the word.

"What?" Sabrina asked.

"Out of control."

"I wouldn't go that far."

"Not like wild out of control." Dionne snarfed down the last of the rum and Coke. "Just not so uptight, like you usually are."

Sabrina frowned. She hated that word. "I'm not uptight. Why does everyone always say that?"

"Who else would have the nerve to tell you that besides me?"

"Clark," Sabrina said, rubbing her eyes. Her body felt light, but her head felt heavy. "That's what he said when he first met me."

"Clark, the cheater. He called you uptight? I'm sure that was a turn-on for you."

"I hated him when I first met him." Sabrina's words slurred into each other. "He showed up at that paper with his brash self. He was only twenty-five, but he thought he owned the world."

"You're older than him?"

"Three years." Sabrina nodded, remembering when she thought that mattered. Maybe that was it. He was just too young to settle down. To be faithful. "He was so careless and cocky. Thought he was the best thing that ever happened to that paper." Sabrina poked herself in her chest with her index finger. "My father's paper."

"That wasn't too bright of him," Dionne said. "To insult the owner's daughter."

"That's the kind of thing Clark did."

"What kind of thing is that?"

Sabrina looked at her with a shrug of her shoulders. "Anything he wanted."

Sabrina could see him watching her from the edge of the cafeteria door. She wasn't a fan of the paper's cafeteria. In her opinion, people seemed to think it was a safe haven from professionalism and acted however they wanted to while there. She had just come to get her lunch out of the refrigerator, but the large television nailed to the wall was on and it caught her attention.

Usually there was one of a few soap operas that the cafeteria crowd preferred, but today the news was on. There had been a car chase up and down Lake Shore Drive, a long stretch of roadway along Lake Michigan in the city. The camera showed the tape as it followed the driver, who came close to hitting several cars before being corralled by the police.

She wasn't sure how long he had been watching her, but she refused to turn her head in his direction. This drove her crazy, his staring at her all of the time. Who did he think she was? Some college girl who would flush from his attention?

Clark Hunter, the new sports reporter. She couldn't stand him. Since showing up less than one month ago, he spent his days walking around with a smirk on his face, flirting with every woman he met, talking louder than anyone in the room, and never passing up an opportunity to stare at her. It made Sabrina uncomfortable and she was certain he knew it. Knew it and liked it. The jerk.

Sabrina wondered when he actually found time to get work done.

She intended to stay there as long as it took, staring at the television as if he didn't exist. He would have to leave eventually. She certainly wasn't going to give him the satisfaction he so obviously—from the smile on his face—got every time she made eye contact with him and turned nervously away.

One of these days she was going to give him a piece of her mind.

"Speed racer makes his return," he said in a deep, confident voice.

Sabrina suddenly realized he was walking toward her. No way!

He stopped only a couple of feet away from her, close enough to force her to turn to him and acknowledge his presence, which she did with the most tepid smile she could form.

Sabrina thought of him as a spoiled child who couldn't stand not getting all of the attention all of the time.

"I'm not a big racing fan," he continued, "but I should write a story about this guy. That was awesome, don't you think?"

Sabrina couldn't hold her tongue. "Did you say awesome?"

"Yeah. That run was awesome." He pointed to the television. "The way he weaved through there."

"You find that entertaining?" Sabrina asked.

"Criminal behavior? He could have killed some-one."

Clark rolled his eyes. "I wouldn't have said that if someone had actually been hurt."

"So as long as no one gets physically hurt, even though they were probably scared to death, it's okay to make fun of it?"

He stared at her, his temporary amusement ob-viously deflated. "Why are you so damn uptight?"

Sabrina's mouth fell open. "How rude!"

"Come on, Sabrina." He smiled a charming, in-credibly charming smile. "Chill out, okay? I was just trying to lighten—"

"Sabrina?" She placed a hand on her hip. "Do you know me? Because you're talking to me like you know me, but I don't think you do."

The charming smile wasn't as charming now, or as wide. "I was hoping to get to know you."

"Is that how you get to know everyone?" she asked. "By insulting them?"

"Okay," he said, laughing now. "I know what your deal is. You're the kind who—"

"I don't think you want to go there," she answered, feeling herself heat up in response to his pompous-ness. "First of all, you don't know what my deal is because, unlike you, Mr. Hunter, I don't yell out my business to everyone in the office."

"I don't yell out my business."

"You yell out everything else."

Clark was serious now. "You've obviously got a problem with me. I don't know why, but since I got here I've only gotten ugly looks from you."

"That's because I don't like being stared at."

"Then maybe you shouldn't be so beautiful."

His words caught her off guard and a victorious smile framed his face at her speechlessness, only angering her more.

"Look," he said, "I was staring at you because . . . I was trying to figure you out."

"What do you need to figure out?"

"What makes you tick." He took a step closer. "I was curious."

"I'm not interested in being an object of your curiosity."

"Well, how about being an object of my affection?"

Sabrina was aghast at his forwardness. "You're way too fresh for the office, Mr. Hunter."

He nodded. "You're right. Look, I'm sorry. That was inappropriate. I just really wanted to introduce myself and find out why you seem to have a particular distaste for me. Is it because your father likes me so much?"

Sabrina's lunch bag almost fell out of her hands as she gave him a hostile stare. "What?"

"I'm very familiar with that whole rich-girl syndrome," he answered. "I've seen it plenty of times before. They always like the guys their daddies hate. Any guy he approves of is automatically out of contention."

This man needed to be taken down a notch. "For your information, Mr. Hunter, you were never, nor will you ever be, in contention. And as for my father liking you so much, I haven't seen any indication that he particularly favors you anyway."

Sabrina knew that wasn't true. Her father spoke nonstop about Clark and how he was a genius to have hired him to the paper. It drove her crazy.

"I think we both know better than that," Clark said with a sly tilt of his head.

That was it.

Sabrina tilted her head to mock him. "I hope you remember this moment, Mr. Hunter. I don't think you will, but I hope you do, because one day when you finally mature, you'll realize how much of a fool you made of yourself."

The smile disappeared completely this time, and Sabrina quietly, head held high, walked past him and out of the cafeteria. She was almost all the way back at her office before she realized that she was feeling that peculiar pull at her belly.

What was that about?

"How in God's name did you two ever get together?" Dionne asked.

"I lost a bet," Sabrina said, feeling the emotions well inside her. "He wouldn't leave me alone. I think it killed him that someone didn't like him. He had become a local celebrity of sorts. Chicago worships its sports, and the most popular reporters are almost as well loved as the athletes. He thought he was so great."

"Every man likes a challenge." Dionne snapped for the bartender. "Jimmy, can we get some peanuts or something over here?"

A challenge. Sabrina had to laugh at the thought. After she had finally given Clark a chance, she had fallen so quickly for him, she couldn't believe she presented any type of a real challenge for him. Maybe that was why he eventually strayed. She had been too easy, too eager to marry him. Then why did he have to propose? Had she forced him into it?

"I need another drink," Sabrina said, raising her hand for the bartender, who nodded.

"So?" Dionne asked. "The bet. How did Clark get in there?"

"It was a trick," Sabrina answered. "One of the oldest in the book probably, but I didn't know about it."

"The sure bet?"

Sabrina looked at Dionne, who shrugged an apology. "So it's just me that didn't know about it?"

Dionne nodded. "A guy makes a bet with a girl that he knows he'll win for whatever reason. It's got to be something she thinks she is certain of the answer to or whatever. He's got an in, already knows the answer, etcetera. It can't be so complicated that it's obvious he has the upper hand. He bets that if she wins, he'll do something innocent for her that doesn't seem like a come-on. Like—"

"He'll owe her twenty bucks." Sabrina filled in the blanks.

"Exactly. Nothing sexy about that. But, if he wins, he says she has to take him to dinner. Now the woman, certain she's going to win, agrees."

Sabrina took a quick swig of her drink. "I was such an idiot. I totally fell for it."

"I'm still surprised you agreed to the bet, hating him like you did."

Sabrina's lips formed a guilty smile. "By that time, I was . . . I don't know. Interested, I guess you could say. He was so dang-gone cute!"

"That'll do it every time," Dionne said. "You need a stronger drink."

"Why? According to you, I'm already drunk."

"Not drunk enough if all you can muster is dang-gone. When you're cussing, then I'll be satisfied you're drunk and ready to really get over this man."

Sabrina picked at the lemon slice on the napkin in front of her, remembering all of the cussing that had gone on. There wasn't a name in several languages she hadn't called him. If it didn't help then, how could it possibly help now?

"So how did you find out?" Dionne asked.

"Find out what?" Sabrina felt the room moving a bit now.

"About him cheating on you and wanting you just for your money?"

Sabrina suddenly felt sick. "The cheating? She was waiting for me outside the paper one day. My job. Just waiting there. I laughed at her, but then I got pictures of them together in the mail."

"From her?"

"I know she sent them."

"So what did he say when you confronted him with the pictures?"

"I didn't show them to him at first."

"Why not?'

Sabrina didn't know she was crying, but she felt the tears running down her cheek. Maybe it was sweat. It was very warm in the bar. "I wanted him to admit to it. To tell me the truth because it was the right thing to do, not because he was caught and cornered and had no other choice."

"We're talking about a man, Sabrina."

"I know that now."

"So this girl. You know her?"

"Never met her," Sabrina said, shaking her head.

The image of the average-looking woman who helped ruin her life was frozen in time in her memory. "Clark claimed not to know her either."

"Before or after the pictures?"

"Both."

Dionne nodded. "He played the you-must-be-going-crazy game. I know that one."

"He never called me crazy. Just kept saying he didn't do it."

"I still can't believe that trick had the nerve to show her face to you."

"Called herself helping me out," Sabrina said bitterly. "She told me that Clark was dumping her, so she wanted to get back at him. When she called me—"

"No, she didn't call you." Dionne seemed amazed.

Sabrina nodded. "Oh yeah, she called. She played this tape of the two of them. Her begging him to stay, but he told her he didn't want to risk missing out on his cash cow."

"He called you a cash cow?"

Sabrina jumped up from her stool at the bar. "Excuse me."

She ran to the bathroom as fast as she could and threw up for the next twenty minutes. She felt as sick about it today as she had when she'd first seen the pictures.

She was remembering now what she learned then. All of the alcohol in the world couldn't cover up for a broken heart.

As he walked down the hallways of the Acropolis, Clark couldn't help himself. Had he promised

Sabrina he would stay away from her? That he would at least try?

What did it matter? She didn't believe he stuck to his promises anyway.

He could always use Levy as an excuse. With no respect for time zones, Levy had woken him up earlier than early, requesting an update. After Clark refused for the fifth time to print what Alicia told him, Levy threatened to fire him if he didn't get an interview with both Tommy Gaxton and Artemis Grove. In her usual lifesaving way, Lauren hopped on the phone with a copy of Tommy's daily schedule, with no explanation for how she had gotten her hands on it.

As he scoured the hallway for his subject, Clark knew who it was he was really looking for. Last night, he'd had the dreams, or fantasies would be more appropriate. Was it possible to have a fantasy if it was replaying something that already happened?

The truth was, Sabrina had always been his fantasy and he had dreamed of her well after they had been together and ever since then. In the past month or so the dreams-fantasies had come less frequently, but now, seeing her again, brought them rearing back, waking him up in the middle of the night drenched in sweat.

"Where are you going?"

Clark stopped, slowly turning around to face the familiar voice. Nick Stewart stood at the end of the hallway looking like an old cowboy ready for a gunfight at high noon. Clark had to suppress the smile that he knew would only anger Nick more.

"What is it, Nick?" he asked. "Last I checked, I

was a guest at this hotel, so I'm allowed to walk around."

Nick slowly started toward him, making some attempt to appear intimidating. Clark couldn't care less. With all that was going on, Nick Stewart wasn't on his mind. That was, unless . . .

"This is the convention area," Nick said. "And there aren't any conventions going on until this afternoon."

"I'm looking for Tommy Gaxton. I am a reporter, remember?"

"Are you sure you aren't looking for Sabrina?"

Clark gave him a once-over, feeling the testosterone rev up. Nick was definitely challenging him. "If I was looking for Sabrina, I would have said I was looking for Sabrina. What business is it of yours?"

"Well, considering that she and I are a couple now, any ex-boyfriend following her around is definitely my business."

Clark couldn't help losing a step as Nick confirmed what he wasn't willing to even contemplate. He refused to let an image of Sabrina with Nick or any other man anywhere near his mind.

Nick was pleased. "Is that your teeth I hear grinding against each other? You had your chance, brother."

Clark kept his arms at his sides as his hands formed into fists. When he was younger, he was quick to fight, but he couldn't be that man anymore. "I'm not concerned with Sabrina's love life. As a matter of fact, that's what we talked about yesterday. I'm surprised she didn't tell you, you being her boyfriend and everything."

Nick's smile faded. "She did tell me. She also told me you agreed to leave her alone."

"I'm not here for her," Clark lied, hating that Sabrina shared their conversation with him. Was it over dinner? In bed? *God, no. Don't start that.*

"Nick! Nick, are you there?"

Nick reached for the radio at his hip. "What is it?"

"We have an incident in the casino," an exasperated woman said. "Stolen money bucket. Security is calling for you. Now!"

Nick turned back to Clark, who smiled with his hands raised innocently in the air.

"Don't let me keep you from your incidents," Clark said.

"I'm keeping an eye on you," Nick said. "You've hurt her enough, Clark. I won't let you hurt her any more."

With one last sneer, Nick turned and walked away. Clark tried to calm himself down. His pulse was pounding at the thought of Sabrina with Nick.

"No," he said as he turned and headed down the hallway. "That's not something I can live with."

With her back to him, Sabrina could still tell that Tommy was staring at her butt. She had agreed to show him the prefight party room set up for Nick's sake, and was quickly regretting it.

"Did you hear me?" she asked, turning around to face him.

He took his time to raise his eyes to her face, lingering for a long time at her chest. "Sorry. I'm just taking in the view."

Sabrina sighed. "Come on, Tommy. After all this time, you can't come up with better crap than my grandfather used? *I'm just taking in the view.* How genuine."

Tommy smiled, showing his gold-capped teeth. "Do I make you nervous?"

"You wish," Sabrina said. "Now, are you going to listen or am I leaving?"

"I just want to know when I'm coming out."

"That's what I was just telling you." Sabrina pointed to the left side of the back stage. "You'll be coming out from there after Nick introduces you. Not less—"

Tommy held up a hand to stop her as he reached for his ringing cell phone.

Sabrina rolled her eyes. She just wanted to get this over with. She bade her time as Tommy spoke incoherently on the phone with his hand over his mouth. As if she cared whom he was talking to.

Sabrina wasn't thinking about Tommy and his private phone calls. She had the career day to plan, which was what she should be doing right now. That day, and the idea of doing something for the local kids, was the only positive thing going on in her life right now and she needed to immerse herself in that project before she went into a deep depression.

Tommy closed the phone, gripping it in his hand. "All right, sweetheart. Go ahead."

Sabrina gritted her teeth. It was almost over. "It'll be less than five minutes."

"What?"

"How long between the time everything gets

started and Nick introduces you." She wasn't repeating another thing.

Tommy looked around the expansive ballroom. "This place is too boring. You better be picking it up a whole bunch."

"Of course we are." *You idiot,* she added to herself. "The decorations just like you and Nick agreed to are going to go up, starting this evening."

"How long do I get?" With his hands behind his back, his chin was pressed forward as he walked toward Sabrina, thinking himself a man of importance.

Don't come near me. I threw up enough last night. "You'll get five minutes to say whatever you want and then you get two-minute introductions for each fighter."

He stopped only inches away from her, with an outdated pimp's smile on his face. Sabrina had to fight not to laugh. Did he actually think he was impressing her?

"What are you wearing?" he asked in almost a whisper as his fingers reached for her hair.

Sabrina leaned her head away, staring him down. "That's none of your business. Are we done?"

"I'm just asking," he said, "because you always dress so conservative. It's a shame because you're swole in all the right places, girl."

"We're definitely done," Sabrina said as she started for the door.

Everything happened suddenly. Sabrina's attention was at the door she wanted to get to and when Clark appeared there suddenly, she was frozen in place. At the same time, she felt Tommy grab her arm tightly to pull her back. Her mind went into self-defense mode, as she realized what was going on.

"Let me go," she said quickly. Looking at Tommy, she saw that his expression showed his anger, and hurt pride was making him dangerous.

"You don't walk away from me when I'm talking to you!" His eyes squinted as he tightened his grip.

"Hey!" Clark pushed for them.

Sabrina took advantage of Tommy's surprise at Clark, who was gunning for them. She grabbed Tommy's arm with her free hand and, stepping to the side, she pulled it, twisting as tight as she could toward her.

"Ahhhhhhhhhhh!" Tommy's screech sounded like a wounded animal as his cell phone fell out of his hand and clanked against the floor.

Sabrina twisted with all of her strength. "I told you to let go."

Tommy let go of her other arm as he fell to his knees, wincing in pain. Finally, she let go as Clark arrived.

Clark was so fueled by the anger that came the second he saw Tommy grab Sabrina, he wanted to kick him. But looking at the man on the ground, crying in pain like a little girl, his rage turned to pity.

"Are you okay?" he asked Sabrina, who was surveying her victim.

"I'm fine." Sabrina could feel and hear herself breathing hard and fast. She was mad as hell, but she was fine.

Clark grabbed Tommy by his shirt collar and pulled him up. "Get up, Gaxton. And stop whining like a baby."

Tommy jerked away as he stood upright, rubbing his arm. "Don't touch me."

"You think that's touching you?" Clark asked. "You better be glad it took me this long to get over here."

Tommy made a smacking sound with his lips as he turned to Sabrina. His embarrassment was obvious. "Who do you think you are?"

"Someone who told you to let go," she answered in half a snarl. He picked the wrong woman.

Tommy pointed his finger at her. "I can get you fired for this."

"Do whatever you have to," Sabrina said carelessly.

Clark slapped Tommy's finger away. "You wouldn't bother. You, the big fight promoter, the ladies' man being taken down by a one-hundred-twenty-pound woman? I'm sure that would make great press. I wonder where my editor is right now."

"You a reporter?" Tommy asked nervously.

"*Vegas Sun,* via the *Chicago Sun Times.*" Clark held his hand out to Tommy. "Clark Hunter."

Tommy looked confused and unsure of what to do. "Nothing happened here, man. You don't need to print anything. I could sue you if you did."

Clark shrugged. "Or you could guarantee I won't tell the world you got beat down by a beautiful woman by granting me an interview about the fight."

Tommy nodded. "I could give you a quote or two."

Clark shook his head. "Not a quote or two. I want a sit-down interview. Today. You're free at three. That's when you like to watch *General Hospital.* You can skip an episode today."

"How do you know that?" Tommy looked around as if he thought he was the center of a cosmic joke.

Sabrina let out an exasperated sigh. "I'm just going to leave you and your new best friend alone."

"No, Sabrina," Clark said. "Tommy was just leaving. He's gotta find his assistant and make sure he sets me up at three. Right?"

Sabrina watched with amusement as Tommy nodded in agreement. He was very uneasy with Clark's confidence and assurance. She could see he wasn't too interested in disagreeing with a man who saw him get taken down by a woman and knew he watched soap operas.

He gave Sabrina one last hateful look, which was returned with equal fire, before strutting past them both.

"What are you doing here?" Sabrina asked. She was holding on to her anger at Tommy for Clark. She would need it for protection.

"Thanks for the appreciation." Clark was just happy to see her again.

"Appreciation for what?"

"I just helped you out here!" He pointed to the door that Tommy had just slammed behind him.

"You helped me?" She laughed. "Just like a man. For your information, I saved myself."

"Yes, but if I hadn't come—"

"I would have saved myself again."

"You still owe me a thank-you."

"For what?" She bit her lower lip to fight the smile that wanted to come. He was so cocky.

"You took care of yourself, yes," he admonished her. "With the self-defense lessons you learned from the class that I talked you into taking."

Sabrina gestured her impatience, slapping her arms at her sides. Clark wasn't going for it. He stared back at her with that very familiar accomplished smile on his face and she couldn't fight it anymore. Her smile came out, cheek to cheek.

"Thank you," she said with a curtsy. "You're right. I remember."

Clark's face softened. He missed her smile. It was so tender, so genuine. "I remember you telling me that you didn't need it."

"I remember you jumping at me from around the kitchen corner in my apartment and scaring the living daylights out of me to make your point that I did."

Clark knew he was making a mistake, but he couldn't help himself. "I remember after you quit hitting me, we made love for two hours."

Sabrina's lips parted, and a sigh escaped them. She remembered that too, and as it flashed before her, the passion seemed to sweep through her body.

Clark was pulled to her as her eyes became wistful and bright. His own unspoken pain responded to the indefinable emotion that traveled between them. His hand reached for her face as if by instinct. He wanted, needed to touch her.

"Sabrina, I . . ."

The sudden vibrations that raced through Sabrina made her step back just in time, before he touched her. She wanted to walk away, but her knees felt weak and she wasn't sure she could.

"You just saw what happened to the last guy who tried to do that."

Clark couldn't ignore the hunger that was swirling

in his gut, in his groin. Sabrina had always been able to get him going in a second.

"But he doesn't know you like I do, Sabrina. He doesn't know that underneath that austere and composed shell is a woman full of fire."

"And ice," she said, her voice catching in her throat. "For you at least."

Sabrina felt a force pulling her to him. Suddenly they were only inches from each other. Had she stepped forward or had he? She wasn't sure and her body didn't care.

"Even your ice is hot," Clark said as his body was urging him to do what his mind told him would only bring him hell. He could never think when he was near this woman.

When his hand touched her waist, Sabrina felt the electricity rush through her. She was helpless to his touch, which was like water after a lifetime in the desert. His hands tightened and he pulled her to him. Sabrina's whole being was filled with wild urgency. The intensity of his manhood flared before her in the passion she could see in his eyes. She was entranced.

When his lips came down on hers, Sabrina's heart jolted and her body pulsed with excitement. Her heart was beating rapidly, hammering in her ears. The warmth of his lips sent tingles all the way down to her toes. The hunger his lips showed her awakened a giant within.

Clark could feel her lips softening, her body melting into his as it was made to do. It only encouraged his desire to ravage her. The moment of touching her full, sensuous lips sent him ablaze with a whisper of insanity. He squeezed her tighter, wanting to mold her body into his as his lips searched further, deeper, harder. His life meant nothing between the last time he had kissed her and now.

The desire overflowing within Sabrina was so intense it felt more like pain than anything else, making her suddenly realize what it was she was doing and where it was they were going. She had only a second before she lost her mind.

When she pushed away, Clark knew not to push back. He took a few steps backward just in case his body wouldn't want to listen to his mind, which it didn't. As he looked at her tortured face, he felt almost blinded by the passion still waving through him.

"I'm sorry, Sabrina. I'm so sorry."

"You promised to stay away from me." Sabrina felt humiliated and embarrassed for letting herself want him, for kissing him. "You promised to keep your distance."

"I didn't come here to do . . ." This wasn't true—Clark knew that. He wasn't going to lie to her. He never had and he never would. "Sabrina, I didn't intend to upset you. That's the truth."

"What do you know about the truth?" she asked.

He could accuse her of wanting him too, but he wasn't that type of man. He took responsibility for his own behavior. She never understood that. "I don't think I'll be able to avoid you. I'm staying at the hotel and I'm going to be at the prefight party Thursday night. We'll be running into each other."

"And you just thought you might hit it for old times' sake?"

"Don't be crass, Sabrina. It doesn't fit you."

"You so sure of that, Clark? I mean, you might

know me better than Tommy Gaxton, but you don't know me as well as you think you do. You didn't know that I wouldn't take your crap. You probably thought you could come back out here and get right back in there."

"I never thought that," Clark said. "I know it's over between us. I know you're with Nick now. I don't—"

"What?"

"I don't want you back," he said. "Not if it means I'll have to live with a guilt I haven't earned."

Sabrina forgot about any mention of Nick in Clark's last words. They stung her more than she could imagine because she knew deep down inside she should have been happy to hear them, but she wasn't.

"That's a good thing," she said, hearing her voice shaking like her stomach. "Because you'll never get me back. And if you come anywhere near me again, what I did to Tommy is going to look like flirting after what I'll do to you!"

Clark was certain the entire Las Vegas strip could hear her slam the door when she left.

He was a jackass. He had known that for quite some time, but for some reason felt compelled to remind himself of it in the most painful way again and again. These were going to be the longest, most painful few days of his life. So why did he not want them to end?

As he headed for the door, hoping to create a safe buffer between himself and Sabrina, Clark noticed the cell phone half hidden by the podium. Picking it up, he read the lighted LED display: CASH MAN.

A smile crossed Clark's face. He flipped open the

phone and pressed the button that displayed the most recent incoming calls: SILVER INC.

"Interesting," he said, his investigative nature building the outline for his suspicion. "Why would Tommy Gaxton be calling one of the most famous sports bookies in the country?"

He was certain there was some law that was being broken. It was generally deemed inappropriate for a promoter or manager to bet on a fight involving his own fighter. If any did, generally all the proceeds went to charity. Clark was sure there were some legal issues around a promoter or manager betting on a fight where both fighters were his, as in this case. He remembered reading about a recent Vegas fight under investigation where a promoter had conspired with one of his fighters to take a dive so one of his other fighters could win because the other fighter's next opportunity was a much more promotable and profitable fight.

Clark cleared the pad and pressed the button displaying the most recent outgoing calls: BANK OF GRAND CAYMAN.

"Hey!"

Clark looked up as Tommy Gaxton flung the ballroom door open. Tommy was rushing for him, but Clark knew he wasn't coming after him. He wanted his phone.

"I'm sorry," Clark said, holding the phone out. "Is this yours? I was just curious."

Tommy snatched the phone from him, looking at it as if to check for damage. "You need to quit messing with what doesn't belong to you."

Clark shrugged innocently. "I didn't know who it belonged to."

Tommy sneered at him. "You reporters."

"You reporters? We reporters have made you famous, Tommy. Which reminds me, what about our interview?"

"I'll get back to you," he called out with his back to Clark as he rushed out of the ballroom.

Clark had no expectation of Tommy getting back to him. Tommy was smarter than he looked. He knew Clark was on to something, and he was right.

FOUR

Sabrina could see his lips moving, but she couldn't hear a word he was saying. Everything that came out of Brad Nagle's mouth sounded garbled and incoherent. She would have canceled her dinner with the man who had agreed to be the architect for her upcoming career day, but Dionne had told her Brad was waffling and it was too late to let anything go wrong for a day that was very important to Sabrina.

Being a local kid, born and raised in the hardest part of Las Vegas, Brad was exactly what the career day was all about. He had battled a fatherless home, an alcoholic mother, and mean streets. He made his way to college, put himself through, and was now working at Las Vegas's top architectural firm and living in a luxury home in the foothills of Southern Highlands, which he designed himself.

This was why Sabrina kept her dinner date with Brad at Brizola, the Acropolis's top-grade steak house. She knew there was still the *O* show at the Bellagio to go. It was the hottest ticket in town and Brad had never seen it. She had promised to garner front-row tickets for him and his wife to join her. She couldn't back out of that.

The problem was, after kissing Clark earlier that day, Sabrina had been a zombie. All she could think of was the way it made her feel. The way kissing him always made her feel. Memories she tried so hard to forget quickly washed back over her, keeping her in a daze and an emotional mess all day.

She was embarrassed, letting a man interfere with her professionalism, but that had no effect. Besides, Sabrina knew that Clark was more than a man. He was *the man*. The man that, no matter what happened, she would love more than she had ever loved or would ever love any other man. The way that kiss made her feel etched that fact in stone.

"That's very interesting," Sabrina said, sensing a pause in the conversation. She hoped her response was relevant. "Tell me more about that."

As he went on about what he would say to the children, Sabrina had to resist the urge to bring her fingers to her lips as she had already done several times that day. She wanted to touch them and feel the warmth rush through her again. Dionne had threatened to slap her if she saw her do it once more. Maybe that was what she needed, a good slap in the face to get her back into the real world.

Be careful what you ask for.

As he slid into the booth just across from the one she was in, Clark appeased the waitress, who giggled and flipped her hair back flirtatiously.

Sabrina felt her heart begin to beat faster and was suddenly uncomfortable in her own skin, which was experiencing a tingling sensation all over. The man had a way to make a plain white T-shirt and a pair of khaki shorts look better than anything in *GQ* magazine. It was the confidence in which he carried himself, knowing he looked good no matter what he had on.

It was that confidence that he could also take too far. Like now, as he casually looked up from his menu and made eye contact with Sabrina. His smile spoke to her, telling her he had always known she was there.

Sabrina wanted to look away, but she couldn't. She wanted to give him the finger, but she didn't. Her body was heating up like a finely stoked ember. She felt her hands beginning to sweat. Her brow.

No! she was screaming to herself, hoping to find the strength to listen. *Don't let him do this to you. The entire relationship, you let this man have power over your body. Be strong! Be strong! Please? Pretty please?*

As difficult as it was, Sabrina finally tore herself away, but it made no difference. She could feel his eyes on her and they were making her heart do cartwheels.

How was it possible to want a man you hated? Sabrina had always thought this was what made being a woman so much better than being a man. Men were led by their penis, which was how they got into so much trouble in the first place. Women, on the other hand, had the ability to reject their urgings for someone they were physically attracted to if the emotional and mental weren't there.

Especially if the emotional and mental were repulsed.

So what was going on here?

As the waitress returned, Sabrina looked in Clark's direction again. The waitress partly shielded him from her, making her feel a little more relaxed. One of Clark's most charming features was the fact that when he spoke to you, no matter who you were, he looked directly at you. He made you feel as if you were all that mattered. It wasn't anything sexual and it worked with men just as well as women. It was just special, and everyone loved someone who made them feel that way.

Sabrina remembered it all too well.

"Sabrina?" Brad stared at her, confused. "Sabrina?"

Sabrina broke from her Clark-induced trance. "Yes?"

"Have you been listening to a word I've said?" he asked, skeptical.

"I . . . Of course I have. I just . . ." *Think, quick!* He'd mentioned something about his childhood, hadn't he? "I was just taking it all in."

Brad's laugh held a little uneasiness. "I just asked if you would excuse me to the men's room for a second."

Idiot! She cursed Clark under her breath. "Sure. I'm sorry. Go right ahead."

Sabrina knew what was going to happen the second Brad left. Her body was filled with the anticipation while she tried to convince herself it wasn't what she wanted. It was and there was nothing she could do about that. So she waited.

She didn't have to wait long.

Clark resisted the urge to slide right next to her and kiss her, which is what he really wanted to do. All he wanted to do. Instead, he slid into the booth across from her with the most harmless smile he could form. It wasn't doing any good.

"Does Nick know about this?" he asked.

"What?"

"Your dinner plans." He couldn't help feeling envious of any man who would have Sabrina's attention for an evening. "Who is he?"

"What are you doing here?"

"I'm getting dinner. I'm a guest here, remember?"

"Please, Clark." She picked at her barely touched plate of food, already feeling her body react to him. "Don't start this again."

Clark knew what she was talking about and it hurt him. "I'm not stalking you, Sabrina. I'm not crazy."

"You're here, aren't you?"

"I can't say that I wasn't looking forward to seeing you again after we kissed, but I'm not stalking you. Back then . . . Back then, you have to understand what I was going through."

"I was a little busy trying to understand what I was going through," she said. "And you wouldn't leave me alone."

"What did you expect me to do? I loved you, Sabrina, and you were leaving me. I may have been a bit aggressive, but I felt like I was fighting for my life. You were my life."

Sabrina's eyes softened. He seemed so sincere. It didn't make any sense. "Then why didn't you just admit to it? Why did you have to make it worse with your lies?"

Clark looked away. He could never win this one. "Sabrina, I've told you why one million times."

"I showed you—"

"You're starting to sound like a broken record, Sabrina." He knew his words were harsh, but he refused to go back to this. "I told you those pictures were doctored. I never heard the tapes, but—"

"It was your voice," she said quickly. "You can't tell me that was a fake. I know your voice, Clark."

"I never ever said those things to Cara."

Sabrina leaned forward. "So you admit to being with her?"

"No." Clark shook his head vehemently. "I only knew Cara from a story I had done on her brother. I spoke with her less than three times. Look, Sabrina, please stop this. I understand why you did what you did. But you can't sit here and tell me that you don't doubt—"

"No, Clark." She held up her hand to stop him. "I don't doubt. I can't."

"Why not?" he asked. "Because it would be too late? Wouldn't it be worth the risk if it wasn't?"

Sabrina looked down as Clark's hand slowly traveled across the table toward her own. Her entire body began to shake. Her heart was screaming inside her and she felt as if she would break down in tears at the possibility.

"Clark Hunter!"

His hand just inches from Sabrina's, Clark looked up to see a sheepishly grinning man, Sabrina's returning dinner date, who seemed uncomfortably excited to see him.

"Do I know you?" Clark asked.

"No, man." He pressed his hand against his forehead. "I'm a big fan of yours. I read your articles in *Sports Illustrated*. You're like my favorite sports reporter. I see you all the time when you do your stuff on ESPN."

Clark received his outstretched hand, familiar with this type of thing in Chicago. It was flattering, although the timing wasn't too great. "Thanks, man. I didn't know I made it all the way out here."

He looked at Sabrina, who was managing a nervous smile. The timing wasn't great at all.

"Clark Hunter," she said, "this is Brad Nagle. He's a local architect who is helping me out with a career day the Acropolis is planning for local high school kids."

Brad slid into the booth next to Sabrina, his hand reaching out to Clark. "I'm really honored to meet you. I've read both of your books. Awesome."

"Thanks," Clark said.

"How do you two know each other?" Brad asked.

"It's a long story," Clark said.

"Not worth going into," Sabrina added, ignoring the quick glare from Clark. "Clark is in town for the fight this weekend."

"So this is a business dinner," Clark said. "I thought I was interrupting a date."

"Geez, no." Brad laughed. "I'm married. Wife is eight months—"

"You're right," Sabrina said. "It is a business dinner. So if you don't mind."

"Hey!" Brad's eyes lit up. "I just had a great idea. What are you doing tonight, man?"

"Nothing," Clark said, knowing what was coming and seeing how uncomfortable it was making Sabrina as she knew it too.

"Brad—" Sabrina tried.

"You should come with us," Brad said, ignoring her. "I just called to check on my wife and she's feeling a little too uncomfortable to join us for *O.*"

"That circus show?"

"It's more than a circus show," Sabrina said. "And I don't think that Clark wants to see that."

"Sure I do." Clark leaned back in the booth. "That was on my list anyway."

Sabrina knew that Clark would rather eat dirt than sit through a theater performance. He was doing this to get to her.

"Great!" Brad looked as if he would leap off the seat. "So it's settled. Hey, man, why don't you order something? We have a little time."

"I'm not that hungry," Clark said. He looked at Sabrina's plate of filet mignon and smashed red potatoes. He was hungry. "I'll just eat what Sabrina's left over."

Sabrina sighed as Clark grabbed her plate and slid it toward him. This was all wrong. She should be upset, worried, anything other than what she was feeling now. It was that same feeling she had had when she first met Clark and he had imposed himself into her life, much to her annoyance.

Sweet anticipation and curiosity.

She couldn't give in to it this time like she had always done before. The stakes were too high.

O was one of the most beautiful performances Sabrina had ever seen. Unique in so many ways, it was performed by the famous Cirque du Soleil group at the luxury, four-star Bellagio Hotel on the strip. The show was an entirely original form of theater. A mixture of circus, theater, and magic performed by over eighty artists in, on, and above 1.5 million gallons of water. It was a fantastic escape for Sabrina, which she badly needed when she first arrived in Vegas. She had already seen the show five times and was able to dream through the entire show.

Until tonight.

Tonight, even with all of the fantasy and drama playing itself out in front of her eyes, Sabrina could only think of the man sitting next to her and the electricity his closeness sparked inside her. As the show went on, the tension between them increased with frightening intensity. The infinity and elegance of the performance were lost in the desire and promise that she once felt for the man next to her. With every second that passed, with every sideways glance exchanged between the two of them, Sabrina felt herself lost in his presence, his masculine scent, and wanting more and more to have his arms around her and his lips touch hers again.

Just as she always had. As if the last five months had never happened. But she knew that was a bigger dream than even Cirque du Soleil could create. A bigger dream than her heart had the courage to wake up from for the moment.

Clark was mesmerized. He wasn't much for theater, always considering himself a meat and potatoes man. He allowed Sabrina to drag him to this place and that out of affection for her. Sometimes he would surprise himself and actually enjoy it. Rarely. But this . . . this show was compelling and drew him in right away. It began as entertainment and curiosity, but its smooth, flawless delivery got inside him just as Sabrina's presence sitting next to him was doing.

Both effects were molding into memories and fantasies of what it had been like, could be like between them. The fluid way in which the actors moved reminded him of how perfection was when he made love to Sabrina. Their bodies had been carved to fit each other, their motions shared telepathically. What he watched before him seemed too perfect to be rehearsed. It had to be natural, just as every moment he and Sabrina touched each other. This was why he didn't like coming to these types of shows. They turned him into a sap.

Still, the emotion won him over and when Clark turned to Sabrina once more, he was warmed by the fact that she was already looking at him. He smiled tenderly, looking into her eyes. "It's beautiful."

"Much more than a circus," Sabrina answered, certain he could hear her heart beat above the noise. Since he was always on the go and looking for excitement, Sabrina appreciated these few moments when Clark's softer side came through.

She turned away, feeling his arm accidentally rub against hers. She didn't move away. She didn't want to. The comfort, the familiarity that had been missing for what seemed like forever felt so perfect, so appropriate right now. Sabrina shut her brain off, not thinking about the implications of her rash behavior. The show would only last another half hour. Reality could wait until then.

Just before the show ended, Brad excused himself to answer his vibrating beeper. Only his wife had the number. It didn't matter. Sabrina and Clark barely noticed he was gone. As the show performed its startling finale, the excitement rushed through the wildly applauding crowd. Sabrina felt like she was coming down from a high, because now reality would set back in and nobody wanted that.

When Brad returned, he had to make his way through an already moving crowd.

"You missed the ending," Sabrina said with an apologetic tone as soon as he reached them. She noticed his expression was harried. "What's wrong?"

"It's my wife," he said. "She's gone into labor. I have to go."

"Do you need a ride to the hospital?" Clark asked.

"I'm fine. I'm catching a cab out front."

"You'd better hurry," Sabrina urged. "With this show letting out, there's going to be a line for cabs in a hurry."

"Thanks, but I have a guy looking out for me," Brad said. "He's going to get me in the next one when I show up. I'm sorry, Sabrina."

"No." She pushed him forward. "Don't even say that. Just go. Hurry and good luck!"

He was waving and yelling something incoherent as he rushed away.

"So," Clark said as Sabrina turned to him. "It's just you and me."

"Does it ever cool down in this town?" Clark asked.

They finally reached the employees' parking lot at the Acropolis, having walked a couple of blocks from the Bellagio, and Clark was building up a sweat.

A block on the strip was a good quarter mile. It was after ten in the evening and it hadn't seemed to him that the heat had let up a bit.

"It's Las Vegas," Sabrina said. As soon as she spotted her car in the distance, she felt the tenseness in her body begin to release. It would soon be over. "It's the desert in June."

"Who would build all of this in the middle of the desert? It has to be miserable here for most of the year."

"I told you that you didn't have to walk me." She stopped in front of her car, knowing that every second with Clark was weakening her. "I can manage a couple of blocks."

"I'm walking this way anyway." The truth was Clark wanted to spend every minute he could manage with Sabrina. "I'm staying at this hotel, remember?"

Sabrina pointed toward the grandly styled entrance. "The hotel is that way. Good night, Clark."

Clark didn't leave. He just stood there, staring at her, and Sabrina knew she was in trouble. Her senses were at full alert as he took one step closer. He had that look on his face that she knew all too well. A look that always made her change her mind.

"It was nice," he said, his voice softer, with an emotional vein to it.

"It was," she offered with a tender smile.

"Just like old times." It became suddenly clearer to Clark than ever before that he had been lying to himself these past few months. He had been doing everything to convince himself that no matter what attraction he still felt for Sabrina, he accepted that it was over. He could never accept it, because

Sabrina was more than a pleasant memory. Times spent with her were more than treasured moments. She was it. She was everything.

"Clark, stop." Sabrina heard her voice in protest sound as weak as the intention behind it.

"Kind of like those Chicago summer nights," Clark continued. "Not quite like this, because we had that smothering humidity. Just hanging out like a couple of kids without a care in the world after a Cubs game, or a long walk down Michigan Avenue."

Sabrina let the memories wash over her, relaxing in the joy of them. Without a care in the world. She had thought it would last forever.

Clark watched as she reacted to his words. She didn't try to hide her feelings. Sabrina wasn't into playing those games. That was one of the many things he loved about her.

"Sabrina?"

"Yes?" Unnerved by her body's signals, Sabrina wasn't thinking straight.

"I forgive you."

A tornado slammed into her chest. If the car hadn't been behind her to lean against, she would have fallen to the ground.

With her eyes wide in disbelief she screamed out, "What?"

"I said I forgive you." Clark knew he was going to get in trouble with this, but he had to do it. He had to pull out all of the stops if this was ever going to be resolved. High stakes, but he was going for the big win.

"You forgive me for what?" Her hands were already on her hips. She felt as if her head were about to explode. She was almost too breathless with rage to speak clearly. "And this better be over something I said or did tonight, because if you—"

"For not trusting me." Clark stayed calm. Nothing would work if they both got excited. "I know that one day you will realize that I never cheated on you and you're going to feel awful."

Sabrina's mouth opened, but there were no words to be found. She felt as if she were suddenly in one of many nightmares she'd had about Clark in the last four months. Was she going crazy?

Clark stayed the storm. "I don't want you to feel that way, so I'm forgiving you ahead of time."

"You son of a bitch!" Sabrina's hand went flying and connected with his left cheek.

Clark felt the sting and, besides the shock of it, he couldn't say he didn't like it. He couldn't say it wasn't worth it to see Sabrina this way. All fired up. It wasn't easy to get her like this. It usually took some getting angry, but the reward was always worth it.

He grabbed her at her waist, the force of his body coming on hers, pushing her against the car. Sabrina felt her body in a panic. Not for fear of what he would do to her, but for fear of her body demanding he do it. Desperate to be saved from her own insatiable need for him, she raised her hand again, but this time Clark's head fell back and her hand breezed by him.

"I'll bite you," she warned.

"You forget," he said, with tunnel vision for nothing but the wine of those lips. "I like that."

When his mouth came down on hers, Sabrina's mind told her she would turn away, but that wasn't what happened. What happened was her mouth met his with a rage of heat, hard and searching for the ecstasy only his lips could bring. Fire raged through her veins as his mouth possessed her body and then her soul.

Sabrina wrapped her arms around him, pulling him toward her even though he couldn't get any closer. Clark's calm had been shattered by the fierceness of her anger at him and now his soul was brought to its knees by the warmth and comfort of her lips. Drugging him as his tongue went deep into her mouth, her womanliness sang through his veins.

Sabrina heard herself moan as Clark's lips left hers and sent slow, torturous kisses down her neck. With his hands, he desperately untucked her silk blouse. When Clark's fingers made contact with the soft hot flesh of her belly, he groaned.

"Clark." His name escaped with a gasp from Sabrina as his heightening passion sent currents of burning desire through her. Her hands were feeling frantically everywhere, her body yearning, begging for what it had always craved and always would.

Clark's arousal threatened to send him over the edge as his hand felt the creamy flesh of her inner thighs. His need was stoked by the sounds Sabrina made as his hand moved up, higher and higher. He felt the edges of her satin panties with his eager fingers.

Lava-hot flames rushed through Sabrina as his fingers brushed against the fabric right at the center of her pleasure. A flush of heat rippled through her entire body before an intense shock hit her when Clark suddenly pulled away.

"No." Sabrina's voice was low and breathy as she reached for him. To feel his body pulling away from hers was like being stripped naked. She didn't want this to end. Ever. "Don't stop, Clark."

"No." Clark stumbled backward several steps, feeling a hot fever rage through him. "Not until you say it."

"Say what?" Sabrina felt as if she would say anything to get those lips back on hers at this point.

"We can't be together until you say that you believe me." He was looking into her eyes with an intensity to match his conviction.

"Clark, not now." She reached for him, but he stepped back farther. She didn't care who was looking. She wanted him. "Don't do this now."

"Right now," he said. "Right here. You tell me you believe me when I swore to you on my mother's grave, on my life, that I never slept with anyone while we were together and that I never wanted you for your money."

Sabrina leaned back against the car again, unable to stand up straight any longer. She felt insanity whisper at her. Wanting, not knowing, believing, unable to think clearly.

"Sabrina." His voice held that hint of desperation he only let her see or hear. "I'm waiting for you. Tell me what you believe."

"I don't know!" This time she was certain she was getting looks. Like every night in Vegas, the streets, parking lots, everywhere anyone could be was full of people, but you had to really do something to get any amount of consideration.

"What do you mean?" Clark asked.

"I don't know what I believe anymore." Sabrina

felt suddenly overwhelmed and terribly emotional. "I can't . . ."

"What?" Clark stepped closer this time. He had to get her to where she did know.

Sabrina looked at him, a tear falling down her left cheek. They all said they didn't do it. They all did, didn't they? It was never true. She had the pictures. What did he want her to give up for him? All sense of reason. *Stop it!* She was yelling at herself now. If she was going to believe something, it had to make sense, didn't it? Believing him made no sense.

"I don't know what I believe," she said. "I can't tell you what you want to hear."

Clark didn't know why he expected so much. Possibly the evening, the time spent together again made him jump ahead of himself. He was prone to that. It had all gotten to his head. This woman had gotten to his head, but he knew he was right. She would know too.

"It doesn't have to be what I want to hear," he said. "But it has to be something. Can you sit here and tell me that you know beyond a doubt that I cheated on you? That you are as certain as you've ever been that I was marrying you just for the money you stand to inherit one day? I'm doing real well myself in that area."

She shook her head, unable to speak the words that she had been so sure of. The words that she was sure would define the rest of her love life no matter how much time had passed. The words she had staked the demise of the dream life she had always wanted on. All she could do was shake her head.

"Good," he said. "So now you have to look into your heart, Sabrina."

"Don't tell me what I have to do," she snapped with all the pride she had left at that moment. "I don't have to do anything."

"Yes, you do. For both of us, Sabrina. Neither of us will ever be able to get on with our lives until you do. I haven't, and no matter who you see, Nick or anyone else, you can't lie to me and tell me you have. That kiss spoke louder than any words you could muster."

Denying himself the touch of what he wanted more than anything in the world, Clark turned and headed for the hotel.

"Clark!" she called after him, but knew he wouldn't turn around.

"You better be dying!"

"Lauren, I need you to do something for me." Clark paused. "Don't hang up."

"When are you telling me that you're dying?"

"I am dying," Clark said. "In a way, I've been dying since February and I need you to help bring me back to life."

"It's after freaking one in the morning, Clark."

"I need you to go by my apartment."

"That sty?"

"Lauren, just listen. You know where my set of spare keys are in my work desk. Go to my place. In my home office, open the bottom drawer of the dresser next to the window. There will be a purple folder in that drawer."

"On who, what?"

"The name is Cara Milton."

"That chick you slept with?"

Clark banged the phone against the night table in his hotel room before returning it to his ear. "Don't mess with me, Lauren."

"You think you can call me at one in the morning on a Wednesday and I'm not going to get anything out of it? Fat chance."

"I was trying to track her down to get her to tell Sabrina the truth, but I couldn't find her and I was too busy trying to get Sabrina's attention. Then I just got stubborn and—"

"Stubborn for what?"

"Because I didn't think I needed that woman to prove me trustworthy. Listen, that's neither here nor there. I need to finish what I started with Cara. I need to find her and find out why she did this."

"Somebody must've made some progress." She formed the words in a song.

"Or I could've put myself further in the hole."

"I don't think that's possible."

"We're talking about me here."

"You're right. Are you doing any actual work? Because as much as I love the drama, Levy's gonna kill you if you don't make a story out of this."

"I've got that end covered. Can I count on you?"

"I'll call you tomorrow."

"When?"

"At a time that I hope will be the most inconvenient for you."

He heard the click and smiled as he hung up. Sitting on the edge of his bed, Clark knew he wasn't getting any sleep that night, but that didn't matter.

The look on Sabrina's face was all he needed to get through to tomorrow.

Doubt.

He was staking everything on it.

Sabrina couldn't resist. She had to look at them. She had placed them in the bottom of a shoe box underneath several other boxes in the back of the closet of her guest bedroom in the condo as if this was the only way to silence them. Since moving to Las Vegas, she only gave in to them twice. That was good, considering how many times she was tempted to.

It was much better than in Chicago, when she would fall asleep drenched in tears with them at the foot of her bed on a nightly basis. So many times she had wanted to throw them away, knew that she should have, but never could.

The pictures.

Sabrina was sweating by the time she reached them. Something compelled her to look at them. The kiss. When she finally composed herself enough to drive home and was safely in her apartment, Sabrina's entire body had been shaking uncontrollably. Not just because of the kiss, although that would have been enough. It was the doubt. That doubt that she had never allowed herself to consider feeling. She had been a woman of reason all of her life. She wasn't going to desert that.

When this mystery woman had appeared out of nowhere claiming to be Clark's other woman,

Sabrina laughed it off. Clark had been a player before he met her. His reputation was well known, but she had changed him. She was certain she had, because he showed her time and time again. She hadn't even mentioned that first encounter to him.

Then the pictures arrived in the mail and Sabrina almost passed out. There were only three, but that was enough. Three pictures of Clark with the woman who gave her name as Cara. One picture was of the two of them eating outside a café, smiling at each other. Another was of them in bed, under the covers, looking at each other with their faces only inches apart. The third showed her still in bed, her hand reaching to caress Clark's back as he sat on the edge of the mattress in nothing but his underwear. There was a sticky attached to the last picture with the words: THEY GET BETTER, IN CASE YOU'RE INTERESTED.

As if on cue, the phone rang. Sabrina could hardly breathe. She stumbled for the phone, hoping it was someone, anyone who could help her, or better yet, wake her up.

"Did you get the pictures?" the female voice asked.

"What?" Sabrina could hardly speak. "Who—"

"You didn't believe me," she continued, "so I sent you some pictures. If you want more, I have more. I told you he was no good."

"You . . ." Sabrina was filled with a scalding fury, but she was too confused to focus it. "How dare you!"

"Don't try to accuse me of taking your man, 'cause he was never your man."

"You think he's yours?"

"He was neither of ours."

"He loves me!" Sabrina had no idea why she was even bothering to say this to this woman. This devil. "You're nothing!"

"I'm doing you a favor, girl. You could have married him and it would have been too late."

"Too late for what?"

"Listen to this."

After a short pause, Sabrina heard a click and a scratchy background came through, followed by voices.

"Clark." It was her voice. "You don't love her. You love me."

"You're wrong on both counts." The voice was clearly Clark's. Sabrina could tell that in a second. "I have to go, Cara."

"Wait," she pleaded. "She doesn't know about us. Why does it have to end?"

"We have to make sacrifices for our goals."

Sabrina's eyes closed in pain as she squeezed the phone tight.

"You haven't gotten caught. She's not suspicious, is she?"

"It's risky, Cara. There's a lot of money involved."

"I can't believe you're willing to give it up and spend your life with that ice princess just for money. She won't even get it all until her father dies."

"The money is there," he said. "It's a matter of waiting."

Sabrina fell to her knees in the middle of her living room.

"Clark, I don't think I can stand to be away from you. No man has ever made love to me like you do."

"It's a cash cow, Cara. Some would say only a fool would pass it up."

Click. There was a short pause.

"He only wanted you for your money." Her voice held a ring of finality.

"Why did you do this?"

"Not to hurt you," she said. "You see, I believe in sisterhood."

"So you slept with my fiancé!"

"Okay, so to hell with sisterhood. I just don't take getting dumped very well. I wanted to make sure Clark doesn't get what he wants. You should thank me."

"I'm gonna tear your eyes out," Sabrina said, meaning every word. "Now how about not being such a coward and tell me who you are and where I can find you?"

"Ask Clark. He knows me." With a loud smirk, she hung up the phone.

That night, Sabrina had stayed for hours in that same spot where she had fallen in her living room. Just like tonight, as she leaned against the closet door, looking at the pictures. The pictures that changed her life, broke her heart, and destroyed everything she always wanted.

How could she doubt?

FIVE

"Your turn."

Clark wasn't listening. Standing against the wall outside the press room of the Acropolis, he was consumed with thoughts of Sabrina and the possibility of being with her again. He would never admit it to a soul, not even to her, how much it mattered to him. He felt like a betrayer of men, needing a woman so much.

Living in a world of professional sports, Clark saw how so many women were treated like dirt. Not that they were all innocent victims in the least, but there was definitely a culture of viewing women as only worth whatever these godlike men wanted to use them for at the moment. The sad thing was that a lot of women accepted that. Either way, the attitude was that they weren't needed or even loved. Clark had never bought into that, but he had lived carelessly when it came to women.

Until he met Sabrina. She changed everything

about him. She made him want to be everything she needed, could rely on and depend on. He wanted her to look at him and know through her heart and soul that she would never need to look any further. Ever.

"Hey!" The tall, dark, and burly bodyguard snapped his fat fingers. "You listening to me?"

Clark jolted back to reality. "What?"

"You're Clark Hunter, right?" He leaned in, his bright eyes drilling into Clark.

"Yeah."

"Get the hell in there, then."

When he entered, Clark saw a familiar scene. Artemis Grove sat stretched in a luxury, leather chair, surrounded by his crew of admirers. A lot of star athletes liked to surround themselves with people who reinforced their royal identity. People who told them everything they did was right. Everything bad that happened was someone else's fault. Everything they wanted, they deserved to have. It was a dangerous thing.

Artemis's almost raven-black skin was shining like crystal and his muscles were taut. He had a masterful body. A scantily clad woman sat on each side of him, manicuring his nails, with another standing behind him, braiding his shoulder-length hair into two braids. Behind him, members of his crew were drinking the expensive liquor and eating the catered food the hotel most likely comped him with.

"Come on in, my brother!" He waved Clark over as another oversized goon directed Clark to a bean-bag type of chair a few feet from Artemis.

"Thanks for taking the time, Artemis." Clark sat down.

With a quick scan of the room, Clark noted that there were at least ten men he could certainly not take on if things got dicey. That wasn't a good sign.

"I'm a fan of yours," Artemis said. "You're becoming a popular guy. You could be bigger than you are if you wanted to. You could be making millions."

"I do all right." Clark sighed, going for his first punch. "If I wanted to get it all, it would mean selling out, and I'm not in that game."

Artemis's expression quickly changed, as his face became darker. He had a broad, commanding nose that flared up a bit. Clark could see a flint of guilt hit him before he covered it up. When Alicia made her front-porch confession, Clark knew the fix was in and that Artemis knew about it. Seeing *Silver Inc.*, as in Benny Silver's name, on Tommy's cell phone was just the icing on the cake.

"You got ten minutes, like the rest of them."

"Where's Tommy?"

"He's conducting business right now. You come to talk to him or me?"

"You of course." Clark knew Tommy was suspicious of him, but wondered how much of that suspicion he shared with Artemis.

"Then talk."

"You seem on edge, Artemis. Nervous?"

Artemis laughed out loud, joined by the women, who had no clue as to what they were laughing at. "You joking, right? That's a joke, because I know you're known as a kind of funny guy."

Clark didn't laugh. "Seriously. You look a little nervous."

Artemis gave him a warning stare. "I'm not nervous for nothing, man. Nobody makes me nervous. Especially not that wimp Rodriguez."

"Of course not." Clark was trying not to show how on edge he was. "You can beat him with your eyes closed."

"Yeah." Artemis scratched his nose, a sign of discomfort.

"Easily," Clark added. "Everybody knows that. I mean, look at the odds. Everyone has you knocking him out by the second round."

"Yeah." He shrugged. "Whatever."

"I mean, anyone betting against you is going to lose big." Clark knew he hit it on the head as Artemis's eyes tightened to slits. "But nobody's gonna do that. It would be crazy to bet against you in that fight."

All expression vanished from Artemis's face as he looked at Clark. He was waiting for the ball to drop, but Clark wasn't ready to drop it just yet.

"What about your wife?"

"What?" Artemis started as if he was going to stand up, and at least four of his crew headed for Clark.

Clark held his hand up, trying to stay calm. "Wait a second! I'm not trying to mess with you, man."

"My wife ain't none of your business!" Artemis sat back in his seat. "I don't talk about my family."

"Everyone knows what happened." Clark leaned away from an approaching bodyguard. "I just want to give you a chance to tell your side of the story."

"Hold up." Artemis waved his men back. "What do you mean?"

"When you don't talk, everyone assumes the worst. What do you have to say about it?"

Artemis was visibly unnerved at this point. He waved away the women around him, leaning forward in his chair. He looked at the floor for what seemed like a full minute. When he looked up, Clark could see the pain in his face. He was suffering inside for what he did. As well he should.

"I don't want to talk about it," Artemis said. "To you or anyone else. I love my wife and we'll work through this."

Clark believed his sincerity, but he knew from experience that love by itself wasn't enough to always work everything out. "I hope so, because it's tearing her up."

Artemis's lips pressed together as he glared at Clark. "What do you . . . What do you know?"

"I'm just saying," Clark said, "that if I had a family problem, I would make sure that every step I took was helping that problem. You fighting this Saturday: will this help or hinder that problem?"

Artemis was out of his chair now, prompting Clark to stand. If he was going to get the snot knocked out of him, he wanted to be standing while it happened.

"Your ten minutes are up."

"I haven't even asked you about your strategy for—"

When Alicia entered the room from a side door, her attention immediately came to Clark and her mouth opened in surprise. She glanced nervously from Clark to Artemis, and then back at Clark, who quickly turned away. Without hesitation, Alicia turned and headed back out the door she had just come from.

Clark looked at Artemis, who had observed every

bit of the awkward exchange. Artemis Grove was not the sharpest knife in the drawer, but neither was he an idiot.

"What in the hell are you up to?" With his fist clenched, he stepped closer to Clark.

Clark braced himself. "What are you talking about?"

"Why did she run out like that?" He grabbed Clark by the arms and backed him up until he was against the wall. "You been talking to my wife?"

"Artemis! Come on, man." Someone that Clark couldn't see was pleading with the fighter. Clark could only hope it would work.

"You don't want to do this, man," Clark said.

"I don't want to do what?" Artemis leaned in, his face only inches from Clark's. "Answer my question. You been talking to my wife?"

"You want to get arrested again?" Clark asked. "Unlike Alicia, I will press charges. The fight is in two days. You won't make it. Am I worth that?"

Artemis's fist, which clenched looked as big as a soccer ball, was raised. Clark ignored it, keeping his eyes locked with the fighter. Artemis suddenly turned away for a second. When his fist came forward, it made a hole in the wall right next to Clark's face.

When Artemis backed up, he didn't even appear fazed or hurt in the least. Clark heard himself let out a heavy sigh as he felt his body relax. He didn't need to be told again.

He was out of there.

Was she trying to sabotage what was left of her life? Sabrina wondered as she made her way to

Nick's office. How could she let that man kiss her? How could she throw herself at him the way she had? That had always been the question, hadn't it? Something about Clark Hunter brought out things in Sabrina that she didn't know she had. She was always one to pride herself on her sensibility, but Clark's touch made her lose all of that and it had frightened her to death at first. So much so, she had broken things off at one point. Clark pursued her vigorously to change her mind and she had eventually bared her soul to him.

"I'm scared!" Sabrina screamed out.

She kept her distance from Clark as they both stood in the kitchen of her Chicago apartment. He had begged his way inside, but she wasn't going to let him seduce her. The safest place she could think of was the kitchen. Everywhere else, she was afraid of being tempted.

"I don't understand," Clark said. The anguished look on his face told the story. He had been pursuing her for two weeks since she called him and said this was not the right relationship for her and she wanted out.

"I can't explain it, okay? You frighten me."

"What did I do to frighten you? I've never even raised my voice with you, Sabrina. I've never hurt a woman in my entire life."

"Not that kind of frightened." Sabrina turned away, ashamed of herself and her own feelings. She felt like a coward. "I mean, sexually."

Clark approached her from behind. When he placed his hands on her arms, Sabrina felt the heat shudder through her. She stepped away.

"This," she said, pointing to his hands. "This is what I'm talking about."

With a second's thought, Clark finally smiled. "I understand, Sabrina."

"No, you don't." She fiddled with nervous hands, unable to look him in the face. "You're so confident and . . . you don't know what it's like to . . ."

"To feel yourself lose control?" he asked. "To feel like you're tumbling into some wild fantasy, but it's real life and you're scared to death because you don't know what the outcome is? Wondering how you can be a good person if you want something so bad you don't care what the consequences are?"

Sabrina looked at him, amazed at his words, the words she had been screaming to herself as she paced her apartment, debating whether or not she should see him again.

"I feel them too, Sabrina. I feel them every time I touch you."

"You don't act like it," she said. "You act like this is nothing for you."

"Are you kidding me?" Clark laughed. "You have no idea how terrifying it is for me to know that one woman has this hold on me. That I'm with someone that could make me do anything she wanted and praying that she treats me right because even if she doesn't, I'm still hers."

"My life made sense before I met you," Sabrina said, feeling such comfort in her words, she couldn't describe. "I need things to make sense."

"Love isn't supposed to make sense," Clark said. "That's what makes it worth doing anything for.

There couldn't be any sense in that or no one would bother with it."

"So what do we do?" Sabrina asked.

Clark walked to her, gently taking her face in his hands. He looked down at her with an affectionate smile. "We go for it."

Sabrina felt her heart leaping in her chest. She was in love and he was just as scared as her. "Then let's go for it."

That night, she found out that one could be seduced in the kitchen.

Nothing has changed, Sabrina thought to herself as she stood at Nick's door. Nothing had changed and her body was still at his mercy.

Sabrina took a second to gather herself together before entering the office. It was a good thing this time. Usually she just walked right in, a privilege reserved only for her. Today, she was still reeling from last night with Clark and wanted to make sure she wasn't giving herself away before Nick saw her. She may have been willing to admit to herself she was having doubts, but she had too much pride to admit it to anyone else.

Just outside the door, Sabrina heard voices and leaned in to listen. She couldn't hear the words very well, but she recognized the tone. Both tones. Nick and Tommy. Good, she thought. Nick promised to take care of things after she told him about the incident in the party room the day before.

When she opened the door, something about the scene in front of Sabrina told her she was witnessing something entirely different than what she expected. It was Nick who appeared upset and distraught as he sat at the end of his office sofa, with Tommy smiling, sitting on the other end.

"I've come too far to lose all of this. I can't . . ." Nick turned to Sabrina as she entered. "Sabrina."

Tommy's jaw clenched at the sight of her as he stood up. "Don't you know how to knock?"

"No," she answered, "but I know how to do a lot of other things. Speaking of which, how is that arm of yours?"

Tommy flashed a grin. "You got lucky."

Sabrina looked him square on. "No, Tommy. You got lucky."

"I'm out of here." Tommy turned to Nick, who looked as if he'd just eaten something bad. "You. You don't wimp out on me now. You can only lose if you do."

Sabrina ignored Tommy's glare as he left, making sure not to walk too close to her. She approached Nick on the sofa, who barely nodded a hello.

"Did you talk to him about it?" she asked.

"About what?"

"About his grabbing me yesterday. You said you would."

"I meant to, but . . ." He looked away, staring at the blank wall. "I got other things I'm worried about. Besides, you took care of the situation. He's not gonna mess with you again."

"That's not the point." Sabrina was confused. Nick was acting peculiar. If she didn't know him better she would say he looked scared. "What's wrong with you?"

"Nothing." He stood up, walking to his desk. He fell into his chair as if it had been a long, hard day, and it was barely noon.

"Something's wrong with you, and it has something to do with that jerk."

"Tommy's just a show man. Being a jerk is par for the course in his business."

"You making excuses for him?"

"It's business, Sabrina."

She knew that, but there was something more to Nick's behavior right now. "What did you mean earlier?"

"When?" His eyes shifted back and forth as he pretended to care about some papers on his desk.

"You said you didn't come this far to lose. What did you mean by that?"

He looked at her as if he wanted to tell her something, but then quickly changed his mind. "Nothing, Sabrina. It was just business. I'm very busy right now. What did you come by for?"

Sabrina came around the desk, leaning against it, placing her hand on his shoulder.

"Nick, something is bothering you and there's no way I'm going to just walk away from you. I owe you too much. You were there for me all the time I was dealing with Clark and needed a shoulder . . ."

Sabrina couldn't even think of Clark without getting emotional. This wasn't about her anyway.

"I'm fine, really." He squeezed her hand, looking up at her with a smile that wasn't convincing.

"What could you lose?" she asked. "Is this about Artemis Grove and his wife? I don't think that's going to get in the way of the fight."

Nick nodded decisively and squeezed her hand tighter. "You're right. This is all going to be worth it."

"Worth what?"

"This fight is going to do great things for the Acropolis. For me."

"What do you mean by worth it?" she asked again, confused at his sudden upturn in mood.

"Tommy," he said. "We'll have Tommy out of our hair after Saturday night and the Acropolis is going to go from being a casino on the strip to *the* casino on the strip."

"I can't wait." Sabrina smiled reassuringly.

"Plus," Nick said with an accomplished grin, "we'll be rid of Clark Hunter."

Sabrina's hand slipped away as her heart pulled at her. "Yeah."

"That's what you want, right?" Nick frowned. "You're not letting him mess with your head, are you? I told him to stay away from you."

"When?"

"Yesterday morning. Have you seen him since?"

"Kind of," she answered, having to smile at her own words. "It's not important. Not to you at least. I can handle Clark Hunter. You just keep Tommy Gaxton in line."

"Saturday can't come soon enough."

Sabrina wasn't too sure about that.

Clark was headed for the casino, where he had already spent too much time since arriving in Vegas, when his cell phone rang. Since he was already down five hundred since hitting the strip, any distraction was welcome.

It was Lauren. Even better.

"Shoot," he said, nodding to the security guard who waved him away. Cell phone conversations didn't mix well with the blackjack table.

"I'm fine, Clark. Thanks for asking. How are you?"

"Sorry," he said. "I'm on the edge."

"Did you just apologize to me? Whoa. So you do have some manners."

"Cut to the chase."

"She's in Scottsdale, Arizona."

"Scottsdale?" Clark didn't need to ask who.

"Yup. It was pretty easy tracking her down."

"Did you talk to her?"

"Didn't really get the chance. I told her who I was and said that I was calling about her brother. That's when she started."

Cara's brother was Michael Milton, who used to be a hot high school basketball prospect. Clark had done a story on Michael, and spent probably three hours at the most with Cara to learn more about the kind of person Michael was. Without a father or mother, Cara played the role of both parents as the head of the house, taking care of Michael and their younger sister.

"What do you mean she got started?" Clark asked.

"How much did you check up on this woman after . . . you know?"

"It's complicated. I didn't even know who she was until Sabrina finally showed me the pictures. Sabrina didn't believe me, but I begged to see the pictures just to know what in the hell she was talking about."

"But you did spend time with her more than that?"

"That was a year before she started this. The pictures Sabrina left me were copies she had made and they weren't that clear. She didn't want to give me the originals. At first I didn't even recognize her. It took me a while studying the pictures before I could remember."

"So, you did something to find her then?"

"I tried to track her down, but she was gone. I called Michael, but he didn't know anything about where she was or what she was trying to do. His life was consumed with college."

"I reread your article about Michael," Lauren said. "You didn't say anything bad about him or his family. You were talking about his life, his fame, and the choices he had as a high school junior. Whether to go pro or go to college. There's no reason for her to be angry at you over that."

"I thought about that at the time too. The article went great, and the little time I can remember I spent with her went great as well."

"Did she hit on you and you rejected her?"

"No."

"You sure?" Lauren seemed to be hinting at something.

"I would remember that," Clark said.

"Sometimes it's subtle and if you don't pick it up the wrong woman can get real offended."

"A year later?"

"Good point. Then what is it?"

"I went over every scenario. She has no reason to be mad at me."

"Obviously she does. Unless she's doing this for someone else."

"What are you getting at?"

"Scratch that. Let's stick with her for now. Do you know where Michael Milton is now?"

"Well, he just graduated in May, so he's either planning to go to college or he's going pro." Clark knew the NBA draft was later this month. "I remember I encouraged him to go to college."

"He went to college, but not like you think."

Clark was frustrated with this direction. "Lauren, I don't care about Michael. What happened when you talked to Cara?"

"She didn't want to talk about her brother either, so I pushed and lied about how we want to do a follow-up on such a promising star athlete. She was livid. Told me he wasn't a star. He was a broke college student and he'd never be a star of any kind."

"What did she mean?"

"She wouldn't explain. She hung up on me. So I did the research myself. He's not even in Chicago anymore. He lives in Champaign-Urbana."

Champaign-Urbana was a college town about two and a half hours south of Chicago. The University of Illinois.

"That makes sense," Clark said. "Illinois was one of the schools that were interested in him."

"Yeah, but he's not down there to start his college basketball career. Come August, he'll be enrolling in the school as a pre-vet-med student."

"A vet student?" That was weird. "Not basketball? He could do both."

"He's not playing hoops, Clark. There was a big article in the paper down there about it. He's giving up basketball. Weird, isn't it?"

"Very weird." Clark remembered the guy was a

shoo-in for a multimillion-dollar contract. He had the skills. "But that doesn't help me with Cara."

"She wouldn't talk to me anymore," Lauren said regretfully. "There's something there. You've got to keep thinking."

"I've been thinking it to death. Trust me. But this new info might help."

"I'm gonna find out the truth. I'll call you back."

Clark hung up. He couldn't say he was satisfied, but he knew Lauren was on it and she would come up with something. He had to work harder at it from his end now that he had some new news. This was his window of opportunity with Sabrina and he had to bring something to the table to keep the momentum going.

From the stage, Sabrina applauded along with the wealthy, carefully selected crowd of party-goers as Nick exited the podium, handing them over to Tommy, who was ready to get them riled up. When Nick approached her, he smiled and winked reassuringly. His eyes were dancing. He was more excited than Sabrina could remember.

"You guys did great," he said. "This place looks incredible."

Sabrina had to admit this was one of her best jobs. Going against Tommy's suggestion of loud colors and shock, Sabrina had opted for a late-spring Hamptons look with a touch of sexy. Champagne glass arches, cocktail charms, streaming curtains, burning bright votive candles, and ten-foot-high ice sculptures of both fighters.

Sabrina thanked him, nodding toward Dionne,

who looked like a James Bond bombshell standing on the other end of the stage between both fighters. This was one of Tommy's ideas as well, but Dionne didn't seem to mind.

"You can give Dionne most of the credit," Sabrina said. "She added that sexy flair."

"Speaking of sexy"—Nick leaned in closer—"You look the most incredible I've ever seen you, and that's saying something."

Sabrina threw him a humble smile, but she had it going on that night. She needed a pick-me-up, anything to make her feel better after the doubt she was feeling threatened to drive her crazy. After work, she had allowed Dionne to drag her to the hotel salon for a facial, pedicure, and manicure.

She was prepared to slink into one of her standard cocktail dresses, but Dionne showed up at her apartment with a knockout lavender silk gown that seemed to be made for Sabrina's body. Dionne explained to her it had been a gift from one of her many male admirers. She had never worn it, but found it too beautiful to give away.

It was an elegant sunburst pleated gown of shimmering satin, halter style with a plunging V neckline that stopped just above her belly button. Sabrina's hair was up with loose tendrils falling at the sides, exposing her slender, regal neck. She looked like ten million bucks. Dionne had gone on and on about how it was necessary. After all, the highly selected list of guests was of all wealthy businessmen and women, athletes, and other celebrities. If she wanted to get some attention she would have to glam it up.

She hadn't mentioned the members of the press

who were also in attendance. To Dionne, they weren't important, but Sabrina couldn't think of anything but them. One member in particular. There was a part of her that wasn't looking forward to running into Clark. He could read her like a book and she didn't want to give away the doubt she was feeling. He would pounce, and she didn't have a death of a chance. Sabrina felt as if she were wearing a big red target on her face, just inviting trouble.

There was that other part of her that wanted to knock his socks off. That part that still hurt like hell and wanted Clark to see what he had lost. Although Sabrina knew she was much more than the way she looked, a nice package could come in handy from time to time.

He was out there somewhere, and he could probably see her now. Refusing to scan the crowd for fear he would catch her looking for him, Sabrina felt her body tingling in anticipation. The tingling was loud enough to cover the sounds of her heart telling her she was being a fool and she would end up paying for it again.

What a fool he had been. That was all Clark could think to himself as he watched Sabrina move across the floor of the ballroom with Nick by her side. They were meeting and greeting the party guests, and everyone lit up as soon as they laid eyes on Sabrina.

What a fool he had been to think he could ever get over a woman like that.

He was mesmerized by her. Not just her beauty, which was enough. She was a very attractive woman, who when she went that extra step became a devastatingly beautiful woman. It was the way she held herself that touched so many parts within him. She had self-respect, dignity, and that touch of class that can't be taught. Then there were the eyes. Those eyes that gave it all away and told you that beneath this conservative vision of perfection was a little girl that wasn't so sure of everything. Of hardly anything. It pulled at the man in him.

After the theatrics, all of the major players exited the stage as the music went up and caterers appeared out of what seemed to be nowhere with trays of expensive champagne, antipasto, artichoke bites, stuffed clams, and California rolls.

Clark watched and waited as Sabrina made her way across the room. She knew where he was. She could feel him. She had to. He felt her as he always had when they were in a crowded room together. There was this thing between them that made them always aware of each other. He thought maybe she had lost it in the press room when he first saw her again, but no—it was still there. He would be patient and let her decide when to look at him. He would be patient and enjoy the view.

"Who else?" Nick asked, as he looked around the room. "Who else do I have to meet?"

Sabrina pointed to an elderly couple sitting at one of the tables lining the walls of the ballroom. "Mr. and Mrs. Tioshi. He owns that new hotel in Reno we were talking about."

"Let's go."

Just as they were set to head for the couple, a man stepped in front of them, holding up his hand to halt them. He was tall, thin, and dressed in an offensive dirt-brown leather suit. Sabrina recognized him as one of Tommy's entourage, but he didn't bother to look at her. He was only interested in Nick. He leaned forward, whispering something into Nick's ear. Sabrina noticed with concern that the smile on Nick's face quickly faded as he looked up and in the direction that the man nodded.

When Sabrina turned she saw Tommy for just a second as he motioned to Nick and disappeared out one of the side doors that she specifically remembered ordering closed for security reasons.

"What's going on?" she asked Nick, holding on to his arm to keep him from leaving. "What does he want and why is he using those doors? They're supposed to be closed."

Nick looked at her, forming a smile that even a five-year-old could tell was forced. "Don't worry about it. He's just nervous about how the night is going."

"Tommy? He's not nervous about anything."

"Make sure you meet everyone, Sabrina. I'll be right back."

Sabrina thought for a second as she watched him walk away. She had a peculiar feeling. Something was wrong and she wasn't going to let Nick get hurt. He was her friend.

When she started after him, Sabrina was surprised as a strong hand gripped her arm. She turned to face the man who stopped her, his expression threatening.

"No," was all he said. His voice held an African-sounding accent.

"No?" Sabrina jerked her hand away. "I don't take orders from you."

"Tommy does not want you anywhere near him." He stepped in front of her to block her.

Sabrina looked him up and down. "You may follow his orders, but I don't."

"Why don't you women ever know your place?"

"You picked the wrong woman to ask that."

The man turned his attention to Clark as he stepped in between him and Sabrina. Sabrina watched as the man assessed the situation and backed off a bit.

"It's a private meeting between them," the man said. "Don't interfere."

He gave Clark a once-over before walking away.

Clark turned around, facing Sabrina. He was happy to be so close to her. His intention to wait until she made contact with him went out the window when he saw that man touch her. He was ready to deck him if necessary.

"What was that about?" he asked.

"Nothing." She was wondering when he would come. She had sensed him since stepping out into the crowd. She would deal with Nick later.

"Sorry," he said.

"Sorry for what?"

The only word that could describe Clark tonight was dashing. It was an old-fashioned romantic word that was out of style, Sabrina knew, but it was accurate. Right on point. He was a great-looking man.

"Sorry for helping you out there." He could smell her. Fresh, clean, soft. Intoxicating. "I know you hate it when men help you out."

"You actually helped him out," she said. "It was about to be on up in here."

"I'd love to see that. You beating him down? I don't think so."

"If I'm pushed," she said, resisting the urge to reach out and touch him. She was mad at him, wasn't she?

"You don't believe in making scenes, Sabrina. I know you."

"Whatever."

"I'll show you."

Without hesitation, Clark took her arm in his and wrapped his other hand around her waist. He felt that surge of energy run through him at the touch as he led her to the dance floor, which was half full at this point. The hired band was playing a funky R&B/pop tune.

"What are you doing?" Sabrina's eyes senses leaped to alarm.

In a second, she was in his arms and as the time switched to a hot salsa sound, Clark jumped into gear. She felt her stomach tighten, knowing what effect his touch and being so close to him would have on her. *Put your seat belt on.*

"Stop it," she said. "I don't want to dance with you."

"If you pull away from me now, you'll cause a scene. You don't want to ruin this party, do you?"

"Clark." She pressed her lips together, wishing she could kick him. "You always do stuff like this."

"Try to have fun? The nerve of me." He placed his hand firmly at her hip as she began to move to the music. She had a fluid way of moving. She was a natural eye-catcher. "You look incredible, Sabrina."

She felt her cheeks warm. "You have no right."

"No right to what?" How he loved touching her.

"Putting this on me."

"What is this?"

She placed her hand on his shoulder and sashayed toward him, looking into his fierce green eyes. "All of this. You know what I'm talking about."

"I was a little harsh last night. I know that. I'm sorry."

"Sorry doesn't cut it after that. You can't just kiss me like that, reject me, and then give me ultimatums."

"I was emotional." It was a lame excuse, but the truth. "I'm not used to that state. I just felt like . . . I don't want us to be together with this thing still between us."

"Who says we were going to be together?" She didn't appreciate his assumptions.

"Sabrina," he said, "what always happens when we start kissing?"

She turned away, biting her lower lip to keep from smiling. This was not funny. This was her heart and he was driving her mad. "Regardless. It doesn't mean we were going to be . . . together. That's never going to happen."

"Never say never."

"Never," she said with as much conviction as she could fake. "And it's just like you to put it all in my hands as if it was my fault. I didn't start this."

"I didn't either, but that's not the point. The point is you have doubts."

"You don't know what I feel." She didn't even know what she was feeling.

"Still, you're right."

"I'm right?" Something was wrong. "You never concede an argument that fast."

"When I've done something wrong, I own up to it." He stopped, looking at her with purpose. "When I haven't, I won't."

"Enough," she said. "Just dance and get this over with."

"She's trying to set me up." Clark saw Sabrina's eyes begin to roll. She had heard that before. "Hear me out."

"You don't know who she is, but she's out to get you. Then you know who she is, but can't quite remember. Then you remember who she is, but you never really knew who she was."

"I've been going over and over my conversations with her. I wish I had the tapes, the ones I used for all my interviews, but I could never find the ones from that particular interview. I'm trying to remember, and I can't put my finger on one thing, but there's something wrong. I had my assistant call her and—"

"When?" Sabrina asked.

"I called her last night after I got home. She's been working on it all day."

"Wait a second." Sabrina stopped, unable to receive the information and move at the same time. "Are you telling me you're still in touch with this woman?"

"No." Clark looked around. "Let's go talk."

Sabrina moved her hand away as he reached for it. She felt anxiety build within her. "No."

"I want to talk to you about this." His eyes were pleading.

"I can't, Clark. I can't do it."

Clark read her eyes. She was scared of the truth.

"Sabrina, I just want to talk to you about this. I know it will help."

"I don't want it to help. I can't . . ." Sabrina knew tears were coming. She had to get away from him. "It's too much and I can't deal with it tonight. Not tonight. I have work to do."

"Sabrina." He reached for her again, but she stepped back. "I need you to meet me halfway here. I'm doing what I can. You have to be open. I know you have doubts."

"It can't be true," she said, her voice catching. "It can't be."

"It is."

Sabrina shook her head. "You heard me. I have work to do tonight, Clark. I want you to leave me alone."

Clark fought the urge to grab her and not let her walk away. He had done that so many times in Chicago and it had only worked to upset her more and make things worse. Still, he wasn't about to give up. Not for a second.

SIX

Sabrina made her way through the doors she had ordered locked, and finally exhaled. She wasn't sure how long she had been holding her breath, but she was just glad to get out of there. On the other side of the doors was a hallway that connected the main kitchen to all of the meeting areas of the hotel. It was brightly lit with a winding hallway that Sabrina began walking without knowing where she was going.

She just needed to walk to keep from falling down. She was feeling dizzy and completely confused at her own reaction. She wasn't ready or willing to accept that Clark had been telling the truth. That the nightmare that ruined her life had never really happened. How could she believe that? She had the pictures. She'd heard the . . .

Sabrina stopped, holding on to the wall beside her to keep her balance. The phone conversation between Clark and that woman. What was making her wonder? When Sabrina told him about what Cara played for her over the phone, he'd sworn to her it was a fake. Someone was impersonating him. He swore he hadn't spoken to her about anything personal and had never said the things Sabrina told him she'd heard.

Sabrina didn't believe him. She could pinpoint Clark's voice anywhere and it was definitely his voice. It was a little scratchy from the tape, but certainly his.

She remembered what was making her wonder. What had Clark just said? *I've been going over and over my conversations with her. I wish I had the tapes, the ones I used for all my interviews, but I could never find the ones from that particular interview.*

What if?

"Don't you punk out on me, brother!"

The sound jolted Sabrina back to the present. Someone was ticked off and the voice was coming from just around the corner.

"I don't punk out!"

"Then what do you call this?"

That last voice was Nick's. Slowly Sabrina peeked around the corner just enough to see with one eye. She watched as Nick and Tommy had Artemis Grove backed against the wall.

"I didn't say I wasn't going through with it," Artemis said, trying to shift to the right, but Tommy stood in his way.

"It's too late to back out," Tommy said, jabbing Nick in the arm with his elbow. "Tell him."

Nick nodded. "Too many people are involved. Too much money."

Sabrina wondered if Artemis didn't want to go

through with the fight because of the stress in his marriage, but it seemed like more than that.

"I don't care about the money," Artemis said. He pumped his fist to his chest. "I'm a man and I have my pride. I can beat this man to a pulp! What am I gonna look like if I—"

"Brother." Tommy smiled, patting Artemis on the shoulder. "Brother, you know I got your back on that. I'm already setting up the rematch."

"Right here at the Acropolis," Nick added. "In less than four months. The odds will be against you that time and we'll make even more money."

Sabrina turned back, leaning against the wall. What in God's name was going on? What was she hearing? She couldn't believe for a second that Nick would be involved in something like this. Like what? Whatever it was and no matter how close she was to Nick, Sabrina had the distinct feeling she was in danger if she stuck around there.

Quietly she headed back for the ballroom, her heart beating as fast as light as she reached the first corner.

"What the—" Sabrina smacked right into Clark, biting the urge to scream out loud. Confusion hit him as she grabbed him and pulled him around the corner.

"What's the matter with you?" Clark asked, noticing the fear in her face. "I really upset you, didn't I? I didn't mean to."

"Keep quiet," she said. "And don't be so self-absorbed. Everything isn't about you."

"Then what's going on?"

"What are you doing out here?"

"I had to come after you. I wanted to tell you

that I understand the implications for you, for both of us, when you realize I've been telling the truth all along."

"Not now, Clark." Sabrina heard footsteps. What could she do? She didn't really know anything for a fact, but her woman's intuition told her to keep her mouth shut.

Clark couldn't help feeling frustrated. He wanted so much more than he had reason to expect from her, but his heart couldn't stop him. "All we have is now, Sabrina. We're both open. Let's talk."

"What are you two doing here?"

Clark's journalist's intuition hit him immediately as Nick, Tommy, and Artemis turned the corner. The look on their suspicious faces gave them away. He knew what they had been up to. What he wanted to know now was what Sabrina had been doing coming from their direction.

"Artemis." He smiled, an outstretched hand extended to the fighter, who didn't even pretend to accept the gesture. "What are you doing out here? That party in there is hopping and it's all for you."

Nick placed a hand on Sabrina's shoulders, his expression cautious. "What's going on? He bothering you again?"

Sabrina thought quickly. "No, Nick. Actually I wanted to talk to him. That's why we came out here. We wanted to get away from the crowd."

She knew something. Clark nodded as Nick looked at him. "It's too loud in there."

"How long have you been out here?" Nick asked.

"Just now," Clark said. "We just got here, so if you don't mind."

Nick looked at Clark with no love lost in his

eyes. "Yes, I do mind. You don't do anything but hurt her. Of course I mind."

"It's not about that." Sabrina knew the sooner she could calm Nick's concerns, the sooner she could get away from him, Tommy, and Artemis. "Trust me, Nick. I have everything under control. There won't be any more problems after tonight."

Nick looked at her in disbelief for a moment. When his face softened a bit, he backed up. "You know I'm here if you need me."

He turned to Tommy and Artemis with a nod.

"See ya at the party." Clark smiled with a wink, which was returned with hateful stares from all three men.

Clark and Sabrina watched as the men made their way down the hall, with Tommy whispering to Nick and Artemis looking back at Clark with distrust.

"First of all," Clark said, "are you okay?"

"I don't know." She had never spoken such truth.

"What happened back there? You were with them?"

"No, I wasn't, but . . ." Sabrina was shaking her head, not sure what to think. After all, it was Nick. He had been her friend since they were kids.

"But you heard something," Clark said. "That's why you were so upset."

"I heard something, but I'm pretty sure I wasn't supposed to. I don't think anyone was."

"They were talking about a scam, weren't they? To take a dive in this fight."

Sabrina looked at the excitement in Clark's eyes. She was very familiar with that look. A big story. "What are you up to?"

"Tell me, Sabrina."

"This is what you came here for?" she asked. "To make up some ridiculous story about fixing a fight?"

"I came here to follow up on the abuse angle, but when I was talking to Alicia Grove, she gave me some hints and I did a little background searching. This is a real story, Sabrina."

"You're shameless," she said. "There is no way—"

"What did you see? What did you hear?"

Sabrina paused with a sigh. Her curiosity was getting the best of her. If she still believed anything about Clark, it was that he had a good nose for a story and he usually didn't pursue one unless he had some proof that it was big.

"I don't know for sure," she said, "but it seemed like Artemis wanted to back out of the fight or not go through with it the way they planned."

"I bet his pride is giving him a hard time."

"Sounded like it. Tommy was telling him everything would be okay because he was setting up a rematch, and . . ."

Clark noticed her hesitation. "And what? Nick. Nick is involved somehow."

"He couldn't be," Sabrina said, knowing it didn't make sense with what she'd heard. "Nick would do a lot of things, but this . . ."

"This is clearly illegal and would involve millions and millions of dollars."

Sabrina remembered what Nick told her when she had last been in his office. This fight was going to change things for the Acropolis. For him. "There must be some explanation."

"Don't go soft just because he's your boyfriend."

"What?" Sabrina shook her head. "First of all I would never go soft on someone who was doing wrong no matter who they were. You should know that more than anyone."

"Ouch." Clark stepped right into that one.

"Secondly," she added, "Nick is not my boyfriend."

"I thought . . ." Clark couldn't fight his smile. "You mean you're not involved with him?"

"No." Sabrina wanted to smack that smile off of his face. He was so smug. "I know this feeds right into your self-absorbed ego. That's right, Clark. I'm not involved with Nick or any other man."

"Sabrina." He was happy at the news, but not at the fact that it was only true because he had hurt her. Or so she'd thought he had. "This is not about my ego. It's about us. Both of us not being able to be with anyone because we're still tied to each other."

"No."

Sabrina tried to move away, but Clark took hold of her at her shoulders.

"Yes," he said. "You can't deny it. Right now when I touch you I can feel it and so can you. What exists between us is strong enough to bring this building down. And I'm not going to make it easy for you to fight me anymore."

"Easy?" she said, almost laughing at the irony of his words. "Do you think it's been easy? To resist you? To pretend as if I wasn't . . . No, Clark, it's been hell staying away from you."

"Like it's been for me." He pulled her to him. "Since we're both in hell, let's go down in flames together."

His lips kissed hers gently and Sabrina felt her

knees weaken again as they always did when he kissed her. She was helpless to resist because nothing inside her wanted to. The sweet warmth and teasing agony of his lips sent her head into the clouds.

Her left hand went up to wrap around his neck, loving the feel of his skin against her fingers as she caressed him. Her tongue entered his mouth, sending a passionate message of desire.

Like a race car tearing through a course, fire ran through Clark as her warm tongue explored his mouth. A euphoric calm clashed with a hot ache in his body, reminding him of how he had planned to spend the rest of his life in this maddening comfort.

"We have about five hundred rooms in this hotel for that kind of thing."

Dionne stood a few feet from them, her face just at the edge of cracking up. She was obviously amused with the scene before her.

Sabrina tried to cool herself down as she reluctantly stepped away from Clark. "Dionne. What's going on?"

"I'm supposed to pretend like I need you for something urgent back at the party, but I didn't have time to come up with something, so I'll go with the truth. Nick told me to come and get you away from Clark, but it doesn't look like you want too much to get away from him."

Clark grinned at Sabrina. "I hope not."

Sabrina smiled nervously. "I just . . . I don't want to, but I think I better."

"We were making some progress," Clark said.

"Progress would be talking, not . . . not what we were just doing."

A SPECIAL "THANK YOU" FROM ARABESQUE JUST FOR YOU!

Send this card back and you'll receive 4 FREE Arabesque Novels—a $25.96 value—absolutely FREE!

The introductory 4 Arabesque Romance books are yours FREE (plus $1.99 shipping & handling). If you wish to continue to receive 4 books every month, do nothing. Each month, we will send you 4 New Arabesque Romance Novels for your free examination. If you wish to keep them, pay just $16* (plus, $1.99 shipping & handling). If you decide not to continue, you owe nothing!

- Send no money now.
- Never an obligation.
- Books delivered to your door!

We hope that after receiving your FREE books you'll want to remain an Arabesque subscriber, but the choice is yours! So why not take advantage of this Arabesque offer, with no risk of any kind. You'll be glad you did!

In fact, we're so sure you will love your Arabesque novels, that we will send you an Arabesque Tote Bag FREE with your first paid shipment.

Call Us TOLL-FREE At 1-888-345-BOOK

* Prices subject to change

THE "THANK YOU" GIFT INCLUDES:

- 4 books absolutely FREE (plus $1.99 for shipping and handling).
- A FREE newsletter, *Arabesque Romance News*, filled with author interviews, book previews, special offers, and more!
- No risks or obligations. You're free to cancel whenever you wish with no questions asked.

INTRODUCTORY OFFER CERTIFICATE

Yes! Please send me 4 FREE Arabesque novels (plus $1.99 for shipping & handling). I understand I am under no obligation to purchase any books, as explained on the back of this card. Send my free tote bag after my first regular paid shipment.

NAME _____

ADDRESS _____ APT. _____

CITY _____ STATE _____ ZIP _____

TELEPHONE ( ) _____

E-MAIL _____

SIGNATURE _____

Offer limited to one per household and not valid to current subscribers. All orders subject to approval. Terms, offer, & price subject to change. Tote bags available while supplies last.

Thank You!

AN014A

ARABESQUE

Accepting the four introductory books for FREE (plus $1.99 to offset the cost of shipping & handling) places you under no obligation to buy anything. You may keep the books and return the shipping statement marked "cancelled". If you do not cancel, about a month later we will send 4 additional Arabesque novels, and you will be billed the preferred subscriber's price of just $4.00 per title. That's $16.00* for all 4 books for a savings of almost 40% off the cover price (Plus $1.99 for shipping and handling). You may cancel at any time, but if you choose to continue, every month we'll send you 4 more books, which you may either purchase at the preferred discount price. . . or return to us and cancel your subscription.

* PRICES SUBJECT TO CHANGE

THE ARABESQUE ROMANCE BOOK CLUB
P.O. BOX 5214
CLIFTON NJ 07015-5214

"Looked like a lot more fun than talking to me," Dionne added.

"Well then, let's talk," Clark said. "Let's go somewhere and talk."

"Tomorrow." Sabrina saw the disappointment in Clark's face. "I need to think, Clark. I promise we'll talk tomorrow. I've got a party to work and this . . . this new situation is going to take some sinking in. If what you say is true."

"I'm sure it is," Clark said. "And I think you know it is."

"I'll ring your room tomorrow."

Clark wanted to protest, but he could tell from the look in her eyes that she meant what she said. Sabrina always kept her word. "There's just one more thing."

"Yes?"

"The pictures," he said, knowing he could reverse all the progress they had just made with this one request. "Do you still have them?"

Sabrina swallowed. "Yes, I do, but I gave you—"

"I need the originals, Sabrina."

"What are you going to do with them?"

"I want to find out how she made them."

Sabrina sighed, wondering how she could so willingly participate in her own fool-making. "Okay. I'll bring them by tomorrow."

"Thanks." Clark gently touched her cheek with the back of his hand, loving the softness of her skin. "I know this is hard for you."

"You have no idea," she answered, loving the comfort of his touch too much. She stepped away. "Good night, Clark."

"Good night."

As he walked away, Clark was filled with promise and hope. This wasn't going to go smoothly. In fact, it was probably going to be pretty rough and painful. Pride had to be swallowed and truths handled delicately, but this was going to happen. There was no doubt in his mind about that.

"What are you doing?" Dionne asked with a naughty smile on her face.

"I'm not sure," Sabrina answered. "I might be getting my life back. I might be making the biggest mistake of my life."

"You're going to forgive him for what he did to you?"

"He might not have done it, Dionne." There, she said it. She said it. Now, there was no going back.

"How is that possible? What about the pictures? What about the conversation you overheard?"

"I don't know," Sabrina said, "but I have to find out the truth."

"What if . . ." Dionne didn't need to finish the question.

"Then I may have made a mistake that I'm not sure we can ever recover from."

Sabrina hoped to God that wasn't true.

When Sabrina opened the door to the executive offices at the Acropolis the next morning, she was not prepared for what she saw. And she was not happy about it at all.

"What are you doing here?" she asked.

Clark waved with a bright smile as he leaned against Dionne's desk. He had that modern-day cowboy offhandedness look about him. Like everything was just fine in his life. He'd been all Sabrina could think about since he left her at the party the night before. She had gone to sleep that night pretending it was his arms that were wrapped around her instead of her bedsheets. That her head had been leaning against his chest instead of the pillow. Remembering the way his lips tasted and his hands felt as they traveled the path of her body, bringing it to life the way only his hands could. Her dreams had been pleasant to say the least.

But Sabrina had set the rules for them meeting again, and if he was going to disregard her wishes with this . . . whatever it was they were doing . . . there was going to be trouble for him.

"I thought the normal way to do this was to say good morning." Clark noted the anxious look on her face. "Don't worry. I'm not here to see you."

"I told you I would call . . ." Sabrina realized what he had just said. "What?"

"He's here to see me." Dionne stuck her tongue out for effect.

"Unless it's none of my business, which I doubt, does somebody want to explain this to me?" Sabrina sat at her desk, placing the yellow envelope with the pictures on the table. She noticed Clark look at them for a second, then look away. His smile never skipped a beat, but she could tell he knew what they were.

"She needed my help," Clark said. "So I had to oblige. I'm using every tool I can to get in your good favor."

"It doesn't work that way," she said, turning to Dionne. "Since he's intent on flirting, you wanna tell me what this is about?"

Dionne nodded. "Brad Nagle canceled on us. You know, with his wife having the baby."

"Was everything all right?" Sabrina had forgotten about Brad. All she could remember from that night was kissing Clark in the parking lot.

"Yeah, but he says she's going through some kind of postpartum depression and he doesn't want to leave her alone right now. Even for a few hours. I judged him wrong. He's a good guy, but . . ."

"But," Sabrina finished, "we're short one."

"So I'm pitching in," Clark said with a politician's smile that made Sabrina laugh. He loved making her laugh. "Graduate of Northwestern University and professional sports journalist."

"I knew you would freak out if I told you someone canceled the night before," Dionne continued, "so I made sure I had a replacement before I told you."

"Good thinking," Sabrina said. "I would have freaked out, but I would have gotten it together in a few minutes and we would have worked something out. It's too bad that Brad can't make it, but I guess Clark will do."

"Thanks," Clark said. "So nice to know I'm useful for something."

Dionne stood up from her desk, pointing her pen at Clark. "So you know where to be and when, right?"

"Got everything." He held up the prep sheet she had given him.

"Thanks!" She blew a kiss at him before heading and turning out. "See you soon."

With Dionne gone, Clark made his way to Sabrina's desk. He wished he could run his fingers through her hair, which was down and a little unruly today. Unusually carefree for Sabrina, but he'd always liked it that way.

"Is that because of me?" he asked, pointing to her hair.

"What?" Sabrina touched her head as if there was something on it.

"The hairstyle. You letting a little loose. Because of my magical lips, as you used to refer to them?"

Sabrina rolled her eyes. "There isn't enough room in this office for your ego, so I'm gonna have to ask you to leave."

"Well, since I'm here . . ."

"I didn't ring your room." She shifted through some papers on her desk, but there was no way she could concentrate. Not with him this close.

"So it's gonna be like that, is it?" He joked with her, knowing just how she liked it. Teasing, but not too aggressive. He was disappointed, but he knew she would keep her word.

"It's gonna be like that, all right." Sabrina slid the yellow envelope toward him. "You requested these."

Clark took the envelope. It was so light. For some reason, in his mind he had pictured them weighing a ton.

"Thanks, Sabrina. I know it hasn't been easy for you holding on to these."

"I . . ." *Fight the emotion.* "They kept me strong, but I'm ready to let them go either way. Do whatever you want with them."

Her words hurt, but there was no time for pitying himself. That was the past. "I understand."

"With the career day today, I have a pretty packed schedule."

Clark's red flags went up. Was she trying to back out? "When is it over?"

"After four," she said, turning on her computer or anything else she could to busy herself. "After that I have to go over some last-minute things for the fight tomorrow night."

"Sabrina."

She looked at him, the fear in his voice reaching her. That was all she had wanted. It was cruel of her, but she needed to hear that. If Clark assumed, Sabrina knew she didn't have a chance. "We should have dinner then."

Clark smiled, relief washing over him. "Dinner it is. I'll get out of your mystery sexy-somehow-today hair now."

Sabrina bit her lower lip to keep from laughing. "Clark, what are you doing about last night?"

"We'll talk at dinner," he answered, a little confused until he saw the hesitant expression on her face. "Oh, that. Yeah. I'm writing a story about it, Sabrina."

"What is the story exactly?" she asked. "You don't know anything for sure."

"We're talking about professional boxing here, so the bet is that I do know for sure even without all of the facts yet. That being said, I'm working on my leads and getting it all together. Nick and Tommy are working with a local bookie to fix this fight and make some extra millions on the side."

Sabrina was confused. "But Nick said that the hotel was already going to make several million bucks off of this legally."

"The hotel will, but that money is going to the owners. Nick's doing the fight for the hotel, but the scam is for himself."

"This is going to hurt him," Sabrina said. "He'll go to jail if it's true, won't he?"

Clark nodded.

"Let me talk to him, Clark."

"No, Sabrina. It's too dangerous. This much money—you never know what someone will do."

"Nick would never hurt me."

"You'd be surprised what people would do for money that they normally wouldn't. Besides, even if he won't hurt you, do you think that Tommy wouldn't? And God only knows who else is involved."

Sabrina acquiesced. "I just wish—"

"I know you do. You're a great friend, Sabrina, but don't push this. If Nick gets suspicious of you, things could get out of hand. I couldn't live with myself if anything happened to you because of a story I'm pursuing."

"I know." She smiled tenderly. "You better be careful too."

"You care?" Clark's lips edged into a smile.

This man was going to drive her crazy. "Enough. I'll see you at the event today."

"You'll be there?" he asked.

"It's my baby. I certainly will be."

As Clark closed the door behind him he wondered if Sabrina really understood what he was saying when he warned her to keep quiet about the scam. She was a stubborn woman and a loyal friend, but she wasn't stupid. Just in case, he was going to have to keep tabs on her.

Sitting on the edge of his bed, Clark stared at the pictures. It had been a while since he'd last seen them. In a fit of rage, he had torn up the copies that Sabrina had given him. Looking at them again, in a different state of mind, Clark had to understand what must have gone through Sabrina's mind. They were fakes, he knew that, but good ones.

The picture of him with Cara outside the café was real. He had met her there to talk to her. Who had taken this picture he could never tell. She must have been planning something from the beginning. But why? For what?

Then there were the two pictures of them in bed. One with the covers up to his neck, but only half covering Cara, revealing a sexy red nightgown. They were smiling at each other. He stared from one to the other, focusing, begging for anything to come through. To show itself.

He imagined an emotional Sabrina, seeing the first photo that was real and just assuming the rest were. Then being played a tape of whatever it was she had heard. He had been so angry that she hadn't just taken his word, that she hadn't known it was a frame-up, but what would he have done? Clark had said from the beginning if it had been the other way around, he would never have believed it. He trusted Sabrina completely and knew she would never do something like that.

Only what if someone had shown him pictures that looked very real and played him tapes of her, confirming his worst thoughts? And what if she had had a not-too-distant past of jumping from man to man?

Clark fixated on the picture of them in bed together. It had to be his head superimposed on . . .

Clark grabbed the café picture again, its inno-

cence making it a foregone conclusion. That had
been his mistake from the beginning. He should
have paid more attention to it. He looked from
one picture to the other, wondering how he could
be so stupid not to have seen it before.

It was the same face, the same expression. Cara
looked different. She looked like a woman who
had just had great sex and was staring in adoration
at her lover. Not Clark. His face held a charming
smile, but it was the same charming smile that it
held in the picture at the café. She had a picture
taken of her in the bed with someone and superimposed his face from the café picture on to it!
Someone had spent time digitally angling it to appear right, but Clark was sure it was the same
photo.

Clark almost ripped the photo he was so excited.
He couldn't wait to show Sabrina. She would have
to believe him. Wouldn't she?

There was still the issue of the last photo.

Clark grabbed it, staring at it intently. It appeared
as if it was supposed to have been taken just moments after the other one, with her caressing his
back as he sat on the edge of her bed. She was
wearing the same nightgown, her hair the same
style. He had on a pair of gray boxers and white
socks. His elbows resting on his thighs and his face
down, he looked exhausted. There were several
beads of sweat noticeably trailing his brow, and
falling down his face.

"No way." Clark couldn't keep his words to himself as he reached for the photo of them in bed together.

His polite, charming smile highlighted a face

without even a hint of sweat. So what could explain him not sweating after making love, but sweating profusely as he was getting out of bed?

Sabrina could argue that the second picture was taken before they had had sex. No, no one just lies there staring at each other before sex. Not anyone having an illicit affair. These types of glances were always reserved for afterglow.

Still, this was definitely him sitting on the edge of her bed. He continued staring at the picture, waiting for the clue to jump out at him. Minutes passed, but Clark wouldn't look away. There had to be something. Then he saw it. His butt was barely on the edge of the bed. With his weight on his thighs like that, he couldn't have sat that close to the end. Unless . . .

Clark reached for his cell phone, pressing the speed dial.

"I've been waiting for you," Lauren said as she picked up.

"I'm looking at the pictures. Sabrina gave me the originals."

"She did? Did she put up a fight or what?"

"How could Cara get a picture of me at the health club?"

"She did that?"

"I'm sure of it. There's a picture that looks like I'm sitting on the edge of her bed in my shorts, but I'm sure it's me sitting on the bench in the locker room of my gym. After I work out, I usually sit there for a few minutes to bring my heart rate down or wait for a shower stall to open up. Pretty religiously."

"Hold on."

She put the phone down and Clark waited with

anticipation. Lauren's tone was excited the way it was when she got something good. He was thinking of Sabrina and wondering how long it would be before he saw her again. It was so nice to look at her, talk to her without animosity, anger, hatred, or pain in her eyes.

"Clark? Still there?"

"Of course."

"You are not going to believe this."

"I'll believe anything you tell me, Lauren."

"Chicago Sports Club on East Illinois, right?"

"That's my club. Don't tell me she was a member."

"No. Even better."

"What could be better than that?"

"She worked there. Up until she left for Arizona, she was an employee at the Chicago Sports Club. Laundry something or other."

Clark couldn't believe that. "She told me she worked at a beauty salon on the West Side."

"She did that too. Both were part-time. She either sneaked into the gym to take a picture of you or more likely paid one of the male laundry workers to do it so she wouldn't be noticed."

"It all makes sense," Clark said, "but then again it doesn't. There's still so much missing."

"Maybe I can make it clearer for you."

"What do you have?"

"I talked to Michael down at school. By the way, he says he's happier studying vet med than basketball ever made him and he has you to thank for it. He also said hi."

"How much did you tell him?"

"I told him everything, Clark. Sorry, I feel bad

that the kid is burdened, but we aren't going to get anywhere without him."

"Did he know?"

"He had no clue. I asked him to think as hard as he could. Like when did she ever mention you at all? He said she never talked about you except that the article by such a famous reporter could only help the money roll in."

"Do you think he can get something more for us?"

"I don't think so. He says he hasn't spoken to her since he decided to give up basketball. She was so mad at him for throwing it all away."

"I think I know what's going on," Clark said.

"I think we both do."

The hotel phone rang and Clark leaped to catch it. "Sabrina?"

"Is this Clark?" the voice asked.

"Yes."

"It's Dionne. Time to roll. You ready?"

"I'm there."

Clark hung up the phone and got back on his cell. "Lauren, you still there?"

"What's up?"

"I've got to go. Let's keep in touch."

"What about your story?"

"What story?"

"Please tell me that was a joke."

Clark laughed. "Sorry. My mind is a little preoccupied right now. I'm on the story. I just need to track down a few more facts."

"It's a domestic abuse case. How difficult can it be?"

"That's not the story, Lauren. I don't have time

now, but I'll call you back. I need to run it by Levy, but the story I have about this fight is gonna blow more than a few people out of the water."

"Will it make them forget you called a group of high school principals pimps?"

"You'll have to wait and see."

SEVEN

Sabrina tried to remember what Clark told her as she stood outside Nick's office. She tried not to act nervous when Nick called and asked her to come see him, and now that she was at his door she was hesitant to just walk in. She knew that if she knocked, it would tip Nick off that something was wrong. Different at least.

So Sabrina just barged in as she always did, but Nick's reaction wasn't as it always had been. He almost jumped out of his chair when he saw her.

"Did I scare you?" Sabrina asked.

Nick acted as if he had not reacted the way he had, appearing suddenly calm. "Not really. Maybe you should knock sometimes though."

"I thought . . ." Sabrina thought better of what she was about to say. "Sorry, I will from now on."

"It's just that, you know." He waved his hand dismissively. "Forget it. I was just into something and you surprised me. Come on in and sit down."

Sabrina did as she was told, sitting in the chair on the other side of Nick's desk, which was half the size of his spacious office. Nick went against the owner's wishes to decorate his office in the theme of the hotel. It was overkill for him, so he hired a feng shui expert and made up an early twentieth-century safari designed for comfort and optimal mind production.

"What were you just doing?" she asked. "Anything I can help with?"

"Look at the marketing whiz trying to take my job. This is how it starts, right? Asking to help out here and there."

Sabrina smiled. "Stop it. I just figured if it was about the fight, I might know something about it."

"It wasn't about that," he said, adding nothing more.

Sabrina decided not to push. "What did you call me here for?"

"To talk about last night."

Sabrina felt her body tense up. *Stay calm. Remember what Clark said.* "Last night? I told you, Clark and I just wanted to talk for a second. It was nothing really."

"You must have given him the business, because I didn't see him after that."

"Yeah, he left," she said nonchalantly. "I wanted him to keep his distance so I could concentrate on the event."

"Good thinking, but I wasn't talking about him really when I said last night. I meant the party itself. It went well, don't you think?"

Sabrina shifted in her seat. "It went great. Did you see the *Vegas Sun* this morning?"

Nick nodded. "They thought it was stupid of us

to have it on a Thursday night, but it was a success. With all of the private parties going on tonight, it wouldn't have turned out as well if we set it for Friday. Besides, for rich people, every night can be a weekend night if they want it to be."

"Everyone who is anyone in Vegas was there," Sabrina said. "And they had their picture taken with you. The new prince of Vegas."

Nick was more than pleased. "Prince of Vegas?"

"That's what the paper called you. That's your new title. The reporter said you might be king if the fight packs some punch."

"It will," he said definitively.

"Do we know for sure?" Innocent enough question, Sabrina told herself.

It was time for Nick to shift in his seat. "Artemis Grove could be a heavyweight. The smallest one out there, but he's got the potential to get much bigger than he is. That's where the real money is at, and they'll all be saying it starting this Saturday at the Acropolis."

Sabrina had to bite her lip to keep from saying something. Waxing poetic about the virtues of an earned dollar would be too obvious at a time like this. Still, she cared for Nick very much and wondered what kind of friend she was if she just sat back and watched him ruin his life.

"And I owe it all to you," Nick said. "You and Dionne planned everything perfectly. That's why I called you up here. Where is Dionne anyway?"

"She's getting the career day started." Sabrina looked at her watch. It was already noon. "Speaking of which, that's where I should be on my way to now."

"You'll work with public relations to make sure

we market that party for all it's worth, right? It's cost us enough. I want to get as much post-publicity out of it as I can."

"We've already set up a meeting Sunday." Sabrina could see Nick's eyes dancing. "You're really excited."

"Aren't you? This is the big time, Sabrina."

"I thought we were just going to be happy to get Tommy Gaxton out of our hair."

Nick frowned. "What's wrong, Sabrina?"

"Nothing, I'm just . . ." *Think of something.* Why was lying so hard for her? It came so easy for everyone else. "I'm just running a little late."

"You can't let sexist pigs like Tommy get to you. The more you let his words upset you, the happier it makes him."

"It was more than words," she reminded him. "He grabbed me. It doesn't really matter anymore. I just want him gone."

Nick grabbed a small grid of his hair and tugged at it—a gesture that told Sabrina he was a little uneasy about something.

"So you told Clark where he could go last night?" he asked.

"Something like that. Why?"

"I don't like that guy at all."

"You're just saying that because you're my friend, but you don't have to anymore. Before I broke up with Clark you got along with him just fine whenever you came back home. He's generally a good guy. Like you."

"What's that supposed to mean?" he asked, his tone defensive.

"Nothing. I . . . I just don't want you to hate him for me. I can handle my own relationships."

"It's not just that. He's being an ass to Tommy and Artie." He leaned forward with an inquisitive frown. "Did he ask you anything about me?"

"You?" Sabrina tried to laugh as if it was silly for him to even ask, but she wasn't sure how well that came across. "No, I can't remember except he asked how you were doing. He seemed to be under the impression that we were dating. Do you have any idea where he got that from?"

Nick laughed, bowing his head. "I thought it would keep him away, but I don't think it worked."

"You know Clark. He's determined."

"That's not always a good thing, Sabrina."

Sabrina could tell he was deadly serious. "How is he messing with Tommy and Artemis?"

Nick paused, looking at nothing in particular on his desk. "I just don't want him here. I'm working on getting him banned."

"He's a guest at the hotel, Nick." Sabrina would have to warn Clark that he was on the way out. When Nick wanted someone out, he always found a way to make it happen.

"I mean I want to ban him from anything related to the fight."

"Why? He is the press and you want press for this event, don't you?"

"Not his kind of press. Besides, he isn't even local. He doesn't belong here and you should stay away from him."

"I beg your pardon?" Sabrina knew he wasn't kidding, but she had to act like she thought he was.

"He's not up to any good, Sabrina. He's trying to make me look bad."

"He can't do that." Sabrina saw her open door.

"Clark would have to make something up to make you look bad and he's not that kind of journalist. Even if he did, he would never be able to back it up. You're a good, honest person and you have too much self-respect and determination to ever take the easy route. You've worked too hard to—"

"Sabrina, stop." Nick sighed heavily.

"What's wrong?"

"Nothing." His eyes were solemn. "Just don't tell him anything about me or share our conversations with him, okay?"

"Fine, but he never asks about you, Tommy, or Artemis. I told him when he came here he wasn't going to be given any exclusives."

Nick smirked as if he was telling himself a joke in his head.

"Is there something else you want to tell me?" Sabrina asked.

"What about?"

"I don't know, Nick. You just look like you have something on your mind that you're trying to get out. Like you want to tell me something."

"No." He stood up. "Just about the party, that was all. Tell Dionne thanks when you see her for me, will you?"

"You tell her. She deserves to hear it from you." Sabrina waited for another response, but Nick's mind was definitely elsewhere.

"You know, Nick," she said, "you can tell me anything. I owe you that much from what you've done for me since I moved out here."

He looked at her with a stone expression. "I

would, but there's nothing else to tell. I have to use the bathroom before I do my next interview. You're going to be late."

"You're right." Sabrina stood up, thoroughly disappointed with herself.

She wished she had never heard that conversation in the hallway. At least then she would only have to worry about Clark, trying to convince her she was a madwoman, which was more than enough. Now, she also had to worry about one of her friends—her best friend in Las Vegas—turning into a white-collar criminal. She didn't even know for sure that what Clark was suggesting was even true.

"Let me know how it goes." Nick was already headed for his private bathroom in the back of his office.

Sabrina stood at his desk, debating whether or not she was going to break her promise to Clark and try to save her friend before it was too late to turn back or risk putting herself and Clark in danger to save that friend.

Looking down at his desk, Sabrina remembered she had seen Nick shuffling some papers around when she entered. Why had that stuck in her mind? It was the deliberateness of the act. He had been looking at her the whole time he was moving the papers around. Something about it reeked of guilt to Sabrina.

She could hear Nick using the bathroom. Taking a second to build up the nerve, Sabrina reached for the papers and lifted some of them up, peeking for clues. It wasn't long before she fell upon something suspicious. Sabrina grabbed the sheet of paper.

BANK OF GRAND CAYMAN
ACCOUNT SETUP FORM

Nick had already begun filling out the form with his Social Security number and personal information. He was a successful man, but Sabrina knew he had nothing that would require something as elaborate as a Cayman Islands account. Not yet at least, but he was preparing to put a lot of money where it wouldn't be bothered or noticed.

The toilet flushed and Sabrina quickly put the form back on the table and rushed out of Nick's office. She hadn't remembered to shuffle the papers back to the way Nick left him. She hadn't thought of what he might think when he returned to his desk and found that form, which he purposefully covered up when she entered the office, now smack on top of the desk.

Sabrina was a woman who wanted to believe the best in all of the people she cared about, but when the evidence stacked up right in front of her eyes, what choice did she have? What could she believe after what she'd overheard last night? After what Clark had told her, and now the Cayman Islands bank account?

It was like a torturous déjà vu. Sabrina remembered Cara confessing her affair with Clark, the pictures, and the taped conversations. What choice did she have then?

Now look at me, she thought as she entered the Downtown Recreation Center in Henderson, where the career day was already in progress. *If you can't count on the facts right in front of your face, what can you count on?*

Meeting all of the guest speakers who were behind the stage, Sabrina did her best to engage them. She had been so excited about this day and still was. Only now, with Clark showing up challenging her and these suspicions about Nick and the fight, Sabrina was starting to lose focus. If Clark was getting into something dangerous, Sabrina had to reset her priorities.

Sabrina made her way toward the stage area, where she saw Dionne standing at the edge watching Clark talk to the crowd of over one hundred fifty teenagers.

"How is it going?" she whispered.

Dionne winked at her. "Great. He's a natural with kids. They think he's so cool. Do you know how hard that is with teenagers these days? To find someone who is actually a good guy that they respect?"

Sabrina grinned. "I'm glad it's working."

Dionne seemed to realize what she'd just said, and the look on her face showed she regretted it. "I meant, of course besides what he did to you. I . . . Well, you know what I meant. He's not out there rapping about murdering somebody, pimpin' girls, or fathering ten babies with eight different women."

"I know what you meant." Sabrina squeezed her elbow reassuringly. "Don't feel like you need to have an opinion about Clark because of what happened between me and him."

"Are you okay?" Dionne asked. "You look like you've lost a little color in your cheeks."

"I'll tell you later." Sabrina didn't think it was a good idea to share what she'd found out earlier that morning with anyone but Clark. She would have to wait until he was done.

"So how much money do you make?" shouted a kid from the back.

Clark smiled. He had just finished his ten-minute lecture on his hard-knocks life and his current state. "You guys get right to the point."

The audience laughed.

Clark rubbed at his chin. "Let me put it this way. You have to earn your dues in journalism just like every other honest living."

"Forget it then, man," came from someone in the front row.

More laughter.

"Wait a second," Clark said, holding his hand up. "I make good money now."

"How much you get for those books you wrote?" someone asked. "My dad got those books. You must've made a million bucks, right?"

"Money, money, money." Clark shook his head, smiling patiently. "Let me tell you guys something. When I started out in journalism, I was at the bottom of the barrel paywise, but I got something much more important than money."

"Ain't nothing more important than money," someone yelled out.

Clark was animated now, engaging the children. "Aw, no, man. You got that wrong. Experience is worth more. At that time, the beginning of your career, it's always worth more than money. Experience is what motivates you, keeps you on your toes, and keeps you working. Experience is what brings the money."

Sabrina surveyed the crowd of kids. All eyes were on Clark. He had that effect on everyone. Even Dionne was staring at him like a child, hanging on to his every word.

"I was broke, yeah," Clark continued. "But I got the chance to travel all over the country to go to away games and got free tickets to all the big home games in Chicago. I got to hang out with the top ballers in the country. Michael Jordan, Scottie Pippen, Frank Thomas, Sammy Sosa. I even played a round of golf with the late Walter Payton."

There were a few ooohs and aaaahs in the crowd.

"Those . . . experiences . . . and connections gave me the knowledge I needed to be useful to those in power. And those contacts I developed got me where I needed to go. Where I am today."

A young boy with braces and an Afro raised his hand. "Look, Mr.—"

"Call me Clark."

He smiled that unique smile a kid makes when he feels like he's been treated with respect by an adult. "Okay, Clark. So, now that you have the experience, the connections, and the money, you must be gettin' all the chickens? You hang out with the athletes and we all know they all have four or five girlfriends each. You rolling like that?"

More than a couple of the boys cheered his question, while more than a couple of girls booed it.

Clark leaned back in his chair. "First of all, they don't all roll like that. There are some professional athletes who are married and are good guys. They love their wives and they stay away from those other women."

Sabrina felt her grip tighten on her purse as the room seemed to close in on her.

"What about you?" one of the kids asked. "Do you play or stay home?"

"When I was a young guy," Clark said, "while getting my work experience, I was an avid dater."

"You were a player, man!" Afro raised his fist and circled it a few times. "I knew you knew the game."

"No, I wasn't a player," Clark said. "I wasn't dogging anyone. I was honest about everything I did."

Sabrina swallowed as Dionne looked at her. She didn't want to make this about her, but she couldn't help being affected. She was tense all over.

"What's the fun in that?" one of the kids asked.

"When I say honest," Clark continued, "I mean everyone knew the deal and was okay with it. But it didn't last long, because in the end, it's not satisfying."

"You lying," came from the back of the group.

"I'm not lying," Clark said. "When you get older, you'll realize that, more than money and a good time, there is nothing more valuable than the love of one person that you can rely on. Having that one person that you know has your back no matter what. That man or woman who will be there for you through thick and thin, lift you up when you're down, and sing your praises to the world whether the world wants to listen or not. When you realize the value of that, giving up the game will pale in comparison."

Sabrina's eyes became misty as she clung to his

every word. She knew now that she was ready to hope for what she hadn't been before. To hope that she had been wrong. She would be willing to deal with all the dirty aftermath of that if it meant she could be with Clark again.

"God," Dionne said. "I'd believe him after hearing that."

"Dionne, please." Sabrina lowered her head. "It's not that simple. There was substantial proof that he cheated on me. Where is the proof that he didn't?"

She turned to Dionne, her eyes clouded with emotion.

"From the look in your eyes right now," Dionne said, "I would think you had all the proof you needed."

"How about a question that doesn't have to do with money?" Clark asked, as he looked briefly to the side as Dionne had asked him to do to check for timing.

He saw Sabrina standing at the edge of the stage, her eyes tender and her smile precious. He winked at her, his heart doing back flips as her smile widened. It was so good to see that face again.

"Is that her?" a girl from the crowd asked.

"Is what her?" Clark returned his attention back to the kids.

"That girl you just looked at. Is that your girlfriend? You just looked at her like she was your girlfriend."

Clark tried to hide his embarrassment. "Uh . . . no. She is not my girlfriend. She's someone I know."

"Can you hook her?" a boy asked.

Sabrina wanted to disappear.

"Can I what?" Clark asked.

"I'm just saying," he answered, "you got the experience. You got the money. Now get the girl."

Clark turned back to Sabrina, who looked as if she was about to pass out. He smiled at her, turning back to the crowd and zeroing in on the young man who challenged him. "I'll see what I can do."

The crowd of kids erupted in applause, joined by Dionne until Sabrina glared at her.

Dionne nervously glanced down at her watch and quickly made her way to the center of the stage. "I think Mr. Hunter has taken enough torture today. Do you have any last words for the group, Mr. Hunter?"

"Call him Clark!" someone yelled from the crowd.

Clark stood up. "I just want to tell you guys that patience is more than a virtue. It's a tool to lasting success. Notice what I said. Lasting . . . success. The kind you want to still be around if God has the grace to grant you old age, not just for now."

He scanned the crowd, pleased that he had their full attention. "I know how you feel right now. Your bones are aching. Your young minds are racing. You want to get out there and do something, be a part of something. Be important. I felt the same way. Life was taking too long to get to the point. But I'm telling you now that college is worth the wait. Not only worth the wait, but it can be a lot of fun, and the feeling that you'll have after you've tossed that cap and gown in the air can't be explained in words. Thank you."

The kids clapped loudly as many of them stood up. Sabrina clapped as well, greeting Clark with a wide smile as he approached her.

"I did okay?" he asked.

"I think you did better than okay."

"Sorry about that girlfriend question."

Sabrina waved her hand away as if it hadn't mattered, even though it had mattered very much.

"Sabrina Scott!"

Sabrina turned as she heard Dionne say her name. She had been so entranced by Clark, she hadn't heard anything. But now, Dionne was waving her onstage.

Sabrina grabbed Clark's arm, feeling the touch pinch at her belly. "Will you wait? I have to talk to you?"

"Anything you want," Clark said. Wild horses couldn't drag him away from her.

As he watched her address the kids and introduce the next speaker, Clark tried hard to keep himself grounded. He had to remember how hard this could be. All worth it of course, but hard.

When Sabrina returned from the stage, her expression was serious and she motioned for him to follow her. "I have to tell you something."

Clark followed her a few steps toward the entrance to the auditorium where they were out of eyesight and earshot of anyone else. "What's going on?"

Sabrina sighed, not relishing the news. "I was in Nick's office this morning."

"Sabrina, please don't tell me you told him what we suspect."

"No, of course not. He wanted to talk about the party last night. By the way, he's trying to get you banned from anything related to the fight."

Clark expected as much. "I could tell from the

looks I got last night that they're talking about me. What did he say?"

"You're trying to make trouble for him and he was very upset about it."

"Okay." Clark was fine with that. He didn't think Nick was his biggest problem anyway. Not yet at least. "Is that what you wanted to tell me?"

"Yes. No. I . . . Well, I don't know what this means, but . . ." She paused for a second, knowing that any further denial wasn't helping Clark or Nick. "No, I do know what it means. When I was in Nick's office, he stepped out to go to the bathroom. From some papers on his desk, I noticed he's in the process of opening up an account at the Bank of Grand Cayman."

"He's got some money coming to him after Saturday night. Money he doesn't want people to know about. Especially the IRS."

"How can you prove that the money is from this fight?"

"I'm on my way to do that right now," Clark said. "You don't need me here anymore, do you?"

"Where are you going?" Sabrina was worried. Whatever was going on, if it was illegal and involved Tommy Gaxton, it had to be dangerous.

"I'm going to find the bookie that I'm sure Tommy and Nick are working with. I've been calling around and using some sports betting sources I have and he's definitely working hard to get people to vote for Artemis."

"Wouldn't he anyway?"

Clark nodded. "But I found from some tighter sources that he's telling a select few to bet on Rodriguez. I'm going to find him."

"He's not going to admit to anything."

"That's where Lauren, my assistant, comes in. She helped me get some information that I think will make him talk."

"I'm not liking the sound of this, Clark. You're a sports reporter, not a detective."

"I'm a journalist, Sabrina. Detective is implied."

"I'm coming with." Sabrina's tone was defiant and unwavering.

Clark shook his head vehemently. "I work alone, Sabrina. Besides, it could get dangerous. A lot of these bookies are tied to the mob and other unsavory entities."

"Clark, I need to know what's going on. I'm involved in this now."

"This has nothing to do with you." Clark noticed her full lips pressing together and that stubborn frown forming lines on her forehead. "No, Sabrina. I'm putting my foot down."

"You're not my man anymore," she said. "You don't get to put your foot down about anything. Either way, I am involved. Nick is my friend, my best friend at this point in my life. I can stop him."

"I know what you want to do. You want to get him to back out of it, but he can't, Sabrina. It's too late. You can't save him."

"Do you even know how to get where you're going?"

She had a point. "I'll find my way. Don't think that my bad sense of direction is going to make me bring you into this."

"I'm going to try and save Nick from making the biggest mistake of his life before the fight starts, with or without you." Hands on hips, Sabrina just waited for him to give in.

Clark rolled his eyes. "I need to keep an eye on

you anyway. Just in case. Now you have to do what I tell you to. I know this deal better than you."

"Whatever." Sabrina said, her mind racing. "Here's what we need to do."

"Sabrina," Clark warned.

"You go mingle with the other speakers while I hand things over to Dionne."

"Sabrina." This was his story, or had she forgotten that?

"Then we'll go." Sabrina was already heading for the stage.

With Clark's rental car boxed in, they took Sabrina's. Her red flags went up when Clark gave her the address of their destination. It was way off the strip and in one of the highest crime areas in the county. On the way, Clark explained to her that they were going to see Benecio Silver, considered a big, midlevel bookie in the sport betting business. Benecio was a bad guy, but a stand-up one, he explained, even though Sabrina didn't understand how that was possible. He had spent time in jail for a variety of small offenses, one of the not so small being taking bets for athletes on their own game.

"You saw this guy's name on Tommy Gaxton's cell phone?" she asked.

"Yeah. He dropped it after you almost broke his arm."

When they entered the area that was referred to by its zip code, 89109 in northern Las Vegas, Clark parked in front of the worst building on the street. It looked two days from being condemned.

"A famous bookie lives here?" Sabrina asked. "I

thought being famous meant successful in that business."

"He's loaded." Clark was a little confused himself with the choice of neighborhood, but his sources were good.

When they entered the building, Sabrina looked back at her little Mercedes, wondering if she would ever see it again. They walked up creaky steps and down a dirty hallway without any light. Just as they reached apartment 2F, Clark turned to Sabrina with cautious eyes.

"I'm in charge here," he said.

Sabrina shrugged. "If you think so."

"I'm serious, Sabrina. This guy is old-school Vegas. He knows some dangerous people. You don't want to upset him."

"Isn't that what you plan on doing to get him to confess?"

"But I'm in the game. He'll know me. He won't know you and he won't want to hear from you."

"Is this your subtle way of telling me that in his world, women need to be seen, not heard?"

Clark nodded with that smile that could make anything okay. "When in Rome."

"Just knock on the door."

"Thanks." Without thinking, Clark leaned forward and kissed Sabrina quickly on the cheek. When he backed away, he looked at the surprise on her face and realized what he had done.

"I'm . . ." He smiled, unable to hide his pleasure at the comfort of being with her like he used to be. "I wasn't thinking."

"It's okay," Sabrina said, knowing from the flutter in her belly that it was more than okay.

She took a moment to fan herself after Clark turned and knocked on the door. The door swung open almost immediately and a tall, wide man as white as snow stood in the expanse. His dark blue eyes zeroed in on Clark with suspicion before shifting to Sabrina. He smiled, looking her up and down in a way that made her feel exposed. He made the top of the wrong woman's dog list.

"We're here to see Benny," Clark said, getting the man's attention back. "He's here, right?"

"Who are you?" His words were mixed with laughter, as if even the thought of Clark and Sabrina getting in to see Benny was such a joke.

"Who are you?" Sabrina asked, already riled up from his disrespectful look.

Clark turned to Sabrina, his brows raised in that *what are you, crazy?* look.

Big Man laughed. "I like the attitude. Who am I? You can call me Daddy."

"Benny knows who I am," Clark said. "Clark Hunter, sports reporter."

The man leaned forward, eyes squinting. "You're Clark Hunter? From Chicago, right?"

Clark smiled, his chin held high. "That's me."

The man held his hand out. "Cool, man. I'm Dorian. I read your pieces all the time."

Clark shook his hand. "Nice to meet you, Dorian."

Sabrina rolled her eyes. This had been par for the course in Chicago. Everyone loved Clark Hunter. "What about Benny?"

"Now Benny," Dorian said, "he ain't so crazy about you."

"It wouldn't have anything to do with my series

on corruption in college basketball betting?" Clark
asked.

While working on that story about five years ago,
Clark had learned the name Benecio Silver for the
first time. Not in a flattering way.

"You got it," Dorian said, as he stepped aside.
"Come on in. He ain't doing nothing right now."

When they entered, Sabrina was floored by what
she saw. It reminded her of those cartoons where
the exterior and interior were polar opposites. Wall-
to-wall plush carpeting framed an expensively, although not too tastefully decorated room. Italian
leather furniture, state-of-the-art stereo equipment,
and a gigantic wide-screen flat television mounted
on the wall. A stark difference from the exterior.

"What in the . . ." Clark said, looking around.

"The place?" Dorian asked. "Benny says it's the
address that counts. As soon as folks hear the address, they don't concern themselves with how he
lives. It's an IRS thing. Besides, he only works here.
He lives in a posh penthouse in east LV."

That sounded more like it. Sabrina had known
eastern Las Vegas had many of the newer condos
and luxury apartments that newcomers were flock-
ing to. Nick lived there, as did many of the county's
richest residents.

"Where is he?" Sabrina asked.

"Down the hallway," Dorian said. "Follow me."

They followed him to a back room that looked
more like a NASA control center than a bookie's
office. Flat-screen monitors were set up side by
side in a half circle, all seeming to be controlled
by one keyboard where someone, sitting in a tall

leather chair with his back to them, was hard at work.

Sabrina had expected a setting resembling the old movies of dark rooms filled with stacks of paper and calculators. The bookie business was as high tech as it got.

"Yo, Benny," Dorian called out.

Sitting in the large leather chair, Benecio Silver swiveled around, not looking at all like the traditional slimy bookie. He was a relatively young man, no more than forty, clean-cut with a preppy dress style.

"What's up?" he asked, looking from Clark to Sabrina.

Dorian introduced Clark along with his credentials, which didn't seem to impress Benny too much. He seemed more intrigued with finding out who Sabrina was than anything else, and Sabrina, wanting to get out of there as soon as possible, decided to take advantage of his interest to get the ball rolling.

"I'm a friend of Nick Stewart," she said, noticing his smile immediately fade to an expressionless stone stare.

"I'm not familiar with that name," he said. "What do you two want?"

Clark looked at Sabrina, his brows drawing together in an angry frown. He should have known she wouldn't listen.

"Of course you know him," Sabrina continued. "He's mentioned you several times."

Benny shifted in his chair; his eyes squinted. "I'm a popular guy in this city. Just because people know my name doesn't mean I know theirs."

"He didn't just mention your name," Sabrina said, helping herself to the sofa on the other side of his desk. "He mentioned what you guys were working on."

Clark joined her on the sofa. This woman couldn't listen if it meant her life. "What my friend is trying to say is that we want in."

Benny laughed. "You must think I'm an idiot. I don't know who you're talking about and I don't know what you want in on. If you want to place a bet on tomorrow's fight, go get on-line. You look computer literate. I have a select clientele."

"How did you know we're here about the fight?" Sabrina asked. "You take bets on everything, right? So how did you know that's what we're here for?"

Clark was about to tape her mouth.

Benny's lips slipped into a sly, thin smile. "Everybody's about the fight. It's the only game in town right now."

Clark threw his plan out the window and decided to go for it. "We know what's up, Benny. We know that you're working with Tommy and Nick and possibly others to fix this fight. We know that you stand to make millions based on the odds."

Benny just kept on smiling. "What are you accusing me of, reporter?"

"You know what I'm here about," Clark said.

"I'm sorry, but I don't know." He was unflinching. "Now I'm very busy, so why don't you get out of my office and take your trick with you?"

Clark grabbed Sabrina just as she jumped up from the sofa and lunged for Benny. He pulled her back and she fell against the sofa.

"Wait a second," he pleaded with her.

"What?" Sabrina was fuming. She felt red all over and was ready for war. "Did you hear what he called me?"

"I'll handle it," Clark said, standing up. He turned to Benny, leaning across his desk. He ignored Dorian, stepping closer to them. "Look, Benny. You just lost your leeway with me."

"I'm supposed to be afraid of you?"

"You should be," Clark said. "I'm doing the story. And if you're thinking of doing anything to me, think again. The entire staff of the *Vegas Sun* and the *Chicago Sun Times* know I'm here, and I know you aren't that stupid."

"Doesn't mean I have to tell you anything."

"I don't need you to do the story, but if you do, I can help you after it's out there."

"You're not that famous."

Sabrina stood up. "Let's just get out of here. Do the story and screw him. He'll go to jail for a long time. Again."

Clark kept his eyes focused on Benny. "What about your little girl?"

Benny's entire body tightened. His lips pressed together and his eyes strained.

"I know about your court battle," Clark continued. "I know what your ex-wife is trying to do to you. This upcoming court date is your last chance, Benny. You haven't seen your daughter in what four years?"

Benny's chest heaved as his breathing picked up steam. He looked as if he wasn't sure whether to cry or blow a gasket. "You trying to blackmail me?"

Clark shook his head. "No way. That's not my

game. Like I said, there isn't anything you can do to keep me from writing this story. But what will look better in court three months from now? You being a major player in an illegal betting scam netting millions, or you being the guy that helped me expose it?"

Moving his head from left to right, Benny cracked his neck. "You've got some balls."

Clark shrugged. "You ready to show me you've got some too?"

"I'm not saying I know what you're talking about," Benny said, "but if I did, I would need more than your word."

"You want protection from prosecution," Clark said. "I can see what I can do."

"You'll have to do better than see," he ordered. "I'm talking about on paper. And you need to look into protection for yourself."

"Is that a threat?" Clark asked.

"Not from me. If what you say is true, and I'm not saying it is or isn't, but if it is, you better watch your back. You think my guys are tough? Tommy Gaxton has the street at his beck and call."

"You think he would kill to keep this from getting out?" Clark could only think of Sabrina, not himself.

"At least," Benny said.

Sabrina shuddered at the thought of Nick being involved with the type of people Benny was alluding to. "I just want to know one thing. How is Nick involved?"

"Where's my paper?" Benny asked. "I don't know nothing until I see some protection in writing."

Sabrina was around the desk in a second, too fast for Dorian to react. All three men were too stunned to react; she grabbed Benny by the collar of his polo.

"Answer me," she ordered.

"Sabrina." Clark checked for Dorian, who seemed to be contemplating whether or not he should do something. "It's okay. We'll get the paper."

"Answer me," Sabrina urged, pulling harder.

Benny grabbed his shirt from her, jerking away. He looked at her determined face as if she were crazy. "I'm not saying I know anything, but if I did, I might be able to say that he needed to be convinced at first, but not too much."

Sabrina turned away.

"But," Benny added, "I'm not saying anything for sure."

Clark retrieved Sabrina from behind the desk, leading her toward the door. "We get it, Benny. We'll be back later today."

"You're nuts," Clark said as soon as they were on the street again. "You know that? You're absolutely nuts."

"He made his bed when he called me a trick." Sabrina stepped into the street, stopping to turn to Clark, who stayed at the curb. "Nobody gets away with that. Not with me."

Clark tried to calm himself. "I can't believe you did that. I had a plan, Sabrina. You agreed to go along."

"We got what we wanted, didn't we?"

"That's not my point," Clark said.

Sabrina felt her nerves tighten. "Do you have to do this, Clark?"

"This story? Of course I do. It's why I'm here."

"I thought you were here to cover the domestic abuse angle? There's a lot of good you could do with that."

Clark approached her. "Don't get me wrong, Sabrina. I know that violence against women is a big issue. I'm not belittling it, but it's not the story. This is the big story. It's the kind of big story journalists get into this business for."

"You heard what he said. This goes beyond Tommy."

"We don't know for sure." Clark was touched by the concern in Sabrina's eyes. He remembered how much her concern comforted him, reached inside him. Changed him. "I wouldn't let you be touched in any way, Sabrina. I promise you that, but I can't back down. I wouldn't have any integrity if I did."

"But you would have your life," she said, her tone matching her anguish. "I couldn't bear it if anything happened to you."

In an act of pure emotion, Clark reached for her. He brought his lips to hers, meaning for nothing but comfort and gratitude. His lips possessed hers as he squeezed her tight and reminded her with his body that he would never tolerate her experiencing a second of inner torment over him. In his heart he knew there weren't words to explain how much he loved this woman and would give his life to keep her from a moment's pain.

"Hey!" a voice from someone nearby yelled out. "Watch out! Hey!"

Both Clark's and Sabrina's heads shot up and

turned toward the voice, but what they saw was a black sedan rushing toward them. Its deliberateness was undeniable. Clark grabbed Sabrina and pulled her with him as they fell backward to the ground near the curb. The car missed them by inches, not stopping for a second and speeding off.

"Are you guys all right?"

Sabrina looked up at a group of teenage boys who were standing over them. She felt disoriented and confused. "What just happened?"

Clark, feeling shook-up himself, stood up and held his hand out to Sabrina. "Are you okay?"

Sabrina nodded, not really feeling anything for a second as she let Clark pull her up.

"Man," one of the boys said, "that car tried to run you over. Maybe it was your husband or something."

"Or something," Clark said. "Thanks for the heads-up. We're fine."

Sabrina held on to Clark. "Did what I think just happened happen?"

Clark nodded. "That wasn't an accident."

"Did you see anyone?"

Clark looked down the street. "No. Tinted windows. Generic black sedan, but I think we know who it is."

"Benny? We just left—"

"Not Benny, Sabrina. Tommy."

"How would he know we were here?"

"They've probably been following me."

"This is it," Sabrina said, picking her purse up from the ground. She reached for her cell phone. "I'm calling the cops."

"I'll tell 'em what I saw," one of the boys said. He

and his crew were still there, standing a few feet away now, staring at Clark and Sabrina as if they expected them to pass out any second. "Half a license plate."

"Great," Sabrina said.

Clark grabbed the phone from Sabrina. "Wait a second. We can use this to our advantage."

"I don't care about your—" Sabrina watched a drop of bright red blood fall onto Clark's pant leg. "Oh my God. You're bleeding."

"Where?" Clark lifted his arms to reveal an inch-long gash starting from his elbow. "I'm so full of adrenaline I can't even feel it."

"We need to get you to the hospital."

"It's not that serious, Sabrina. We don't have time for that kind of thing."

"So what do we do?" she asked. "We have to do something. You're bleeding. If you won't go the hospital, you have to at least come to my house, so I can wrap you up."

"Go ahead and call the police," Clark said. "But I don't need the hospital."

He had to think of how he was going to play this. Now that Sabrina was in danger, the stakes were higher. He couldn't make a mistake. No story was worth her being harmed.

"Then you'll come home with me so I can fix that?" she asked.

Clark hesitated, knowing all the trouble that could come from this.

"What are you waiting for, man?" one of the boys asked. "A fine lady invites you to her house for any reason, you need to get to it."

EIGHT

It took a while for the police to show up, but after they arrived things went rather quickly. Both Sabrina and Clark gave their statements and one of the young men gave the partial license plate he had seen. Including everyone, the description of the black sedan was pretty solid.

What wasn't solid was Clark's explanation for why he thought it was deliberate as opposed to the officer's opinion that it was just a couple of kids having a little too much fun.

Sabrina watched with admiration as Clark convinced the reluctant officer that this was a big enough deal to call in a detective. Within minutes, the officer was Clark's best buddy and assured him that a detective would meet them at Sabrina's house in less than an hour.

It was a quiet drive back to Sabrina's house as they both let it sink in. Clark had been threatened before, due to stories he had written or threatened to write, but no one had tried to kill him. Really, it was Sabrina he was worried about. This had never happened to her and it was his fault. All he wanted was to be a part of her life again and all he had accomplished was placing her life in danger.

"Straight to the kitchen," Sabrina ordered as soon as they entered the apartment. "Don't get any blood on my carpet."

Clark did as he was ordered, feeling the tension rise the second he closed the front door behind him. He was in Sabrina's new home, a symbol of the life she was building without him. He didn't care to let it sink in, instead rushing to the kitchen as told.

"Put this on it." Sabrina tossed him a hand towel.

"I think the bleeding stopped a while ago," Clark said, even though the pain seemed to be picking up.

She wasn't listening to him. Next to the sink, she was carefully arranging a selection of first-aid materials that Clark had seen only on medical television shows.

"What is all this?" he asked.

Sabrina waved him closer. "My downstairs neighbor is a nurse. She had an idea to put together these first-aid kits, so I worked with her and got the Acropolis to sponsor and market the event for the community."

Clark admired her heart. "That was a great thing to do."

"They're really great kits." Sabrina turned away from him, not wanting him to see how the slightest compliment from him made her feel.

"They look a little complicated for an everyday person."

"They aren't. They come with instructions on the top of the box on how to use everything, in English and Spanish."

"All right," he said. "Hook me up."

"First, take the shirt off."

Clark smiled at her as if he thought she was kidding, but she wasn't. The tension of the moment was kicking up a notch. He was alone with Sabrina in her home and he was about to take his shirt off. What could that lead to?

"What are you thinking?" Sabrina asked. "You're covered in blood, Clark. You don't have to worry about me being taken over by passion at the sight of your bare chest."

His ego deflated, Clark rolled his eyes and removed his shirt. "Where?"

"Toss it on the floor with that towel." Sabrina gripped the edge of the sink a little tighter. Boy, had she been wrong! The sight of Clark's tight, muscled chest did give her a little tingle. More than a little. *Just stay focused. He is bleeding, after all, and you were both almost killed. Why would sex be on your mind right now?*

Sabrina couldn't really remember anything but sex on her mind when she and Clark were alone together and somebody was half clothed.

"Next?" Clark asked, the pain distracting him from what he wanted to concentrate on: Sabrina.

"Just lean over this sink so I can wipe you down." Sabrina heard the words come from her mouth and knew they were innocent in nature, but somehow didn't sound so.

Clark just stood there. He didn't really know what to do. His mind told him that she was trying to treat his injury, but her words only excited him.

"Turn around," Sabrina said, hearing her voice crack just a little. "I need the back of your arm."

Clark turned around and leaned into the sink. He tried to control his breathing, looking around the classically decorated kitchen, as Sabrina turned the water on. He noticed the Italian touch, which Sabrina had taken to after the two of them vacationed in Venice. Clark tried to find something to focus on as his body braced in anticipation of her touch.

He flinched when he finally felt the hot rag rub gently down the back of his arm. Images of showers and baths taken together flashed before him, making his body heat up.

"Is it too hot?" Sabrina asked, feeling her throat become dry.

"No," Clark answered. The irony.

Clark was grateful he had his back to her, allowing him to close his eyes and bite his lower lip as she continued. The movements were almost painful in themselves as they were so nurturing, so gentle, so like the way only Sabrina knew how to touch him.

He could smell her perfume and feel her body heat just inches from his and it made Clark weak in the best and worst ways. This woman. Clark did all he could to keep from acting on his desire for Sabrina right now. It was hard, but he knew this wasn't the time. Because of him, she had almost been hurt, possibly killed, and now they were both in danger. Trying to make a move right now would not be a smart idea.

Later, after this could be resolved, maybe he could—

"Ahhhhhhh!" Clark felt cold, sharp pain rip through his entire body. He swung around, jerking his arm away from a surprised Sabrina. "What are you doing to me?"

"It's to stave off infection," she answered. "It's an open cut, Clark. Don't be such a baby."

"That feels like acid."

"An infection feels worse. Now turn around."

Clark gritted his teeth as she finished wiping him down with what he was sure was battery acid no matter what she said. So much for fighting the passion.

"Now I have to wrap it." Sabrina reached for the gauze, feeling grateful that Clark was being as difficult as he was. Her annoyance with him was keeping her from thinking about how her body was reacting to having him standing half dressed so close to her.

After she finished, Sabrina gave him a glass of water and a pill for his pain before ordering him into the living room so she could clean up. Alone again, Clark sat on the sofa observing her handiwork.

"I think you did too much, Sabrina." He held his arm up to her as she passed by. "It's kind of tight."

"Quit your complaining."

A sense of familiarity and comfort fell over Clark at her dismissal of his whining. Like old times. As he looked around Sabrina's living room, Clark saw the familiar decorations from her apartment in Chicago, where he had spent so many nights. The lamps she purchased at an estate sale in suburban Glencoe. The painting she won at a charity auction for a youth center in Chicago. The wall clock she treasured so much, which her father brought back from a trip to England.

For her being such a conservative woman, Clark had always found Sabrina's home to be warm and welcoming. It reflected the woman she really was, and Clark had felt it such a privilege to be one of the exclusive group of people to see the way she let herself go when she was in the comfort of her own home.

He wanted this. He wanted this all back. It didn't matter where it was—wherever Sabrina lived was where he wanted to be. Where he belonged. He had been in this home for mere minutes and already had an overwhelming feeling that he had been there for years, that this was his home, the place where he could rest his head, his heart, and feel like a man. He felt this way because everywhere he looked were images of Sabrina's style, her taste, and her heart. Any other home, no matter how nice, would always seem less than.

Sabrina looked at her reflection in the medicine cabinet mirror as she stood alone in her bathroom. The smile on her face wasn't by choice. It was as if her heart had a mind of its own and had decided to go on enjoying this experience with or without her.

She was too happy, too comfortable with Clark back in her life. She was supposed to be filled with rage, anger, and resentment toward him. He had broken her heart and only come back to almost get her killed. She was supposed to break down and cry at the thought of him, wasn't she? He had betrayed her in the worst way a man could betray a woman. Hadn't he?

But here she was, not only talking to him, spending time with, but inviting him to her home and dressing his wounds. She was taking care of him like she always had as if nothing had ever happened. And she was liking it. Loving just the feeling her home had with him in it.

The first kiss, she could understand. It was a moment of weakness and emotion. She hadn't been prepared for him and allowed him to catch her off guard.

Then there was that second time. Sabrina shrugged, looking closer into the mirror as if she could find something in the face on the other side that explained that to her. Why had she allowed him to even walk her to her car, let alone kiss her, and kiss her like that? Like he used to when he knew what he wanted and had no doubt he was going to get it.

Sabrina knew there was nothing in that mirror that could come up with an excuse for why she kissed Clark today. That was all inside her, the real Sabrina, not the mirrored image that held no responsibility or accountability for her feelings, her actions. She kissed him because she wanted to feel his lips on hers. Not for passion, but for love. At that one moment, the thought of him being in the kind of danger that Benny Silver insinuated wiped everything else away, including what little faith she still had in the reason she left Clark in the first place.

Sabrina didn't trust anything about herself or what she was feeling right now. Wondering if her best friend was a criminal, believing that he just tried to kill her or harm her at best, and now wanting to be with the man who she was certain had destroyed her life and not knowing how she could possibly get her life back if she had made a mistake about it all.

This past Monday morning, which seemed like a year ago now, she woke up dreading another long, lonely week with only her pride and principles to keep her warm at night. A few days later, her turned-upside-down life had been flipped over yet again by the person she thought once would make everything right.

"Therein lies the issue."

Sabrina blinked as she saw the lips of her mirrored image move and heard the words. "What?"

"It's not up to a man to make everything right for you," her image said. "It's up to you. When you figure that out, you'll know whether or not he deserves to be in your life."

Sabrina blinked again, wondering if she was going crazy. Sometimes the desert sun could get to a girl. Not to mention an attempt on her life. "What is going on here?"

Nothing. The image was her again, mimicking her every expression and word. Sabrina turned the faucet on, splashing her face with water. She looked at herself again, feeling a little more levelheaded.

"Must have been my imagination," she said out loud, watching to make sure every movement of her lips was repeated. "Must have been."

When Sabrina returned to her living room she was caught by surprise as the voices she thought was Clark watching television was actually Clark talking to another man sitting across from him on the sofa. Dressed in a pale beige suit that looked way too thick for the season, the man didn't look a day over twenty-five. He had sandy blond hair and a country-boy way about him that made you think he was straightforward and honest.

"Hello." Sabrina approached them.

Both men turned to her, Clark with a concerned look on his face.

"What have you been doing?" Clark asked. "I was about to come looking for you any second now."

"I was in the bathroom cleaning up," she answered. *Trying to get my head back on straight after being so close to you.* She wasn't even sure how long she'd been gone. "I got you this."

She tossed an oversized University of Nevada at Las Vegas sweatshirt at him, hoping that the covering of his glowing, perfect skin would calm her libido. She doubted it, but it was worth a try.

"You were gone for a long time," Clark said, noticing that the color in her face was a little weak. Maybe their encounter with the deadly car was really hitting her. He had to make sure she was going to be okay.

"Sabrina," he said, "this is Detective Sean Donovan."

The detective stood up, holding his hand out to her. "Mrs. Hunter?"

"What?" Sabrina felt something like a burst of heavy air hit her chest, halting her breathing for a second. It was just a simple mistake.

"Sabrina isn't my wife," Clark said, embarrassed. "She's a friend of mine. Her last name is Scott. It's in the report."

"Sorry." Detective Donovan seemed to realize that Sabrina wasn't going to shake his hand, so he sat back down. "Are you all right?"

"I didn't hear you come in," Sabrina said, nodding. She hurried to the recliner across from the sofa just in case her knees got weak again. Mrs. Hunter.

"I was explaining our situation with Benny to Detective Donovan here," Clark explained.

"Can you do anything?" Sabrina asked.

Donovan shrugged. "I'll have to see. Benny Silver has a lot to offer. My lieutenant isn't going to flip him just for you. We'll want more from him than this fight."

"But the fight is a big deal," Clark said. "Bigger than you might think. We're talking Tommy Gaxton. You know he's been caught up in this type of thing before."

"And he got out of it," Donovan said. "He played the race card and had the only viable witness deported."

"So you know what we're dealing with here," Clark said. "Your lieutenant should be happy to hear that."

"And I don't think Benny is enough to bring someone like him down. Now if we had Artemis . . ."

"He doesn't have the balls," Clark said. "What if Benny had some really strong proof?"

"Does he?" Donovan asked.

"I don't know yet."

"That's a problem."

"What time line are we looking at?" Sabrina asked wondering if there was still time to save Nick, al though she wasn't so sure if she wanted to at this point.

"I can't promise anything before tomorrow," Donovan said.

"The fight is tomorrow night." Clark's mind was racing through alternatives if Benny didn't pan out. The accusation was too dangerous without a solid informant on his side.

"Exactly," Donovan said. "Fight weekend brings a lot of freaks to Vegas. And that's saying a lot for this town. We're backed up on investigating domestic disputes, underage betting, and the like."

"Will tomorrow be too late?" Sabrina asked Clark.

"As long as we get enough proof before the fight, we can possibly stop it from happening." Clark turned to Donovan. "Right?"

"It depends on what type of proof you have. Tommy Gaxton isn't as stupid as he looks. What kind of paper trail are we talking about? It would have to be strong."

Sabrina wondered, if she told Nick any of this, would it change his mind? They didn't have anything on him yet. Then again, there was the attempt to run her and Clark over, but Sabrina couldn't let go of the hope that Nick wasn't behind that.

Detective Donovan stood up. "I have to go back to the station and talk to my lieutenant about this. Can I reach you here?"

"I'm staying at the Acropolis." Clark stood up, putting the sweatshirt on.

Donovan frowned. "Is that such a good idea after what you've told me?"

Clark nodded. "You're right. I'll get a room somewhere else. I'll call you when I know."

"Here's my card," Donovan said, handing it to him. "I'll check on where we are with that partial plate."

Sabrina felt her stomach tightening around the reality of what was happening. She was so torn. She was angry over what had happened, but at the core of who she was, her loyalty urged her to make things right for Nick.

"Don't do that," Clark said the second he returned from showing Detective Donovan out. He was quick to notice Sabrina reaching for the phone.

"What?" She pulled away like a child caught with her hand just at the edge of the cookie jar. "I was just—"

"You were going to call Nick. Don't lie to me, Sabrina."

"I'm not lying to you, Clark. I never have."

Clark checked himself. He was tense right now. He couldn't let everything she said upset him. She was just as upset. "I know that you care about Nick. He's been your friend in the past, but he just tried to kill us."

"We don't know if that was Nick and we don't know if the intent was to kill."

"Do you think that was an accident?" Clark felt his temper rise.

"No, but I don't think Nick was behind it. Tommy, yes, but not Nick. He wouldn't let anyone hurt me."

Clark eyed her skeptically. "Why are you so adamant he's still the man you thought he was?"

Sabrina blinked, looking into Clark's green eyes. He was angry and she could feel the tension coming from him as he stood only a few feet away.

"He's my friend. I don't want to believe the worst about him."

"Yet you were willing to believe the worst about me and I was more than your friend." Clark couldn't help it, as he realized what was really irking him.

"Stop it," Sabrina said. "I don't want to talk about this now."

"You talk about evidence," Clark said, not listening to her. "You saw the Cayman account form on his desk, and you tasted the asphalt a couple of hours ago just like me, yet . . ."

"I didn't say I don't believe he's involved in the scheme. I've admitted that. I just don't believe he would try to have me hurt or killed." Sabrina threw her hands in the air, not wanting to feel the tears that were screaming in her throat. "I'm not going to argue with you about this."

Jumping up from her seat, she headed for the kitchen. She didn't want Clark to see how upset his attack made her. She had wondered if they would ever be able to overcome what had happened between them if it was true that she was wrong. Or, would it always be between them as her unforgivable lack of faith?

"Where are you going?" Clark asked, already feeling guilty for his unwarranted outburst.

"I'm getting something to eat."

He didn't bother to follow her, knowing it would only make her angrier. He was such a fool to slap her in the face with that comparison. Even if it was gnawing at him, he should have kept it to himself and worked it out alone. What chance did he ever have of getting Sabrina back if she was afraid he would throw her mistake right back in her face?

The only chance he had of making things better was to give her the proof she needed. Reaching for his cell phone, Clark noticed that the batteries had run out so he chose Sabrina's phone instead. Much more technically literate than he, Lauren recently showed him a way to check his cell phone's messages whether or not the phone was alive.

"You have two messages," the automated voice said.

Clark hoped at least one was from Lauren and he was rewarded right away.

"Where in the hell are you, Clark? I've been calling your cell and your hotel room all day. You're not at the *Sun* either, where you should be getting some work done. You better not be hurt or dead or anything. I've got great news. You've got to call me back. You're not going to believe what I did. Call me at 602-555-7788."

Clark was confused. Why would she want him to call her back at a number in . . . Where was the 602 area code?

"Damn!" Clark was ready to hang up before the next message started.

"Mr. Hunter, I'm sorry. Look, I'm sorry."

Clark couldn't recognize the woman's voice. It was shaky and whoever it was, she was crying while she spoke.

"Mr. Hunter, look . . . I didn't mean it. I was . . . I thought you had taken everything I wanted and . . ."

As realization hit him, Clark had to hold on to the wall to keep from falling over. Lauren had been calling him from Arizona!

"And I wanted to take what you had." A few sniffs. "She seemed to be the only thing that really mattered to you from what I could see. I worked my whole life so much harder than I should have and Michael was going to be a way out for all of us. After he spoke to you, he started doubting. . . ."

Clark understood now. After he interviewed Michael, Michael began doubting what he wanted and Cara blamed Clark for it. He had encouraged Michael to give college a second look for the valuable experience, but he had no idea Michael would desert basketball altogether. Whatever happened, Cara must have wanted the money and she blamed Clark for not getting it.

"Well, things didn't work out like I'd hoped," she continued, "and . . . you have a good friend in that woman who came by today with Michael. She was ready to take on hell in order to get me to listen to her and . . ."

Clark was shaking his head in disbelief. This wasn't happening. Lauren had somehow gotten Michael to come to Scottsdale with her and the two of them worked together to get Cara to confess.

"I'm sorry. I just . . . I'm sorry. I hope you work it out with her."

Clark stood there, staring into space as he listened to the voice prompt him to press the seven key if he wanted to erase.

"Hell no," he said.

"Who are you talking to?" Sabrina asked as she returned with the intention of apologizing. She was alarmed by the look on his face. He seemed half dazed. "What's wrong with you?"

A wide smile stretched from cheek to cheek. "Sabrina, you aren't going to believe . . ."

Locked in its recharger, Sabrina's cell phone

was ringing, taking her attention away as she reached for it. She looked at the LED display, taking a deep breath as she saw who it was before turning it on.

"Nick?" She tried to maintain some calm in her voice.

Clark hung up the phone, walking over to Sabrina. "Sabrina, don't—"

Sabrina held her hand up to silence him. "What is it, Nick?"

"Where are you, Sabrina?" Nick's voice sounded guarded. "I just tried to call you at home, but I'm getting your machine."

"I'm not at my house," she lied.

"Where are you? I need you here."

"I'm safe, in case you were wondering."

A short pause. "What are you talking about?"

"I'm with Clark and I'm safe."

A longer pause. "You've been with Clark?"

"Yes, I've been with him all day."

"I thought you were at the career day, Sabrina. I would never have—"

"Never what?" Sabrina looked at Clark, conveying with her eyes that Nick was guilty as hell. "You would never have what, Nick?"

"Sabrina." Nick sighed heavily. "What you saw in my office this morning. You told Tommy, didn't you?"

"I don't know what you're talking about." Sabrina felt fear creep through her. He couldn't possibly have been watching her while he was in the bathroom. Maybe he had cameras in his office that she didn't know about.

"Never mind, Sabrina. Don't worry about anything."

"I think it's gotten past that. Don't you, Nick?"

"Sabrina, don't . . . Look, I promise nothing will happen to you."

"Why would anything happen to me?" She wanted him to admit it. She wanted him to tell her the truth. She felt she deserved it.

"Just know that nothing will," Nick said flatly before hanging up.

Sabrina turned to Clark. "He says that I'm safe."

"So he admitted to it?"

"Not in those words. He thought I was at career day. He knows what I saw in his office somehow and I think he told Tommy."

"He thought Tommy was just going to go after me."

Sabrina nodded with a defeated sigh. "I can't believe he would agree to do that to anyone. You could have been killed. He had to know that."

"I'm sorry, Sabrina."

Clark compassionately wrapped his arm around her as her head fell onto his chest. She was more tired than anything. She always cried when she got to the point of exhaustion. Clark listened to her whispered crying, running his fingers through her hair to soothe her. She always liked that. It reminded her of how her mother used to calm her when she was a little girl.

"Little Sabrina," he said, smiling with joy at her closeness and her vulnerability. She was a strong woman and these moments were a gift.

"What?" Sabrina looked up at him, feeling so at home in his arms.

"You carefully select the people you let into your

heart. That's why it tears you apart so much when they hurt you."

"I'm so stupid," she said, meaning more than what she thought about Nick.

Clark held her away, looking intently into her eyes. "Don't ever say that. You aren't stupid, Sabrina. You're the smartest woman I know."

"How can you, of all people, not think I'm a fool?"

Clark gently wiped the tears from her cheek with his finger, smiling at her. "Because I love you, and I wouldn't love a fool."

A powerful current ripped through them both and they lunged for each other. Their potent magnetism, which had been there from day one, brought their lips together in a fiery possession.

Sabrina wrapped her arms around him, grabbing at him desperately as his lips captivated hers, making her dizzy and intoxicated. The strength of him broke down everything that mattered and that was the way she wanted. She escaped in his lips, from the good and the bad—escaped it all into fantasy.

Clark's lips held a savage intensity and they demanded a response. The delicious sensation of her soft touch and hungry hands were creating an unbearable heat inside him.

As his lips traveled over her neck and shoulders, Sabrina pulled at his shirt. She felt her limbs trembling, her body quivering as he lifted her blouse above her head.

Her head fell back with a lusty groan as Clark undid the front hook of her bra. When his warm, caressing hand cupped her breast, her flesh prickled everywhere at the touch.

"Clark!"

Her outcry of delight caused their eyes to meet. With her senses spinning and her body aching, Sabrina knew one more second and she would lose all reason.

"Protection," she said, breathlessly, looking into his dark, smoldering eyes.

He drank in the sweetness, the seduction of her desire. Nothing turned Clark on more than seeing Sabrina turned on.

"I can take care of that," he answered.

"The bedroom is down the hall," she said, pointing with shaky fingers.

"We're right here," Clark said. With care for his injury, he lifted the sweatshirt over his head.

They were on the sofa in seconds, sharing, teasing, and promising with torturous kisses in between disrobing.

Naked with her, Clark leaned back to take in the body that made his knees weak every time he saw it. Pleasure radiated from him as he took in the delicately dangerous curves of her full breasts, her shapely hips, and the shining glow of her perfectly browned skin. Her slim waist rolled into rounded hips that invited him to ecstasy as she lay back.

"What are you waiting for?" Sabrina asked, biting her lower lip.

Clark gave her a wicked smile. "I think we've both waited long enough for this."

With demanding mastery, his lips came to the core of her belly, leaving kisses strategically, deliberately placed to induce madness in her. Each kiss was like a coaxing whisper, bringing her body closer and closer to abandon.

As her fingers dug into the flesh of his back, Clark felt a guttural moan escape him. Every place on her body was like wine and he wanted to drink in every inch of her. As he slowly, purposefully moved up, he begged himself to be patient. He had waited for what seemed like a decade to touch her again. He wanted to savor every moment, every second of what was his own personal heaven.

When his lips first touched her breast, Sabrina couldn't breathe. Electric shock couldn't have had a stronger effect. The tease, always the tease, and how she missed it as his tongue left a bubbling hot circle around her taut nipple before his mouth encompassed her.

"Oh God." Her body wriggled in agony underneath his warmth, his strength. As he explored both her breasts, Sabrina succumbed to the passion that pounded throughout her body.

As he tasted the sweetness of her soft, silky breast, Clark's hand caressed her thighs. His whole being was flooded with desire and he knew he had only one second more before he'd forget about protection, and he couldn't do that.

Sabrina's apparent arousal at the sight of his hard erectness as he applied the protection urged Clark to work faster than he ever had. One second away from Sabrina was two seconds too many.

Positioned on top of her, Clark looked into Sabrina's waiting eyes. There was no disguise, no resentment, no anguish there. Just the surrender she'd always offered him. The surrender that said, *Make me your woman.*

This is what he did.

As he entered her, Sabrina was filled with an amazing completeness. Her body burst into a golden wave of pleasure and pain. With each thrust, she met him and together they sent searing flames through each other. Ebb and flow. Their passionate lovemaking, their turbulent lovemaking filled the room, the world, and their souls.

Beyond the point of no return, tremors ripped through them as the sensations went higher and higher, sending them both into a hysteria until gusts of fire exploded inside them. Together, they cried out in surrender to the trembling, consuming joy that made everything in the world worth it. Everything.

Sabrina's eyes opened as the bright sun rays streamed through her bedroom curtains. Her lips fluidly stretched into a warm, honest smile as the memory of last night returned to her. They had made love three times before their starvation forced them to eat something. Later, holding each other silently in bed, they fell asleep in each other's arms.

Sabrina rolled around in bed, expecting to see a gently sleeping Clark, but was surprised when she saw him lying up in bed, head resting sideways on his hand, staring at her.

"Morning," Clark said, happy she was awake even though he enjoyed watching her sleep for that short while. "I love the way you wake up."

"You do?"

"Yes. Most people wake up all cranky and confused, looking like death just missed them. Not you. You always open your eyes with a smile on your beautiful face. You look so fresh."

The way this man made her feel was sometimes unreal. "How long have you been awake?"

"Just a few minutes." His fingers gently touched strands of her hair, moving them from in front of her face. He couldn't imagine ever loving anyone the way he loved Sabrina Scott.

"We have a big day in front of us." Sabrina noticed a few lines on his forehead. He was worried about something. "Everything will work out, Clark. I'm sure Benny will get what he wants and he'll tell the cops everything."

"That's not what I'm thinking about right now."

Sabrina tenderly touched his cheek, caressing it with care. "I know, Clark. I'm really okay with Nick. I'm disappointed and I'm hurt, but I'm okay. I won't cause any problems there. I'm going to let you do what you have to do and stay out of it."

"I'm not worried about Nick." Clark sat up. "I'm thinking about us."

Sabrina felt anxiety reach within her. "If you're worried about last night, don't be. I wasn't coerced into anything. I wanted you just as much as you wanted me."

"But what now?" Clark asked, knowing he should probably have left well enough alone, but that wasn't his style.

Sabrina sat up, unable to look directly at him. "I don't know, Clark. I really needed you last night. I really . . ."

"Missed me?" His hand lay on her soft bare shoulder. Just touching her did something incredible to him. "I've missed you too, Sabrina. More than you could imagine. But that doesn't solve our problem."

"Can anything?" she asked, finally looking at him. The strain in his face matched hers.

"What if I had complete proof that everything I said was true? That Cara set me up and lied to you just to hurt me?"

"For what reason?" Sabrina didn't even want to talk about this. It had been so nice just moments ago.

"Because she believed I had influenced her brother to give up going pro and go to college. She wanted him to go pro so the family could get the money right away. She thought I—"

"Stop." Sabrina held her hand up. "You're speculating and I don't . . . I don't want to go over that again. The reality of what we're doing right now is hard enough. Every time she comes up, the past comes rushing back to me and I don't want to go back to it."

"Even if it means we could resolve it?"

"Even if I were to believe you," Sabrina said, "what does that mean? The damage has been done, hasn't it? I failed the test."

"Sabrina, don't—"

"I broke the trust, didn't I?" Sabrina shook her head. "No, I can't deal with this right now. God, Clark. We were supposed to get married today!"

Silence fell over them as the reality of Sabrina's words sucked all the air out of the room. This was to be their wedding day, and the trail of shattered dreams had a paralyzing effect on them both.

"You're leaving tomorrow morning," she said in almost a whisper. "The day we were supposed to leave for Fiji, you're leaving for Chicago. Why can't we just enjoy last night and move on with our lives?"

"Do you think that it would be possible for us to just compartmentalize what happened between us last night?" Clark asked.

Sabrina didn't believe that for a second. "I don't see another choice."

"You'll never convince me you want to let it go."

"I could never let it go." A runaway tear trailed down her left cheek as she looked at him. "I will always remember the pain and betrayal I felt. My world crashed down around me and my heart and mind were trying to kill each other."

"I know my frantic behavior didn't make it any easier," Clark said.

"There was no way to make that easier, but the fact still remains. I don't think I could ever let it go. Whether it was true or not."

Her words felt like a bullet shot through his heart and Clark could only turn away. He could play the message Cara left for him, but that wouldn't do any good. This was what tore at him.

"You don't believe I cheated on you, Sabrina. Not anymore, I don't think you do. I could show you all the proof in the world and it wouldn't make any difference."

Sabrina's tears picked up pace. "Don't make me the bad guy."

"I haven't made you the bad guy, Sabrina. You have and you can't get past that. This isn't about what I did or didn't do to you anymore. It's about you getting over what you did."

"You can't look at me and tell me you don't have anger toward me," she pressed. "I saw it in your eyes the second you showed up in that press room Tuesday."

"I felt anger for a long time," Clark said. "But I can see more clearly now what you went through. I had been caught up in my own feelings and I failed to see that you did what you had to do."

"I did," she claimed. "That's all I could do."

"I know. Coming here and seeing you, Sabrina." Clark shook his head. "Damn, I mean just looking at you, talking to you began to ease my anger. Then last night, making love to you again wiped it all away. I swear on my mother's grave."

"Clark." He could never know what his words were doing to her right now.

"I would do anything to have you back, Sabrina. But that's not what you want. You want what happened to just disappear. In your neat orderly life, you can't move past your own mistakes."

"Stop it!" Sabrina stood up, wrapping a bedsheet around her. "You have no right to come back into my life and judge me. A big part of me died inside that day."

"Every part of me wishes I could take that away," Clark said. "Make it disappear and never have happened, but I can't. We hit a glitch. We had a test and we both failed. The question is, are you strong enough to try again?"

"I need more time," she answered. "I'm sorry, Clark, but I've been spending the last four months in Vegas trying to pull my life together and deal with the fact that the one time I let a man mean more to me than anything else I paid the ultimate price for it. Now, you come back and tell me it was all—"

"We don't have to solve everything today," he said. "All we have to do is agree to give everything we have into trying."

"I can't agree to anything right now." Sabrina felt a complete breakdown coming on. "I can't do this anymore. I have to take a shower. Today may not be my wedding day, but it's still a very important one."

Clark felt like slamming his fist into the wall. Sabrina was a woman. She had the luxury of crying to let it all out. He couldn't bring himself to do that. He had cried only once in this ordeal and that was the night that Sabrina left Chicago and Clark thought he couldn't go on without her.

He was so angry. This renewed chance to prove he hadn't cheated on Sabrina had filled him with hope that he hadn't thought he would have a chance to feel ever again. He had been making progress, spurring on her doubt, and finally the bomb had dropped. A taped confession and the most incredible night of lovemaking they had ever shared!

It all meant nothing. Nothing. It wasn't proof Sabrina needed, it was faith, and that wasn't something he could find and deliver to her. She had to find it herself and Clark wasn't so sure she wanted to.

He had to figure out a way to make it worth it to her to try. It didn't matter how long he had to stay in Vegas or how long he had to wait. He would have Sabrina back and together they would work through whatever they needed to in order to get back what they had. It was a tough bet, but one he was willing to place everything he was as a man on.

* * *

Sabrina let the tears stream with the water down her face as she stood in the shower. Her hands pressed against the wall, she leaned forward, wanting to feel cleansed of all the conflicting emotions she was feeling. How could she be acting like this? Here was Clark holding his hand, his heart out to her, promising to give her everything back that was ripped from her. Promising to give her back everything she always wanted: real love that could last forever.

A voice in the back of her mind tried to convince Sabrina there was still that matter of the pictures and the taped conversations, but she wasn't buying it anymore. She'd had the doubt since Clark arrived in Las Vegas, not to mention the words he spoke just moments ago. It all just fed into what ultimately convinced her of the truth, which was when he held her in his arms last night and made love to her. The way he touched her, looked into her eyes let Sabrina know that man had never lied to her. Would never have lied to her.

But that was then. That was when she deserved that from a man. She broke his heart and destroyed her own. She let reason win over years of love and trust. "Win over" wasn't even the right phrase, because she never even let them fight it out. For all he had done for her, meant to her, Clark deserved more than she had given him. She let her heart and hurt pride shut him up and out. She accepted from a stranger that the man who had made her believe that everything was possible would betray her when he promised her with his love he never would. Proof or not, Clark had deserved more than Sabrina had given him and that was what was killing her.

She had betrayed their love.

This fact, this failure was what tore at her and kept her from accepting the promise he offered. Was it pride? Not really, but something like it. She had made such a huge mistake and was scared to death to live with it. What they'd had was so real and she gave it up for fear of being made a fool. That fear paralyzed her now and she couldn't look to anyone but herself to get out of it.

A fool walks in pride. That was something her mother told her a long time ago. A fool walks in pride and usually walks alone.

There had been something about Clark Hunter that opened Sabrina up. She held back from such emotion, such true deep love before him. Sabrina remembered how, only weeks after they had gotten engaged, she had written the vows she wanted to say on their wedding night. She had memorized them and sketched them into her heart.

There was a reason my view of love changed when I met you. There was a reason you were the one that made me open up completely, made me willing to risk everything to feel. We were meant to be together and God wasn't going to let even my inborn stubbornness get in the way of something He meant to happen.

"No!" Sabrina yelled out loud, feeling all of her senses coming awake.

Leaving the water running, she jumped out of the shower with only time to grab a towel. She almost slipped on the bathroom floor, but grabbed the doorknob just in time to save herself. She couldn't wait. Dripping wet, she ran into her bedroom.

"Clark, I'm sorry!"

Only no one was there. Sabrina looked frantically around, but her bedroom was empty. She rushed into the living room, but Clark wasn't there either.

"Clark." She called his name wistfully because she knew it was for nothing.

Heading back for her bathroom, Sabrina wondered if her words had turned Clark away from her for good. Had her stupid hesitation cost her her last chance?

Just as she reached the bathroom, a piece of white paper laid delicately on her oversized peach pillow caught her eye. Sabrina ran to it, grabbing the sheet of paper as her towel fell from her naked body. She didn't care.

> *Sabrina*
>
> *I understand everything. I promise. It will all be okay. I'm going to press Detective Donovan on Benny. Be careful today and I'll come to the Acropolis later. We'll have lunch and talk. No pressure.*
>
> ❤ *Clark*

Sabrina held the note to her chest, soaking it. She was acting like a high school girl, but it had been a long time since she'd felt hope. There was a chance for her and Clark. She accepted some time ago that she would and could form some type of life and go on without him, but believing now that she didn't have to was opening up a new world for her.

Now if only Clark could keep himself from getting killed so they could have a chance at the world.

NINE

"They got to you!" Clark slammed his fist on Benny Silver's desk.

Clark was fuming. He had spent all morning with Detective Donovan convincing his lieutenant to speed up the process with Benny. Finally convinced, the lieutenant gave Donovan permission to see what Benny had to say. Only when they arrived, Clark witnessed Benny qualify for an Oscar as he played innocent, denying any such knowledge of Tommy, Nick, or any rumor of a fixed fight.

Benny shrugged his shoulders with a tilt of his head. "Look, Hunter, I told you yesterday I didn't know anything. Why would I know something today?"

"You stand to make a lot of money, Benny," Detective Donovan said.

"I stand to make a lot of money either way," Benny said. "I'm a bookie."

"Most people are going to bet on Artemis Grove,"

Donovan countered. "You can stack it in your favor if you encourage them to do that."

"Artemis is gonna beat that guy to a pulp," Benny said. "Everyone knows that. They don't need my advice. Besides, there are some people betting on the other guy. I'll make money either way. The legal way."

"Let's go." Detective Donovan rolled his eyes as he shoved his notepad back into his back pocket. "This is a waste of my time."

"Wait a second," Clark said. "Benny, what about your little girl?"

Benny blinked, showing a second's worth of emotion. It was then that Clark realized what was going on. What was really going on. He had been stupid not to think of it before.

"They haven't threatened you," he said to Benny. "They've threatened your daughter, haven't they?"

"What's this about the daughter?" Donovan asked, seeming curious again.

Benny pushed away from his desk, his lips pressed together in anger. "Look, I told you what I know and it's nothing that can help you. My daughter isn't any of your business and she's got nothing to do with nothing."

Clark shook his head. "I'm sorry, Benny. I didn't mean for this to happen."

"Just get out," Benny said. "It's fight day. I don't have time to talk to you guys about something I don't know nothing about no way."

Clark looked at him, seeing in Benny's eyes something he wasn't supposed to. There was fear. This was a dead end. They would get nothing from Benny Silver.

"I'm busy today too," Donovan said, already turning to leave. "Hunter, let's go."

"Can I have a second?" Clark asked.

Donovan turned to him with skeptical eyes. "I'll be downstairs for five minutes. Then I'm driving off with or without you."

"Thanks."

Donovan took a second to look around. "Pretty nice place you got here, Silver. Is it all clean?"

"Got receipts right in this drawer," Benny said, tapping his desk. "Any time you want to check."

Donovan looked at Clark again. "Five minutes."

Clark turned to Benny, who was apparently done with the facade. He stared Clark down with a snarling curl to his upper lip.

"You brought a damn detective to my place!"

"I told you I was going to work something out for you."

"That stuff is supposed to be on the down low."

"I didn't think we had time for that. I told you what happened to me and Sabrina outside here yesterday."

"You could have warned me about that."

"I'm sorry, Benny. I was a little concerned with my own life and the life of the woman I love."

"This is the last thing I need."

"What did they say to you?" Clark asked. "Tommy, Nick."

"I'm not talking to you anymore. Nothing is worth what this could cost me."

"You could end up going to jail if I get proof somewhere else."

Benny sighed, looking at the picture of the wide-eyed little girl on his desk. With wild ponytails going in every direction, she was smiling from cheek to cheek with less than three teeth in her mouth.

"That's acceptable," Benny said.

Clark wished he could do more. "I understand."

"Now get out of my office. You've already done enough damage."

Standing outside Benny's building, Clark was filled with regret. His eagerness to get a story had made him forget the consequences. Now, he had to make things right for Benny as well. As he made his way toward Donovan's unmarked Taurus, a shining glare caught the corner of his eyes. When he turned toward it, Clark was amazed at what he saw.

"It's the car!" He pointed in the direction of the black sedan. There wasn't any doubt in his mind that this was the same car that tried to bowl him and Sabrina over the day before and it was back for more.

Donovan whipped his head around. "You sure?"

The engine from the car, about half a block away, roared and the car began to move in reverse.

"That's him!" Clark said, rushing toward the car. "I bet they're keeping an eye on Benny."

The car sped up in reverse, doing a half circle before tearing off into the opposite direction.

"I'll get him!" Donovan screamed as he sped up, his tires screeching as the car turned around and headed down the street.

Clark tried to reach for the passenger-side door just as he pulled away, but he missed it by an inch. Donovan was gone and Clark was on his own. He could only hope that Donovan would catch whoever it was. Now he had to figure out how he was going to get out of there.

His cell phone useless, Clark turned and headed back for Benny's office. He had to get to the Acropolis. If Tommy was willing to threaten Benny's child, then there was no way Nick could prevent him from hurting Sabrina if he felt she was really a threat. Clark would give his life to prevent that from happening.

Sabrina had been on edge all morning. Nothing seemed to be going wrong and everyone was so busy because of the fight later that night that few people noticed her strange behavior, but she couldn't help herself. Despite his promising note, she was feeling anxious about how Clark would react to her change of heart about them trying to recapture what they once had. She was telling her sensible self to shut up about him living in Chicago and her in Las Vegas. None of that mattered in the face of true love.

She hadn't run into Nick at all that day, and it was already one in the afternoon. He had left a message with one of the administrative assistants for her to meet him after his lunch with the media in his office. Sabrina wasn't sure how she would handle that, but there was no way she was going anywhere with Nick. From the tone of his voice on the phone yesterday, she believed he'd meant it when he told her not to worry, but she also believed that Nick wasn't the decision maker in this game anymore, if he ever was. She would trust no one but Clark.

Sabrina jumped out of her seat as the door to the executive offices opened. When Dionne entered, she tried to calm herself down, but she was way too obvious to avoid suspicion from someone who knew her that well.

"What in God's name is wrong with you?" Dionne asked, as she approached Sabrina's desk. "You've been acting weird all day."

"Nothing." Sabrina tried to avoid eye contact with her, knowing she could give herself away. She had been avoiding Dionne as much as possible today. "I'm just nervous about tonight going right."

"You're more than nervous. What's going on?"

"Dionne, a big fight is going on. Haven't you heard?"

"Something is definitely wrong with you, Sabrina, and it has nothing to do with this fight."

"You sure of that?" Sabrina tried to laugh, but it sounded more as if she were choking.

"Yes, I'm sure. Because you totally blew off career day and that's been the most important thing to you in these last few months."

Sabrina looked up at her. "I'm so sorry, Dionne. I know I let you down with that. How did it go?"

"It went great, thanks solely to me."

"I'll make it up to you, but now I've really got to get to work."

"This is about Clark, isn't it?"

"I don't want to talk about that." Sabrina sighed. "Really, Dionne, today I just want to focus on getting through this day and making it a successful one for the hotel and for Nick."

"Speaking of who, Nick was looking for you this morning."

Sabrina did her best *so what?* expression. "And?"

"He seemed really anxious. I guess because he expected you to come in early today of all days."

"Sorry. I was tied up."

"The good kind of tied up?"

Sabrina smiled in response to the innuendo. *The best kind.*

"You were with Clark, weren't you?" Dionne asked.

Sabrina ignored Dionne's salacious smile. She wanted steamy details. "None of your business."

"Come on," Dionne pleaded.

"Maybe I'll give you a bit later if you tell me what Nick said about Clark."

"He asked me what I knew about the two of you. I basically told him that Clark was trying to get you back, trying to convince you he never messed around on you, but you were reluctant."

"Good."

"Except . . ."

"Except what?"

"Except for yesterday. I told him I thought Clark was winning because you bagged on career day to be with him."

"You trying to get me fired?"

Dionne laughed. "Yeah, like Nick would ever fire you. You'd have to turn on him big time before he even got mad at you."

Sabrina's eyes widened. "What do you mean? What has he said to you?"

Dionne leaned back, staring confused at Sabrina. "Calm down. I was just saying he's crazy about you. He was really concerned this morning. He told me that he didn't think you were safe with Clark."

"Why not?"

"My question exactly. I was like, what? I mean, I know the guy played you, but Nick made it sound like you were in physical danger being with him."

Sabrina felt a chill run down her spine. Hopefully with Detective Donovan by his side, Clark was safe for now. But for how long?

"What did he say specifically?"

"Nothing. I asked for more detail, but he just warned me to stay away from Clark and to tell you to do the same if I saw you. And . . . I'm supposed to tell him the second I see you or Clark, or both. As a matter of fact, I heard him telling everyone to keep an eye out for Clark. I can call him and—"

"Don't bother." Sabrina held up the message she had from Nick. "I'm on my way to see him now."

"Am I missing something?" Dionne asked.

"I don't think so." Sabrina was pretty certain she could trust Dionne, but didn't want to take the chance. Clark being in danger was enough. "Clark and I just had a good time. He's leaving tomorrow and things will get back to normal."

"You seem to be uncharacteristically fine with that."

Sabrina shrugged. "You told me once that some things are just physical, right?"

"Yeah, I said it, but you looked at me like I was crazy."

Sabrina smiled. "Maybe you were right."

Sabrina stood up, grabbing her purse. She headed for the door, feeling Dionne's suspicious eyes on her.

"Why are you taking your purse?" Dionne asked after her.

Sabrina turned around. "I'm . . ."

"Why do you need your purse to walk upstairs to Nick's office?"

Sabrina, think fast! You're a smart girl. "I'm gonna stop by the gift shop. I have to buy a gift for all the people who participated in yesterday's career day."

"Oh." Dionne nodded, seeming satisfied. "Get them some of the expensive stuff."

"I will."

Sabrina sighed, leaning against the door the second she was out of the office. She had to pull it together for Clark's sake and her own. Most importantly, she had to find Clark and stop him before he got into the Acropolis. Nick and Tommy had something planned for him and Sabrina had to get to him first or it could be too late for all of them.

Looking around for Nick, Sabrina was satisfied that he wasn't nearby. She hastily made her way down the hallway toward the entrance. Like all the other hotels on the strip, the Acropolis was enormous, and it was times like this, when one wanted to get out, that this fact became all too clear.

Sabrina turned the corner slowly, looking down the next hallway, which was lined with a gift shop and a photo shop on one side and some maintenance and housekeeping closets on the other. No Nick.

She walked briskly, but not too fast. If Nick was asking around about her, the last thing she needed was for someone to report that she was seen running like a bat out of hell out of the hotel.

Halfway down the hallway, Sabrina's heartbeat slowed. She was almost there. She had to pass the lobby, then the casino, and she would be outside, where she could catch—

A housekeeping closet door on Sabrina's left swung open and Sabrina jumped a foot backward. She wanted to scream, but luckily her voice caught in her throat and nothing came out as Clark emerged from the closet.

"I've been waiting for you," Clark said, closing the door. "Are you okay?"

Sabrina slapped him on the arm. "You scared the hell out of me. What were you doing in there?"

"Waiting for the clear to come get you."

"That door is supposed to be locked. I can't believe it's open. That is strictly against safety regulations. I'm going to talk to—"

"Sabrina." Clark grabbed her by the shoulders. "Is that really what's important right now?"

Sabrina calmed down. "Sorry. I'm just agitated. I was worried about you."

"You got my note?"

Sabrina smiled. "Yes, and I wanted to—"

"I just wanted to make sure you didn't think I was leaving angry at you."

"I know you aren't angry with me, but you have a right to be. I was just worried because you said lunch and it's after—"

"I got here as fast as I could."

"I have so much to tell you, Clark."

"First, I've got some bad news."

"Me first," Sabrina said. "You've got to get out of here. I'm pretty sure Nick and Tommy have something planned for you. He's got everyone looking for you."

"That's why I'm hiding in the closet. I got a couple of bad looks from some security guys when I entered and one of them got on his radio the second he saw me."

"Did they come after you?"

He nodded. "But I used a rowdy group of seniors to evade them."

"They must know Benny is turning on them. They're desperate."

"That's my bad news," Clark said. "Benny's not turning on them. They got to him. They used the same ploy I did."

"His daughter?"

"Only they threatened to actually hurt her."

Sabrina gasped. "Oh my God. There's no way he's gonna help us now. What did Detective Donovan say?"

"Lost cause there, but he went after the car."

"What car?"

"The one that tried to run us over yesterday. It was outside Benny's office again this morning. I think it was there to keep an eye on him. When we noticed it, whoever it was sped off and Donovan went after him. I don't know what's happened since. I think we need to head to the police station."

"Okay."

Clark held his hand out to Sabrina and she took it, squeezing tight. He took an incredible sense of comfort in this, despite the situation they were in.

"I don't think we're going to be able to stop this, Sabrina. Not without Benny's help."

"What about your story?"

"That doesn't matter now. All that matters is that the people in danger get out of danger. If I keep my mouth shut, no one will get hurt. I'm the only real threat to them now."

"What do you think Donovan can do for us?"

"I don't know, but I don't think they'll go after us if we're around the cops."

"There he is!"

Clark and Sabrina stopped in their tracks as soon as they reached the lobby. There was Nick, his finger pointed accusingly at Clark, with five security guards around him. Sabrina squeezed Clark's hand as the men started for them.

"What are they gonna do?" she asked.

"Stay calm," Clark said, his insides screaming. He had to get news to Lauren. "My assistant's name is Lauren Schuller. Remember that."

"Lauren Schuller," Sabrina repeated. "Why would I—"

"Stay right there," one of the guards said to Clark as they approached. He turned to Sabrina. "Both of you."

"No," Nick said, rushing from behind them. "Not Sabrina. She's not a part of it."

The guard nodded. "Then you need to step away, ma'am."

"Can someone tell me what is going on here?" Clark asked, letting go of Sabrina's hand. She was determined to hold on to him, but he knew he had to let go.

"We're holding you for the police," Nick said with a victorious smile. "They're on their way. You're going to be arrested for theft."

"What?" Sabrina stood back, amazed at what she was hearing. "What are you talking about?"

"There have been several complaints of theft on the sixth floor since Monday."

"The day I checked in," Clark said, knowing exactly what was going on. He was being framed.

"I hadn't heard of anything," Sabrina said.

"You wouldn't, of course," Nick answered. "I'm the manager. I know about everything. We've been wondering who was behind it."

"You don't think Clark possibly stole something," Sabrina said. "He doesn't need to steal."

"Come on, Sabrina." Nick's tone was admonishing. "We all know that's not why people steal. He's a thrill seeker. A wild man. That's how you described him yourself, remember?"

"What proof do you claim to have?" Clark asked.

"The cleaning lady found the items you had hidden in the bottom drawer in your hotel room. She called security and they alerted me."

Clark looked at Sabrina, their eyes locked on each other. Things were about to get much worse, they both knew that. Sabrina nodded to him, letting him know that she knew exactly what was going on and she was going to help him. What was important now was making sure she got the chance to.

"How could you, Clark?" Sabrina put her hand to her chest, appearing baffled. "How could you do something like this?"

Clark wasn't sure what she was doing, but he decided to play along. "I didn't do this, Sabrina. You know that. They're setting me up."

"Oh, come on," she answered, shaking her head. "I . . . I don't know what to think. I just want to get away from this."

"It's fine," Nick said, placing his hand on Sabrina's shoulder. "You won't be bothered with him anymore. Take him away."

"Where is he going?" Sabrina asked.

"To the security office, for now," Nick said. "Then they'll take him to the police station."

Two security guards grabbed Clark and began leading him away, with several onlookers gazing at him. Clark looked back at Sabrina, who was turned away from him now. Whatever she was up to, he had complete faith that everything was going to be okay. Sabrina Scott was the smartest woman he knew.

"Are you okay?" Nick asked.

Sabrina shook her head. "I don't know how I feel. I just can't believe he would do something like this."

"What has he been telling you?"

"He had this idea that you and Tommy were planning to fix the fight so you could bet on Rodriguez and make a ton of money."

Nick frowned at her, focusing on her eyes. "Do you believe that?"

"I did at first." Sabrina ran her fingers through her hair, trying her best to appear flustered. "He was saying that you were working with this bookie, but the bookie denied everything. Then he claimed that you were trying to run us over, but now I don't know."

"He probably set it up so someone would pretend to try to run you over, but he would save you. That way you would feel indebted to him, Sabrina. All the more reason to believe whatever he said."

Think of Clark, Sabrina told herself. *No matter how angry Nick's lies make you, play along for Clark's sake.* "I thought . . . He was telling me so many things about us and how he never cheated on me and . . . but now . . ."

"You know he was lying about that," Nick said. "You've seen the proof."

"I know, but, Nick, this guy . . . He has a way of

making me believe whatever he says. I can't believe I was falling back under his spell."

"It's okay, Sabrina. Clark isn't going to mess with you or the Acropolis ever again."

"Thank you, Nick." Sabrina smiled as she looked up at him. "I've been acting like a fool and you're not using that against me."

Nick grinned at her. "You had me scared for a while there, but I can tell you see what the real story is now."

Sabrina nodded, holding up the message she had from him. "I was on my way to see you now. You wanted to meet?"

Nick nodded. "I wanted to make sure we were gonna go down to the fight together."

"Sure thing." Sabrina glanced at her watch. "We still have time."

"I need a break. It's been a crazy day. Why don't you come to the bar with me? We can both use a winding down."

"I need to go to the ladies' room first," Sabrina said, having no intention of spending another second with Nick. She had to act fast if she was going to help Clark. "I'll meet you at the Agora."

"Are you sure?" Nick asked. "I can wait for you."

"I'm fine." She rubbed his arm. "You've done enough for me already, Nick. I'll be there in ten minutes."

"Okay." Nick stepped back a bit with an excited expression. "Tonight is the night, Sabrina. Tomorrow will be a new day for the Acropolis."

Sabrina smiled, waving a happy fist in the air. She kept smiling until Nick was well out of view. She dropped her hand to her side, gripping her purse to her chest. She didn't hesitate to make her way out of there. When she reached the front entrance, she grabbed her cell phone.

She dialed information and held the phone to her ear. Looking behind her, she picked up the pace toward the employee parking lot and her car.

"Yes, I need the number to the *Chicago Sun Times* in Chicago, Illinois. I need the sports desk."

"Is it you, Clark?"

"No, it's not Clark," Sabrina yelled into the phone as she drove down the noisy Vegas strip. It was packed with tourists braving the hellish hot summer sun. "Are you Lauren Schuller?"

There was a short pause before: "Yes, I am. Who is this?"

"Lauren, my name is Sabrina Scott. I'm a . . . a friend of Clark Hunter."

"Sabrina? Yeah, I know who you are."

Was that a good thing or not? Sabrina couldn't tell from her tone. "Clark told me to call you. Do you know what's been going on down here?"

"You mean what's going on with the fight-fixing or with you?"

"So you know about me."

"Oh, sugar, yes."

Sabrina wasn't sure what to say to that, but it wasn't important right now. "I'm calling you because Clark is in trouble."

"What did he do now?"

"He didn't do anything, but Nick is trying to frame him for theft."

"Your boyfriend is trying to frame him?"

"Nick is not my boyfriend," Sabrina exclaimed. "What did Clark tell you?"

"Never mind. Just go on with the Clark-is-in-trouble thing. Last time I talked to him, I gave him all the info on Benny Silver and he told me why he wanted to talk to him. Benny was supposed to save everything."

"He almost did, but Benny did a one-eighty after Tommy threatened his daughter."

"Tommy is dirtier than we thought."

"And more dangerous than I think anyone thought," Sabrina said. "Now all he has to fear is Clark, so they're trying to get him out of the way by having him arrested."

"What are they saying he stole?"

"Several guests had items taken from their rooms and they were planted in Clark's room."

"When was he arrested?" Lauren sounded very alarmed.

"They're holding him at the hotel right now, but he's on his way to the police station. He'll probably be there in a half hour."

"It's going to take some time, but I'll take care of it."

"What are you going to do?" They didn't have a lot of time. The fight was gonna start at seven.

"The paper has an entire legal team that specializes in getting our writers out of jail."

"Even if they are accused of theft?"

"Usually it's because they won't reveal a source, but I'll work with what I have. What are you doing now?"

"I just had to get away from the hotel, but I don't

know what to do next. I've got to help Clark, so I thought I'd go to the station."

"No," Lauren said. "If you really want to help him, get another source for his story."

"Benny was the only . . ." Sabrina thought for a second, remembering what Clark had told her about working the story.

"If I know Clark," Lauren continued, "and I do, he'll do this story no matter what. He needs a reliable source before he commits professional suicide. If he doesn't have a strong source, he won't get the police protection he needs and it'll look like he's just making something up to get out of trouble."

"I have an idea," Sabrina said, making a sharp right turn. "I won't let him down."

"I'm so glad things got cleared up yesterday so you could be on his side today."

"What do you mean?" Sabrina couldn't imagine that Clark would tell this woman, no matter how close he was to her, that he and Sabrina had slept together.

"I mean that the reason you're in his camp now is the message from Cara. You know, how she confessed to framing him and everything."

"What are you—"

"Hmmm, that's weird. What is it about Clark that makes him a magnet for frame-ups? I'll have to tease him about it after I get him out of jail."

Sabrina had to pull over to keep from ramming into the car in front of her. She was floored. "You mean that was a frame-up? She confessed?"

"I've said too much." Lauren spoke slowly, cautiously. "I didn't mean to get all in your business. All that matters is that we're working to save Clark."

"You're right," Sabrina said. "I'll keep in touch."

Sabrina turned the phone off and placed it in her lap as she stared into the vacant space in front of her. Clark had asked her what if . . . And she had told him it was all speculation. He really had proof, but he didn't show it to her. He understood before she had what the real issue was.

Sabrina just sat there. For how long, she wasn't sure. It was a bit much to ponder and she knew she was out of time. So, finally pulling herself together, she gauged the space around her and swung back into traffic.

"Right now," she said out loud, "we're going to go back to the beginning."

TEN

"Can I at least get my phone call?" Clark pleaded with the guard outside his holding cell.

The officer turned to him with an annoyed expression on his face. He was surely sick of Clark by now. "I told you, man, you'll get the call after you've been processed downstairs."

"Then how soon can I get out of here after that?"

Clark had been in jail before. Once while he was in college, and again in his early twenties. Both times for acting like an idiot under the influence of alcohol. At the time, the experiences had seemed somewhat adventurous, but not anymore. This place was cold and gray and it was away from Sabrina.

She was planning something and he needed to know what it was. She was probably putting herself in danger and Clark couldn't stand not being able to watch out for her. He hoped she remembered to call Lauren and wondered if Lauren was trying to reach him.

The officer was a young Latino, tall and skinny with more than a few pimples still on his face.

"You're being brought up on grand theft charges," he said. "Don't hold your breath."

"Grand theft?"

"Dude, I heard the guys downstairs saying it was over fifteen hundred bucks' worth of stuff they found in your room."

Clark should have figured this. Nick didn't just want him out of the way for one night. He wanted him in jail for a long time. "What does that mean?"

"It means don't hold your breath."

"I'll have to get a chance to bail myself out, don't I?"

"It's Saturday night. Fight night. I don't think there are any judges interested in taking time off for you. Trust me, you need to make yourself comfortable."

"I was set up!" Clark slammed his fist against the concrete wall, trying to hide the pain it caused him.

"Oh, really?" The officer looked wide-eyed. "In that case, I guess I should let you out."

Clark smiled sarcastically. "Thanks for all your help, man. I told you the truth. I told you all the truth and my woman is in danger."

The door to the holding area opened and Detective Donovan entered with a half-disgusted look on his face as he approached Clark's cell. He was holding a manila folder in his hand, fanning himself with it. "So it is true."

Clark sighed in relief. "Thank God you're here, Donovan. You've got to get me out of here."

Donovan nodded for the young officer to leave them alone, which he promptly did. Donovan sat on the bench on the other side of the cell, leaning toward Clark. "You're telling everyone you've been set up."

"I have and you know it," Clark said.

"I don't know it." He opened up the folder and began looking through it. "They found this stuff in your room."

"You know what's going on. They're framing me. You got the guy in the black sedan, right?"

Donovan shook his head. "He got away, but I got the full plates."

"He got away?"

"He drove into a pretty populated area. I'm not going to risk civilians to chase someone down because I really need to know who they are. We're working on the plates. We'll get them."

"Nick has set me up to get me out of the way for the fight and away from Sabrina." Clark spoke as Donovan continued reading. "I don't care about the fight anymore. You've got to help me get her away from him."

"Where is she?" Donovan asked.

"I left her at the hotel, but I don't think she's going to stick around there."

"That's what you want, right?"

"I know Sabrina, though. She's a determined woman. And since she isn't here, I know she's out there trying to stop that fight."

Clark watched impatiently as Donovan skimmed through another sheet. He was about to reach through the bars and snatch the folder away from him, but he saw a sudden change in expression on Donovan's face. He'd found something.

"What is it?" Clark asked.

"Wait a second." Donovan read for a few seconds longer before turning to Clark. "This last report was made by a Mr. and Mrs. Woods from Beverly Hills. A necklace was stolen from their room."

"So?"

"Mrs. Woods said the last time she saw the necklace was when she put it in her drawer at two in the afternoon. When she went to retrieve it to dress for their dinner at four, it was gone."

Clark got the slipup. "So I had to have stolen it between two and four. Which is the time I was outside Benny's giving my report to the officer and later, talking to you at Sabrina's house."

Donovan frowned, looking at the report again as if searching for something to explain the complication. "You could have run over to the hotel right after I left and—"

"I was at Sabrina's all night, Donovan. I was never out of her sight. She lives at least twenty minutes from the hotel."

"I still can't let you go," Donovan said. "It just means we have to clarify this one statement."

"Well, what can you do?"

"We have the maid coming down to the station. Maybe she can help out."

"If she can't get me out of here before the fight, then she can't help." Clark wondered where Lauren was. Lauren could get him out.

"So you lose your story." Donovan shrugged. "That's not the end of the world."

"But what if I lose Sabrina?" Clark asked, feeling a heavy chest. "That would be the end of the world."

Bending his head slightly, Donovan asked, "You really think she's in danger, don't you?"

Clark spoke with all the sincerity he could muster. "Grave."

When Sabrina opened the door to her Chicago apartment she had to fight to keep a pleased smile from forming on her lips. Clark looked devastating in a cinnamon-brown linen shirt and black slacks. The clothes hung on him as if they were made just for him. Sabrina was definitely pleased, but she couldn't show him that. Especially not with that already smug look on his face. She knew then that she would have to ration out the compliments to this guy.

"Right on time," she said, stepping aside to let him in.

"I'm always on time when it's something I want." Clark entered her apartment, looking around. "Nice place."

"Thank you." Sabrina felt the butterflies in her stomach, but wasn't sure why they were there. After all, this was just a bet date. He'd won a date on a bet and there would be nothing more to it.

Then he looked at her. Time seemed to stand still as he swung around to face her and his eyes traveled from her feet to her face, settling on her eyes. There was nothing rude about it—neither was there any mistaking it. Sabrina was frozen in place, but frozen only figuratively, because literally she was suddenly running a body fever. So maybe this was more than a bet date.

* * *

How could she have known what she was getting into that night? She knew no matter what little attraction she felt for Clark, he was not her type. Okay, there was more than a little attraction then, but he was far too careless and free for her. He made her nervous and too self-conscious. Nothing could ever come of this.

Or so she'd thought. Little did she know that what began as an exciting curiosity would turn into a passion of a lifetime that would awaken her body, a love that made her heart bloom, and basically the best time a girl could have. The best of everything, ripped from her in the most painful way, leaving her with nothing to hope for in her heart.

Could she get it back?

Vegas summer evenings never let up. Sabrina was baking as she sat in her car, but she knew she had made the right decision as she watched the flower delivery driver across the street. He got back into his truck and quickly drove off, exposing the front of Alicia Grove's mother's house. It was surprisingly quiet for the late afternoon of a fight night, but Sabrina assumed that recent events in their marriage played a part in the toned-down display.

There were a couple of older women at least in their sixties sitting on the porch, fanning themselves while talking to each other. They would occasionally throw distrustful glances at the man standing at the doorway. He was so big he practically blocked the entire entry. He was going to be a challenge, Sabrina thought to herself as she grabbed her own flowers and got out of the car.

Sabrina caught stares from everyone as she started across the street. She refused to act the least bit nervous, which would only lead to suspicion. This had to work. Alicia Grove was her only chance. When Sabrina considered the best way to help Clark, she remembered Clark telling her that Alicia was his first source and she had given him his first clues. As much as he'd felt he connected with her, Sabrina was certain there was an opportunity there for her to reach her, woman to woman.

Sabrina nodded to the women, who smiled as they took in the immense bouquet of colorful flowers she was carrying, before turning to the guard at the door.

"You don't look like a delivery person," he said.

Sabrina could see that he wasn't sure whether he wanted to interrogate her or flirt with her. Men. "Well, I am today. I'm with the hotel, bringing Alicia flowers personally from Nick Stewart."

Sabrina held her Acropolis ID up as he leaned forward, eyes squinting. It showed her face, her name and title. Director of marketing sounded senior enough. At least Sabrina hoped it did.

"Very nice," came from one of the ladies with an approving nod.

"Nick wants to make sure I give these to her before she leaves for the fight."

The man shrugged as if he didn't care either way before stepping aside and letting Sabrina in.

The house was already filled with flowers and food. Sabrina searched the room for the woman she would find to be Alicia. It wasn't easy. There were about seven women floating between the kitchen and living room who could pass for Alicia Grove. Young, attractive, a little flashy, and wearing a lot of makeup.

"Can I help you?"

Sabrina had missed one. She was sitting on the living room sofa, turned halfway around to face her. She had been leaning over to attend to one of two small children who were sitting on the floor watching cartoons. She had a pensive look on her face and one pretty big black eye.

"Mrs. Grove, I have flowers for you." Sabrina approached. She was going to start sneezing out of control if she didn't get rid of these flowers. "From the hotel."

Alicia frowned. "Who are you?"

"I'm Sabrina Scott." Sabrina stood at the edge of the sofa, handing the flowers to one of the women, who reached for them and took them away. "I work for Nick Stewart."

"I don't want flowers from him." Alicia turned away.

Sabrina felt for her, but couldn't help being happy to see her reaction to Nick. It only worked in her favor. "I'm not really here for Nick. I'm here for Clark Hunter."

Alicia turned back to Sabrina as the name recognition slowly came back to her. "The reporter?"

Sabrina's eyes veered toward the children. "Can we talk privately?"

"I don't have time for that," Alicia said. "I want you to leave."

"I was hoping for one last chance to get your help. Before this fight happens."

Alicia looked nervously behind her. She obviously didn't want any of the other women to hear. She stood up, walking toward the dining room windows, gesturing for Sabrina to follow her, which she did.

"You weren't invited into this house," Alicia said. "So you can please leave now and stop talking about the fight."

Sabrina kept her voice just above a whisper. "Alicia, I know you have enough to deal with right now, but—"

"I don't need your pity." She folded her arms across her chest.

"I'm not pitying you," Sabrina said. "I know you're a woman who can take care of herself. For now at least."

"What do you mean, for now?"

"I mean that I'm a very, very close friend of Clark's and I know he told you about his mother and father."

"He gave me his sob story, but that had nothing to do with me."

Sabrina sighed. "You say that now, but what if it doesn't stop? The violence in Clark's home has scarred him for life. He is still angry about it. He hates his father to this day and still bears some resentment for his mother for staying with him. Is that what you want your children to feel? What good could they possibly learn from this?"

"You leave my children out of this." Alicia looked away, staring at the children as they watched television. "I'm going to fix this. I'm going to fix my family."

"How can you do that with your husband in jail?"

"I don't know what you're talking about."

"Clark has all the proof he needs." Lying was getting a little too easy for Sabrina's comfort. She couldn't wait until this was over. "He knows that Artemis is going to take a dive for Tommy and Nick. You know it too. It took you a while, but you've got it."

Alicia began rubbing her hands together vigorously. "I don't know where you heard that. It's not true."

"That's what started the fight, isn't it?" Sabrina asked. "You were trying to get it out of him. What he didn't want to do. I heard him trying to back out too, but Tommy kept pushing him."

"I should have left him alone. I was pushing him too much." Alicia's tone relayed her guilt.

"You didn't do anything wrong," Sabrina said. "You were doing what was best for your family. And you still can."

"I don't have to talk to you," Alicia said with a burst of seemingly newfound energy. "Now get out."

This time she was loud enough to get everyone's attention.

"Alicia, you can do three things," Sabrina said in an authoritative tone. "You can do nothing and let this happen and see your husband go to jail and see your family go further down the drain. Or you can go to the police and tell them what you know in exchange for leniency on your husband. Or you can go to your husband and convince him to fight the fight and let fate lead you to the next step you take toward rebuilding your trust and commitment to your family."

"Get out!" Alicia stepped back as the bodyguard

entered the house. "You don't know anything about my family!"

Sabrina knew her time was up and she had gone too far, but she didn't have much of a choice. "I'm going, but, Alicia, you're making one of those choices whether or not you do anything."

"Let's go." The bodyguard reached for Sabrina, who eluded his grasp.

"Artemis is at the hotel right now," she said to Alicia. "You still have time."

Alicia waved Sabrina away, turning and heading back for her children, who were staring at her with wide eyes and opened mouths.

"All right, all right," Sabrina said as the bodyguard tried again to grab her.

As she reached her car, Sabrina looked back at the house. Everyone was inside now talking about her, she was sure. She hadn't said all she wanted to, but she had to believe it was enough. If not, Sabrina would have to work from within the deception to bring it out and that was not the preferred method.

As she drove off, Sabrina dialed the number information had given her for the local police precinct.

"Las Vegas Police Department," a voice said clearly and calmly.

"I'm trying to track down a man by the name of Clark Hunter. He was arrested this afternoon and sent to the precinct. He needs me to bail him out. Is he still there?"

"Hold on." A few minutes passed. "He's not here anymore. He was bailed out just a few minutes ago by someone from the *Chicago Sun Times.*"

"Thank you." Sabrina hung up, grateful that

Lauren had done her job. Hopefully Lauren knew where Clark was. Sabrina couldn't stand being away from him any longer.

Standing behind the two-way glass mirror, Clark was quickly losing patience with Donovan's interrogation of the maid who supposedly found the stolen jewelry in his room. Her name was Anisa, she was in her mid-forties and didn't speak English very well. She was ringing her hands together, but Clark wasn't sure if she was genuinely nervous or guilty. She didn't look like the type of person Tommy and Nick would try to bring into the game.

Donovan carefully read Anisa's statement back to her. "So you were refilling the minibar, which is right next to the smaller drawers underneath the television, right?"

She nodded, shifting in the uncomfortable wooden chair. "Yes. That's when I found them."

"The stolen jewelry?"

She nodded again.

"Anisa." Donovan leaned forward with a sympathetic tone to his voice. "You just told me that you saw the jewelry in the drawer, but the drawer wasn't open."

She blinked and Clark knew that something was about to happen. This woman had no idea what Tommy and Nick were up to.

"Did you open the drawer?" Donovan asked.

She took a deep breath and then nodded slowly. "Yes, I open."

"Why did you open the drawer, Anisa? I don't believe you're supposed to."

"Well, I . . ." She pressed her lips together, seeming to take a second to calm herself down. Or maybe remember what she was supposed to say. "The drawer. It has a little opening at the top in the center."

"You looked through the opening?"

"Yes, I . . . Yes, I saw something shining."

"So you opened the drawer?"

She nodded, her brows centering with uncertainty.

Donovan shook his head, leaning back. "I'm not sure what to say, Anisa. I have to commend you for finding these stolen goods, but I'm not happy to hear that you're opening drawers just because you see something shiny."

"I'm not a thief," she protested. "I have never done anything wrong."

"I'm not accusing you of anything, I just find it . . ."

Donovan stopped as Anisa lowered her face into her hands and began crying. Clark stepped closer to the glass, wondering what was coming next.

"I . . ." She spoke through sobs. "I . . . I am not a thief."

"Anisa, I can't understand you. You'll have to look up and speak clearly." Donovan glanced at the mirror for just a second. "What's wrong?"

Anisa looked up, her face stained with tears. "He said if I didn't say he would say I stole it."

"Go on," Donovan said, grabbing the yellow pad in front of him.

Clark watched as an almost hysterical Anisa

confessed that Nick asked her to go clean the room even though it wasn't her floor. He told her they were suspicious of this person, so she was instructed to keep her eye open. She had done so, but saw nothing. When she returned with nothing, Nick became angry with her and told her to go back and look in the drawers. She didn't want to do that because it was against hotel policy for staff to open guest drawers or luggage.

Anisa described Nick on the verge of a temper tantrum as he practically dragged her back to the room. Showing her the drawer with the stolen jewelry in it, he ordered her to call security and alert them to what she had found and ask them to contact Nick. In the end, Nick threatened to take the jewelry and tell security he'd found it in her housecleaning cart. There had been an incident two years ago when Anisa's ten-year-old grandson accompanied her to work and taken an item out of a room, which Anisa promptly returned when she'd found out. Nick threatened to bring that back up.

Clark sighed with relief as Donovan escorted Anisa out of the interrogation room. Finally, someone unrelated to him to prove that something was going on.

"I told you," Clark said the second Donovan entered the dark viewing room.

"He's definitely trying to set you up for something."

"You know what that something is." Clark grudgingly noticed Donovan's resistance. "It's like pulling teeth to get you to admit that what I'm saying is right."

"Look, Hunter. You better be glad I even let you

listen in. You have no right to be here. When your paper bailed you out we're supposed to kick you out."

Clark acquiesced. "I know, but I'm acting as my own lawyer, so that qualifies me to listen in."

"You know who gets in here?" Donovan asked. "Real lawyers, cops, and witnesses. That's it. You're practically a perp."

Clark smiled, patting Donovan on the shoulder. "You're killing me, man. Admit it. You like me and you believe me. Anisa just clarified it for you. Now, will you help me find Sabrina?"

"I'm not in the business of finding girlfriends missing for only a few hours," Donovan said. He feigned annoyance. "But I will bring Nick in for questioning on suspicion of coercing a false report."

"Let's go." Clark headed for the door.

"Don't even try it," Donovan said. "You're not going back to that hotel. As of now, you are still a suspect in a theft there. You can't go back there."

"Is there a restraining order against me?" Clark opened the door.

"There might be. The officers on the scene suggested that Nick wanted you as far away from the hotel as possible. I'll check on that. Then I have to call my partner. I'll be back in a few minutes and we'll talk about what you can and can't do."

"Be quick about it," Clark said, ducking out of the way as Donovan went for him on his way out.

Clark really liked the guy. Which was what made t all the more difficult to ditch him like he did the second he was out of sight. He couldn't take the chance of any restrictions on his ability to find Sabrina and stop her before she got into some real danger. He knew she was going to go back to the hotel and he had to get over there now.

Sabrina felt the muscles in her stomach contract as she pulled into the employee parking lot of the Acropolis. She shouldn't be here and it took her a long time to muster up the courage to come, but her conversation with Lauren spurred her on.

After hearing that Clark had been bailed out of jail, Sabrina called Lauren to thank her and to find out where Clark was now. Lauren had spoken to Clark for only seconds, in which time he asked if Sabrina was all right and wanted to know where she was. When Lauren couldn't tell him, Clark told her he was going back to the hotel because that's where he figured Sabrina would be. He also instructed Lauren that if Sabrina were to call, Clark had orders for her to stay away from the hotel.

Sabrina didn't take well to orders.

Before Lauren could get any more information from him, Clark said he had to go because he'd seen a woman enter the police station who might be able to help his case. With his cell phone dead, Lauren had to rely on him contacting her again. Hindsight being twenty-twenty, they both realized that giving him Sabrina's cell phone number would have been helpful, but Lauren hadn't had it at the time.

Not willing to bet everything on Alicia Grove, Sabrina decided she had to do something to get the attention of the vast amounts of media that would be there tonight before the fight. If Clark was going down for this, she would have to go down with him. At least he wouldn't be alone against the world.

Sabrina was cautious as she made her way toward the hotel's entrance. She wasn't sure what Nick had told the employees about her. She had skipped out on him and their drink at the bar, so he had to suspect she had been lying to him all along. For all she knew, security was looking for her now.

The sound of a car skidding up the long driveway to the hotel caught everyone off guard. People everywhere froze in place, looking around for the car heading their way. A few jumped out of the way as the car in question slammed on its brakes in front of the valet belt of the hotel.

After a few seconds and a couple of rolled eyes, everyone went about their business. Everyone but Sabrina, that is.

There was no mistaking the black sedan that tried to run her and Clark over yesterday. She had seen the car for only a second before Clark grabbed her and pulled her away, but the image was etched in her mind. The fact that it came roaring up the driveway didn't hurt her memory either. She remembered Clark saying that Detective Donovan had gone after the car outside Benny's apartment. Apparently something had gone wrong.

Sabrina slipped behind one of thick white columns that graced the front entrance to the Acropolis, which was designed like the outside of an ancient Greek forum hall. She waited and watched as the door to the sedan opened and the driver got out.

She recognized him immediately. It was the man who had approached her and Nick the night of the prefight party, sending Nick in Tommy's direction and attempting to keep Sabrina from following after him. After he tossed his key to the valet and with a haughty stride headed into the hotel, Sabrina took a deep breath and followed him.

She kept her distance as she tracked him through the hotel, trying to blend in with this group here or there. He never looked back, never seemed to be concerned. As he made his way away from the guest areas, toward the private party rooms that surrounded the arena where the fight would be held, Sabrina knew she wouldn't be able to hide from him anymore. Security was too tight. She had to cut the suspicious act and show the ID.

It was okay that she lost him because she knew where he was heading anyway. The fighters each had a hospitality suite upstairs and a hospitality party room downstairs. The party rooms were set up with the most expensive food, champagne, and French wine for the fighter's entourage to hang out with him up to about an hour before the fight, after which he would go off to prepare with only the most faithful. The rest would stay and keep the party going.

Sabrina looked down at her watch. The fight would be starting in an hour. It seemed early for the West Coast, but because some of the biggest players were on the East Coast, the fight had to happen by ten o'clock their time.

Sabrina showed her badge at two stages before making her way to the private area for the fighters' posses. The outer area was pretty subdued, with no one visible except one gentleman in a loud yellow suit who seemed to want the silence so he could talk on his cell phone.

Sabrina pulled out her cell phone and held it to her ear, pretending she was in a conversation of her own while trying to figure out what to do next. She stepped closer and closer to the other man until she could hear what he was saying.

"Something's wrong, man," he said into the tiny receiver, shaking his head. He was too caught up in his conversation to even notice Sabrina was there, let alone listening in. "What am I talking about? What do you mean? Artie, man, Artie. No, man, he's gone down to the prep room about an hour ago with Tommy, but he was here earlier and he wasn't talking to nobody. He wasn't himself. You know he likes to put on the show before a fight. Something is wrong."

He turned his back to Sabrina, allowing her to step even closer. She needed Alicia to be here. If Artemis was wavering, maybe she could be the last straw.

"What?" the man asked. "No, man. It's not about Alicia. It's something else. Tommy was in the corner with him and he was frustrated. He was whispering into Artie's ear, but Artie was shaking his head like he was . . . like he didn't know. You know what I mean, like he wasn't so sure."

Caught up in the man's conversation, Sabrina hadn't heard the footsteps behind her, but her heart jumped out of her chest when a strong hand gripped her shoulder. She whipped around, backing up as the man whom she had followed into the hotel stood behind her.

So maybe it wasn't okay that she lost him.

He was looking down at her with slits for eyes and a snarl of his upper lip that made it seem as if Sabrina had done something to him or his family. Sabrina couldn't remember being so scared.

She swallowed hard. "I was just . . . I was stopping by to see Nick."

He smiled, seemingly amused by her attempt at normalcy. "You were? Well, that's good, because he's been looking for you."

"Is he . . . is he in . . . in there?" She pointed a shaky finger at the room behind her.

By this time the man on the phone was off and his attention was fully on Sabrina and her newfound friend.

"No." He sneered at her with amused eyes.

"Okay then." Sabrina hoped she could walk. She could barely feel her legs, she was so frightened. "He must be in his office. I'll just go—"

As she turned to pass him, he grabbed her by the arm, tossing her backward with so much force that her body slammed against the wall. Sabrina was too shocked to even speak.

"Rod, what in the hell is wrong with you?" the other man said, seeming amazed at the violence.

"Greg, it's her," Rod said. "The one that Nick was talking about. That Tommy was talking about."

"Ohhh." Greg seemed to have enough confirmation to accept the scene he just witnessed. Apparently violence against women was okay if the orders came from Tommy.

Sabrina was about to use the bathroom on herself. She was angry and scared to death. Her back was killing her, but she had to get away from there. She tried again to run past him, but this time Rod grabbed her left arm and Greg, the telephone man, grabbed the other, pulling her back.

"Let me go!" She struggled desperately.

"Let her go," Rod said, nodding to Greg. "I got this."

Greg did as he was told, letting go and backing off.

Sabrina gasped when Rod let go with one hand to pull a gun out of his jacket with the other.

"Look." She held her hands up, palms out in an attempt to calm the situation even though she seemed to be the only one who was freaking out. "I don't want to start anything. I just need to talk to Nick. I can explain everything to him."

"That's good," he answered, hiding the gun halfway in his jacket. "Because I'm going to take you to him. And he's not in his office. Now, you're going to come with me and keep it real quiet."

Sabrina nodded, saying a little prayer for herself. She was going to get out of this. The last thing Tommy and Nick needed was a murder on the night of the fight at the hotel. She just had to keep her head together and she would be fine.

While she was walking down the hallway with a

gun only inches from her, Sabrina's life began to flash in front of her eyes. Her father, her mother, Clark. She was not going to let this end. She had too much to look forward to.

She didn't have the chance to look behind her and see Alicia Grove arrive and, after catching a glimpse of Sabrina and Rod, walk away before entering the party room.

Dreadlocks purchased at a cheap gag store and a pair of sunglasses seemed to do the trick. Clark did garner a few stares from security as he entered the Acropolis, but he was okay with these kinds of stares. Wearing a tacky Hawaiian shirt he'd purchased at that same gag store, Clark strode through the hotel as if he were a regular.

He went straight for the casino, which is what the hotel liked to see, and played a few slots just in case anyone wanted to keep an eye on him. He ordered a drink from the passing waitress, acting as if he were settling in for the long haul. After about fifteen minutes, he started a slow, short tour past the roulette and crap tables.

In the hallway now, Clark knew he was in the danger zone. Security was much tighter because of the fight, and the only credentials he had—his press pass—revealed his true identity, which wouldn't help him get anywhere but out the front door. If he was lucky. Sabrina told him earlier that Nick had everyone looking for him. Clark wasn't sure if his arrest would make security put their guard down in looking out for him. He hoped it did.

"Excuse me," a female voice from behind called

out to him as he headed toward the executive offices. "What are you doing here?"

Slowly Clark turned around. He was ready to play the slightly drunk, mostly lost tourist with the undecipherable accent, but when he saw who it was another plan came quickly into play.

"Dionne." Walking toward her, Clark pulled off the wig and glasses, revealing himself, to her surprise.

"What are you doing here?" Dionne looked around nervously. "You're not supposed to be here. You're supposed to be in jail. I thought you'd been arrested."

"I got out," Clark said.

"You broke out of jail?"

"No, Dionne, I was let out on bail."

"That was quick."

"Because the charges are false and the police know that."

"You're not supposed to be here either way." She folded her arms across her chest. Dionne was decked out in a sexy silver pantsuit, obviously on her way to the stadium. "What have you done with Sabrina?" she asked with a threatening glare. "Where is she?"

"I'm not sure, but I think she's here. That's why I need your help."

Dionne smirked. "Why would I help you? You're a thief and a cheat."

"I'm neither, Dionne, but I can understand why you'd think that. If you were able to talk to Sabrina, she would tell you."

"Key word there being 'if.' There is no way Sabrina would bail on this event. Something has happened and I want to know what is going on or I'll yell for security."

"I don't have time to explain everything, but you've answered your own question. If Sabrina could be here, working this night, she would. But something is keeping her away and it's Nick. He and Tommy are involved in something dirty and she's in danger because she's going to try and stop them."

Dionne frowned with a disbelieving roll of her eyes. "Nick would never hurt Sabrina."

"But Tommy would and I think you know that."

"You're lying," Dionne said. "Cheaters lie."

Clark sighed. He didn't have time for this. "I love Sabrina and I've never cheated on her. I would give my life for her and I know she's in danger. I need your help. I've got to find Nick. I'm sure she's gone to him."

Dionne looked around again, seeming tempted to call security.

"Dionne," Clark pleaded. "Tommy had someone try to run us over yesterday. Tried to kill us. You can call the police station and find out for sure. Ask for Detective Donovan. He'll tell you the truth. I'm sure you have a cell phone on you now. Call him."

"Why didn't she tell me?" Dionne asked, seeming hurt by the exclusion.

"Because we didn't know who we could trust. But I'm trusting you now, Dionne. I need you to help me save her. Is Nick in his office?"

She shook her head. "He should be down by the party rooms where the fighters' families are. It's down this hallway, to the left and at the end of that trail, but security is tight."

"You could loosen it up for me." Clark smiled his most charming smile. He couldn't lose with it.

ELEVEN

This was not good. Instead of heading toward Nick's office, Sabrina was led down the opposite end of the second-floor executive offices, which were currently unoccupied. The empty offices were used for storage of supplies and marketing goody give-aways.

Sabrina was led to the end of the hallway where the door to the left was open and waiting.

Nick was leaning against the wall comfortably when Sabrina was pushed into the room. He didn't seem surprised or upset to see her or the way she was being treated. He was surrounded by big boxes of bubble wrap. In the middle of the room was an old wooden desk and a chair that looked like polyester.

Sabrina was most bothered by the look on Nick's face. It was so stone, so cold and emotionless. She wasn't very hopeful, but she had to play it as long as she could. She needed time.

Sabrina approached him with a very disappointed look on her face. "Nick, what in the hell is going on? I'm being treated like a criminal in my workplace. That man pulled a gun on me."

Nick looked at the other man who was still standing in the doorway. "Rod? He can be a little aggressive at times."

Rod smiled, closing the door behind him as he made his way for something that was in the corner of the room. Sabrina swallowed hard. That was not the response she was hoping for.

"You didn't answer my question," she said impatiently.

Nick frowned. "You stood me up, Sabrina. I waited for you for our drink."

Sabrina's eyes widened as she smacked herself on her head. "Oh my God, Nick. I'm so sorry. I forgot all about that. I—"

"You forgot?" He wasn't buying it.

"I guess I did." Sabrina did her best to pretend as if she was racking her brain, trying to remember. "I think I . . . Yes, I went to the bathroom to freshen up and Dionne came in. She was asking me questions about Clark and I got so upset that I left. I just went for a drive to clear my head, and—"

"I've got two problems with that," Nick said as he approached the lonely chair. "Have a seat, Sabrina."

"That's okay, I'll—"

"Sit down!" He pointed to the chair.

Sabrina dropped into the chair. "Nick, what is wrong with you?"

"First problem," he continued, pacing the floor behind her. "That was four hours ago. It's not like you to take a four-hour drive, forgetting that you agreed to meet me and that today was the most important day for myself as well as the hotel in the history of its short existence."

"I am sorry." Sabrina knew she was talking too fast, but she couldn't help it. "I wasn't thinking about anything but how betrayed I felt by Clark and how stupid I had been and then I tried to get back here, but traffic was so jammed. You know strip traffic on a Saturday night. Plus the fight and—"

"Second problem," Nick interrupted. "I spoke to Dionne earlier today when I came looking for you. She swore to me that she hadn't seen you since before you left to meet me."

"She must have forgotten."

"Maybe I should call her and have her brought up here as well. That way we can—"

"No!" Sabrina didn't want any more people in danger. "Just . . . Look, Nick. I just needed to get away. I'm sorry."

Nick leaned over her, looking down at Sabrina with a curious smile on his face. "How's Alicia?"

Sabrina looked up at him, screaming to herself not to blink. "Who?"

"You went to visit her today at her mother's house. How is she?"

Sabrina turned away with a sigh. *Okay. We'll have to work with this.* "I wanted to see how she was doing. I was thinking about her."

"You were?" He pulled at his chin, seeming to enjoy this game.

"Yes. I was thinking of how Clark had wronged me, and . . . I thought of what had happened to her. You know, with her husband hitting her and all that. Then I realized that no one at the hotel had reached out to her, so I brought her some flowers."

Nick paused, appearing to work her words through his mind. "Good. You're very smart, Sabrina. I've always thought that. That's why I brought you to the Acropolis. I'm standing here now, with all I know, still almost believing you."

"What do you—"

"But almost doesn't cut it," he said, his eyes growing dark. "I didn't deserve this from you. You made a fool out of me. I bought your game this morning. I always buy your game because Sabrina is always honest."

"Nick, I—"

"Thank God Tommy had Alicia monitored just in case she wanted to start something tonight. Last I heard she was on her way over here and Tommy's not too happy about that."

Sabrina hoped she was coming for the right reasons and prayed she would be safe. She had endured enough already.

"You work for the Acropolis," Sabrina said. "Not Tommy Gaxton."

"The Acropolis has done nothing for me," he retorted. "They ask for more and more from me and give me less and less."

"They pay you a lot of money, Nick." Last she had heard, he was in the middle six figures in salary, not to mention bonuses.

"And they continue to threaten to take it away from me if I don't compete more. I'm bombarded with complaints about how the other hotels on the strip are doing this and that better. Tonight is my chance. My chance to put the Acropolis on the map and secure my future as a player in Las Vegas."

"You're breaking the law," Sabrina said. "You can't expect people to ignore that."

He looked at her with hurt eyes. "I think I had a right to expect it from you. You were the one that went on and on about loyalty. How much it meant to you and how it destroyed you when it was betrayed. Yet you turn to the man who betrayed you the most against me. The one who has been here for you."

"This isn't about me and Clark," Sabrina said. "This is about you, Nick, and what you're about to enter into. Something you can't get out of."

"Who says I want to get out? I was reluctant at first, yes. But the fact is, Tommy has placed a blessing in my lap. A way for me to secure my future at the Acropolis and make millions of dollars on the side."

"Getting in bed with someone like Tommy Gaxton is going to cost you more than all the money you'll make."

"No one gets hurt here, Sabrina. Artemis takes a dive and we make money off the bets. Then they have a rematch and Artemis reams him in a fair fight and everything is back on track. No one is forced to bet. They know going in they could lose. There are no innocents in gambling."

"However you choose to justify it," Sabrina said, "it still doesn't change the fact that you're entering into a pact with a person who is willing to kill for money. You know he tried to kill me and Clark, and he threatened Benny Silver's family."

"Benny knows the game. And I'm sorry, but you

and Clark brought that part on yourselves. I can't believe you allowed yourself to get hooked up with that loser again."

"Clark is not a loser. With all of his mistakes, he's still a better man than you could ever be on your best day. And he's going to expose this. All of it, and not only will you not get what you want, but you'll lose everything you already have. Is it worth that?"

Nick laughed. "Clark is going to jail, honey. We've got him dead to rights and he's going down for grand larceny."

"There are holes in that frame-up and Clark will blow through them."

Nick shrugged. "No, he won't. We have everything we need to send him to jail and ruin his reputation. He'll be in jail at least tonight, so he won't mess up the fight. He can cry wolf all he wants. There will be no one to back him and he'll be a suspected criminal."

Nick looked at Rod and sharply nodded his head. Sabrina turned around just as Rod started for her with rope in one hand and duct tape in another. Sabrina jumped out of her chair.

"No, you don't." Nick grabbed her, forcing her back into the chair. He looked at Rod. "The tape first."

Sabrina started screaming, pushing Nick away as he tried to cover her mouth. She didn't know who could hear her. There was no one on the floor at either end of the offices, and the offices beneath her were closed. She was certain everyone was either at the arena or on their way. Still, she was going to scream as loud as she could for as long as she could.

Nick held her back as Rod placed the duct tape on her mouth. Sabrina felt her adrenaline pick up pace. She was on fire with panic right now. She continued to fight a losing battle as Nick and Rod tied her to the chair. She could not, would not let this happen to her.

Exhausted and barely able to move an inch, Sabrina finally calmed down. She looked up at Nick, mumbling every curse word she could think of.

"I'm doing this for your own good," Nick said. "Tommy wanted me to take you to Clark's room and make it look like he killed you. I was going to leave a message on your voice mail asking you to reconsider asking Clark to stay out of your life because he had just told me if he couldn't get you back, he would kill you."

Sabrina stared at him in disgust.

"But I'm not," Nick said. "I'm going to keep you here, out of the way for tonight. No one is coming up here. This entire area is off-limits until Monday morning. Meanwhile, I'm going to enjoy the most important night of my professional life and then figure out a way to keep you quiet and let you live."

"Why would we do that?" Rod asked, seeming disappointed that he wasn't going to have more fun.

"Because I know that Sabrina won't tell anyone a thing if we promise to free her cheating lover in exchange for her silence. His reputation will be ruined by this, so we don't need to send him away for good." He smiled at Sabrina. "See how nice I am to you? See how loyal I've stayed to you? You should take a lesson."

Sabrina winced as Nick's face came toward hers. She turned away, trying to move, but couldn't avoid his lips touching her cheek. His kiss was quick and meaningless, but it made her sick to her stomach.

Rod turned the lights off, leaving the office completely dark. Sabrina felt desperation rush through her as both men left the office and closed the door behind them. The second she heard the door lock, Sabrina began jerking her body left and right, wildly trying to move toward a structure of any kind, so she could start banging herself against it and make enough noise to be heard by security.

She wasn't going anywhere. The polyester chair seemed to weigh a ton. She couldn't have moved it with all of her strength available. Sabrina knew she had to come up with something else or everything was lost.

With minimal complications, Clark and Dionne made their way past security toward the party rooms. During that time, Clark told Dionne the who, what, where, when, and why of the whole story, pressing the importance of finding Sabrina. Dionne still seemed a little doubtful, but willing to hold out until they found Sabrina and she could ask her own questions.

They were too late. The second they arrived, they could both see that the double doors to the party room for Artemis Grove's crew were wide open and a cleaning crew was already getting started.

"Sorry," Dionne said. "They've all made their way to the fight."

"You need to head that way," Clark said. "If you're

missing, Nick and Tommy might start to suspect you. They've got to be hella' paranoid right now."

"What are you going to do?" Dionne seemed genuinely concerned.

"I'm going to keep looking."

Dionne took her cell phone out of her purse. "I'm going to try and call her one last time," she said. "I've got her on speed dial."

They both jumped with a start as they heard a cell phone ringing.

"Sabrina?" Clark looked around, trying to figure out where the noise was coming from.

"Oh my God." Dionne ran a few feet down the hallway and picked the ringing cell phone off the floor.

Bringing it back to Clark, she tossed it at him as if it were a burning coal.

"It's hers," she said.

Clark felt dread as he saw Dionne's name on the LED display of the phone. He looked at Dionne, who was trying to smile.

"She's okay," Dionne said in more of a question than a statement. "I'm sure of it. Sabrina is a tough girl. She's not stupid either."

Clark smiled reassuringly. He could never accept what this phone was trying to say to him. "I know. I just want to find her and I know she's here."

Dionne looked as if she was about to cry. "What do we do now?"

Clark placed his hand on her shoulder, gripping it tightly. "Dionne, I need you to go to the fight. I need you to go to the fight as if you didn't know anything. Trust me. She's okay and I will find her. I stake my life on it."

"Be careful," Dionne said, before slowly, reluctantly turning and heading swiftly down the hallway.

"She's not here."

Alicia Grove was leaning against the one of the double doors to the party room. With sunglasses on, wearing a white silk pantsuit that was a size too small for her curvy body, she sipped a martini with earnest.

"Alicia." Clark couldn't tell what her mood was. She seemed a little drunk or maybe just very sad. "You've seen Sabrina?"

"She was in this hallway earlier. Like a half hour ago. Right when I got here."

"Who was she with? Did she go down to the fight?"

"She tried to get me to come here to talk Artemis out of taking a dive." Alicia acted as if she hadn't even heard Clark. "I don't want my kids to suffer from this."

"Alicia."

"So I get up the nerve to come down here, but I can't do it."

"Alicia, I need your help. You've got to focus. I know you're going through a lot right now, but I need to find Sabrina. She could be in danger."

Alicia pointed down the hallway in the opposite direction Dionne had gone. "She went that way with what's his name."

"What's his name?" Clark didn't like the sound of that. "Who was it, Nick? Tommy? One of their guys?"

"I don't know what his name is." She shrugged, handing the martini to the passing housekeeper.

"I have to go to the fight. My husband is fighting tonight."

Clark grabbed Alicia as she passed him by, swinging her around to face him. "Alicia, tell me who was with Sabrina when you saw her in the hallway."

"I said I don't know. I . . . He's the one that's always screeching around in that black car like it's a Porsche or something. A damn family sedan, but he thinks he's on NASCAR with it."

Black sedan.

Without words, Clark turned with the intention of heading down the hallway, but ran smack into Detective Donovan.

"I thought I'd find you here," Donovan said, not at all pleased. "You've used up all my free rides today, Hunter."

"I'm glad to see you," Clark said honestly.

"Forget it, Hunter. You're in my doghouse. You aren't exonerated, you know. You're out on bail for a crime allegedly committed in this very building. Stupid move."

"Did you hear what she just said?" Clark turned, pointing to Alicia, who was already down the hallway and headed for the fight.

"Alicia! Alicia!" Clark knew it was useless. She wasn't coming back.

"Isn't that Grove's wife?" Donovan asked.

Clark was feeling a little frantic, but stayed under control. "She saw some guy taking Sabrina that way. She described him as a man who drove a black sedan like it was a sports car."

Donovan took a second before saying, "Let's go."

*   *   *

Sabrina stopped struggling to get out of the ropes. She was too exhausted to do any more. She felt sweat dripping down the sides of her face. She had been struggling in intervals, until her energy wore out. Then she would rest and try again. The fight had surely started by now. Who knew how long the plan was for it to go before Artemis hit the deck?

She couldn't risk being here when Nick came back with Tommy. No matter what Nick may have promised in his warped view of loyalty, Sabrina had no faith that Tommy would let her get away alive or unharmed. She believed Rod would be all too happy to get rid of her.

She couldn't afford these breaks she was taking, but she couldn't keep going on. She was having a hard time breathing and was starting to feel soreness everywhere the rope pressed against her skin when she moved. She had used the last of her energy and this fact brought on tears as she lowered her head.

It couldn't be like this, she thought to herself. Not now. Not after she had been given a second chance with Clark. A second chance to build the trust and respect that they had lost and rediscover the passion and love that they had shared and still did. So much was possible.

"What are you thinking?" Sabrina asked.

They had spent the day looking for the perfect place for a reception. It had been a harrowing day that concluded with more choices than they'd begun with. After getting home, Sabrina suggested they both write down their top five and select from whichever locations they both had in common. At least that way they would still be haggling, but over places they both liked.

Not one of their choices matched and Clark gave up, falling backward onto the living room sofa in his apartment. Sabrina jumped on him, wrapping her arms around him.

"Don't start that 'what are you thinking?' thing with me," Clark said. "That's a trap."

"I don't want us to fight about this stuff. People always fight over wedding plans and it turns what should be a joyous time into a miserable one." She tugged at his chin, making him smile. "I want us to be able to look back on this and laugh."

"Fat chance."

"What are you thinking?"

He sighed, wrapping his hands around her waist and planting them on her rear end. Looking into her eyes, he said, "I'm thinking I can't believe this woman is actually marrying me."

"Stop it," Sabrina said, unable to let anything he said not get to her. He was macho man in public, but a softy behind closed doors.

"You asked."

"Seriously, Clark."

"Seriously," he said. "I'm thinking that I can't believe I spent the day with a woman like you, let alone spent that day looking for a reception for our wedding night. The day we're going to begin the rest of our lives together. I'm not going to get mad over where it is. All I care about is that it's happening."

"Oh, Clark." Sabrina's eyes filled with tears of joy as she hugged him tightly. "You're so full of crap."

"That's why you love me, baby."

The first kiss was a quick tease. The second was for real and Sabrina let herself fall under its spell.

Sabrina slowly came back to the present with renewed hope and a second wind. She had the energy. All the energy she would need to get out of here and back to Clark. She began struggling harder than ever before.

"Sabrina!"

Sabrina stopped. Had she heard something?

"Sabrina!"

It was faint, but she'd recognize that voice anywhere. Clark!

Sabrina gave one last full twist, and with the strength that only love could bring she lifted the chair almost half a foot, which was all the distance she needed. Her feet could reach the old desk, and the little loosening she was able to get in all the time she had been there had freed her legs enough for her to hit the desk with force.

Bang!

"Stop!" Clark held his hand up to Donovan, who froze in place.

They both looked at each other, listening in the silence.

Bang!

"It's her!" Clark leaned against the wall, trying to find out where it was coming from by the vibrations. "What area is this?"

Donovan shrugged. "I don't know. It's dark as hell and I can't find the lights. More offices, I think, but they aren't being used. We've searched everywhere they could have gone if they walked this way. She's got to be here."

Bang!

Clark could feel the vibration clearly now. "She's right here. Sabrina!"

Bang! Bang!

Clark grabbed the office door, but it was locked. He struggled, kicking at it again and again until the door busted open.

Clark was overwhelmed with rage when he saw Sabrina in the chair, struggling through the ropes and the tape on her mouth. Rushing to her, he stripped the tape from her mouth and held her as she let out a desperate breath.

"I'll kill him!" Clark said. "I'll kill them all."

"Clark." Sabrina leaned her head on his shoulder. "I'm so glad you're here. It was Nick and that goon that tried to run us over. Rod. He had a gun and he made me come here and they tied me up. They were keeping me out of the way until the fight was over. They think you're still in jail."

"I'm calling for backup," Donovan said, reaching for his radio.

"I'm so sorry, baby." Clark grabbed her face by the cheeks and kissed her desperately. "This is all my fault."

"Stop it," she said. "You told me to stay away. I didn't listen. I couldn't stand the idea of you going down like that. Letting them frame you and ruin your reputation. You've worked too hard for it."

"It's good to know my woman has my back," Clark said as he began untying her. "But I think you may have taken this one too far."

"I'm fine, now that you're here."

"He's not going to get away with this. I'm going to make him pay."

"You might want to watch what you say in front of a detective," Donovan said. "Besides, we have all we need right here. We're going to arrest Nick and whoever this Rod guy is for aggravated kidnapping and unlawful restraint."

Finally free, Sabrina fell into Clark's arms. He held her tight and she held him tighter. "I thought this was it."

"Never," Clark said. "As long as I'm alive, you will be."

"We need to get you to a hospital," Donovan said.

"No," Sabrina refused. "I'm fine."

"I'll get her out of here," Clark said. "You just make sure Nick doesn't enjoy one more minute of that sham of a fight."

"I'm getting my backup." Donovan headed for the door. "You get her and yourself out of this hotel where you're safe."

Clark nodded, still holding on to Sabrina. He wouldn't let her go until she made him. All that mattered to him was that she felt safe again.

"Are you okay?" Sabrina asked as she separated from him.

"Am I okay?" Clark stood up. "Look who's talking. Can you walk?"

"I'm fine," she said. "Just a little sore. What are we going to do now?"

"We're going to get you out of here."

"What about the fight?" Sabrina said.

"It's already started," Clark said. "That doesn't even matter anymore."

Sabrina didn't want to accept that. "No, Clark. We can still do something."

"Sabrina, please."

"Please my ass," she said. "I'm angry. Who knows how this will all turn out? The one way we can get back at them is to keep them from making their dirty money."

"What do you propose we do?" Clark asked, knowing better than to even bother.

"Come on," Sabrina said, as she headed out of the office. "I've got an idea."

Sabrina used her hotel ID to get herself and Clark past security and into the arena that was bustling with energy and life. Lights were flashing, people were screaming. There was an incredible electricity in the air.

The fight was in the first round and the people were on their feet. Artemis hit Rodriguez with a hard left hook and the crowd cheered as Sabrina was making her way to the front with Clark close behind.

"I'm telling you," he said, "Alicia was drunk. Or close to it when I saw her."

"She did tell you that she came to talk him out of it." Sabrina stopped briefly, standing on the tips of her toes to look around. Where was Alicia?

"But couldn't work up the nerve." Clark showed his press pass to a curious security agent. The man didn't seem to bother to look for more than a second, probably having dealt with so much press. Clark was surprised at the lax scrutiny.

"She came here and that's ninety percent," Sabrina said. "I'll get the rest. Do you see her any-where?"

They were on the floor of the arena where only VIPs were allowed, but with everyone standing, cameras flashing, and the lights so bright, it was hard to concentrate.

"I'm not looking for Alicia," Clark said. "I'm looking for Tommy and Nick. They're the ones we need to be worried about."

"Donovan will handle them."

"I don't see him either."

Their attention turned to the ring as the crowd erupted in screams and gasps. They had missed the hit, but Artemis was leaning back and Rodriguez had a big smile on his face.

"It's starting," Clark said. "He's starting to take his dive."

"We've got to hurry," Sabrina said.

"There!" Clark pointed.

Sabrina looked in the direction he was pointing, but she didn't see Alicia. She saw Tommy sitting in the front row, flanked by two very young, barely dressed women and Rod sitting to the left of one of the women. A few seats down, Benny Silver sat looking uncomfortable and anxious as he watched the fight.

"That's him," Sabrina said, pointing at Rod. "That's the man that pulled the gun on me. The one in the red suit. He's the one I saw getting out of the car that tried to run us over too."

Clark's hands clenched in fists. "He's going to be sorry he laid a hand on you."

Sabrina placed her hand on his chest. She could feel his heart beating fast and see rage in his eyes. "Let Donovan deal with that."

"Until Donovan gets here, I'm going to make sure he doesn't get near you. Look behind Tommy."

Sabrina leaned, peering closer. "Nick."

The crowd cheered as Artemis hit Rodriguez with another major left hook. Sabrina watched as Tommy's eyes squinted in anger for a second before cheering.

"He's resisting," she said. "Artemis is resisting."

"Why isn't Alicia over there?"

"She doesn't want anything to do with them." Sabrina looked to the left again and with a line clearing, found whom she was looking for. "She's over here."

"Go on," Clark said. "I'm going to stay here and run interference if they decide to come visit you again."

"Clark, don't play a hero, okay? They aren't going to do anything on the floor of the arena."

"Just go." He nodded in Alicia's direction. "Before I change my mind about all of this."

The crowd groaned as Rodriguez planted an uppercut on Artemis that made him stumble back two steps. The bell rang and a subdued, somewhat stunned, overflowing crowd slowly took their seats as the fighters went to their corners.

Sabrina made her way for Alicia, who was sitting in the front row, gripping her diamond-studded purse so tight it looked as if she could rip it apart any second. Even with sunglasses on, when she saw Sabrina sit in the empty seat next to her, the expression on her face was obvious. Annoyance.

"What are you doing here?" she asked with a smack of her lips.

"I'm glad you came," Sabrina said. "I knew you were a courageous woman."

"Stop it, okay?" She motioned toward the ring. "You can see for yourself it's too late. He's already starting to go down."

"He's being stubborn. You saw that left hook."

A brief smile formed at the edges of Alicia's lips but quickly disappeared. "I saw it."

"That is still your husband, Alicia." Sabrina placed a firm hand on Alicia's arm. "This is still your family. Not Tommy Gaxton's."

"It's too late."

"It's never too late for what's right," Sabrina said. "I've learned that the hard way too. There are things thrown in front of us that trip us up where we think we could never have been taken down. We lose a step, but we can always get it back if we believe it's worth fighting for."

"What do you expect me to do?"

"Fight for what matters." Alicia pointed to the stage. "This is your family right here, right now. Are you going to let Tommy Gaxton decide what happens to it?"

Alicia's head lowered as she looked down at her lap, squeezing her purse even tighter. She took a deep breath before looking back up. Sabrina watched as she slowly removed her sunglasses, revealing her bruised eye. Her eyes were set on Artemis, who was being attended to by his handlers.

There was something between these two, Sabrina could see it. She could feel it and it filled her with hope. She watched as Artemis looked up, appearing as if he could sense Alicia's eyes on him. When he turned, his eyes set straight on hers and the entire arena seemed to pause.

Sabrina wasn't sure when Alicia stood up, but she was standing now and everyone seemed to be looking from her to Artemis. Photographers from all over the arena swarmed to Alicia and began flashing pictures of her as the noise level in the room picked up.

Alicia and Artemis didn't see anyone, hear anyone. They just stared at each other and, with the look on their faces, Sabrina knew she and Clark had accomplished their goal. Looking across the ring, she saw Rod, Nick, and Tommy staring at her with awe and surprise. Rod nudged Tommy's shoulder and pointed toward Clark.

Clark smiled as Tommy's disgusted expression could not be contained at the sight of him. Clark waved at the three men with a boyish, careless smile on his face. They were helpless to do anything and they were scared.

Benny Silver looked at Clark, switching to Tommy and then Clark again. He shook his head in a gesture that told Clark he thought he was a fool. Clark shrugged in response.

The ringing bell ignited the crowd again and everyone's attention turned from Alicia to the ring. After another second, Artemis turned away from Alicia, who remained standing, staring.

Sabrina's heart was doing cartwheels as she turned to Clark, who winked at her. She smiled, loving him for standing by her. He could have, probably should have ushered her out of this hotel. She would have to show him her appreciation for his faith in her.

She turned back to the fight just in time.

The crowd seemed to anticipate it as Artemis's left arm went back in almost slow motion. Rodriguez seemed to know what was coming as well. When Artemis's glove connected with Rodriguez's right cheek, the sound reverberated through the entire arena. The crowd screamed as Rodriguez's wilting body hit the floor. The place was a madhouse as the referee knelt down and began counting. Rodriguez's head turned from left to right. His right arm lifted halfway in the air and fell flat on the ring floor. His left leg pushed as if it could do something, but went limp.

Artemis Grove didn't see any of this. He was turned away from Rodriguez, his eyes only on his wife as she beamed with pride and love. His eyes begged for forgiveness and her smile awarded it.

Sabrina was now a boxing fan.

"Ten!"

Everyone screamed and cheered as Tommy Gaxton stood with his mouth wide open, zeroed in on the ring. Clark would remember this feeling for the rest of his life. He had to say he probably felt better than Artemis did as he was paraded around the ring by those oblivious of the previous plans that meant nothing now. Nothing.

An enraged Tommy turned to Rod, pushing him and raising his hands in the air. Rod shrugged, claiming his innocence. With looks of murder on their faces, they both turned to Nick, who was already heading out of the aisle for anywhere that was as far away from Tommy and Rod as possible.

"No way," Clark said as he rushed to the edge of the aisle, blocking Nick from leaving. "You can't walk away from this one."

Nick was steaming. "Get out of my way, Clark.

This isn't a game anymore. They're going to kill me."

"Like you were going to do with Sabrina?"

"I was trying to save her!"

"You're going to pay for what you did to her."

Clark felt some satisfaction at the sight of Nick's chin shaking. He was definitely more scared of Tommy than of anything Clark could to do him, but all Clark needed to see was that Nick knew life as he had lived it up until this point was over.

"Thank God." Nick sighed as he looked behind Clark.

Clark turned around just as Donovan pushed him out of the way.

"You're supposed to be out of here," Donovan said. "But I should have known better."

"It's the stubborn one." Clark pointed toward Sabrina, who was heading his way. "There's no stopping her."

Donovan rolled his eyes before turning to Nick and showing his badge. "Nick Stewart?"

"Detective." Nick's voice was shaking as his eyes held his desperation. "You've got to get me out of here. I'm not safe."

"You'll be safe in jail," Donovan said. "You're under arrest for the illegal abduction and restraint of Sabrina Scott. Turn around please."

Clark had seen enough as he left Donovan and Nick to meet Sabrina. The entire stadium was now focused on what was happening to Nick and now Rod as another officer approached and began cuffing him. All Clark could see was the beautiful woman, the love of his life, coming toward him.

"Oh, Clark." Sabrina rushed into his arms, hold-

ing him tight. To her side, she could see the venge-
ful stare of Tommy Gaxton. "I'm scared."

"Scared?" Clark asked.

"Nick and Rod are getting arrested, but what
about Tommy?"

"It's just a matter of time. He'll be going down
by the end of the night. He's through. They all are."
Clark looked into her eyes. "Everything is going to
be fine. I have you in my arms."

"Can you ever forgive me?" she asked, desperate
with love in her heart.

"You did what you had to," Clark said. "You're a
strong, black woman who wouldn't accept anything
less than the respect she deserved. You were given
proof that your man had been unfaithful to you
and you did what you had to for your dignity and
self-respect."

"I should have given you a chance," she said. "At
least more of one than I gave you. I'm so sorry,
Clark. I almost ruined both our futures."

"But you didn't." Clark took her face gently in
his hands. "Love is forgiveness. Forgiveness is love.
Why whatever happened to us happened, I don't
know. But we can figure it all out. Right now, let's
just enjoy what we have."

Sabrina looked around. "What we have is a lot
of trouble. Look at what we've caused."

Clark waved away the almost hysterical crowd,
which was cheering as Alicia approached the ring
and jumped into Artemis's arms. "What are you
talking about, trouble? You just saved the world.
My little Sabrina is an American hero."

Sabrina's head fell back in uproarious laughter
as she felt herself finally able to be happy for the

first time in what seemed like forever. Clark pulled her closer and planted a kiss on her lips like never before. Surrounded by madness and mayhem, they both hugged each other tightly, feeling peace and completeness sweep over them.

EPILOGUE

Sabrina handed the last picture to Clark. Never taking his eyes away from hers, Clark tossed the manufactured picture into his fireplace. After a few sparks, it quickly melted into the fire, along with the past that it so firmly had taken control of. But that was no more. It was all behind them now and Clark and Sabrina were looking toward the future. A future together.

"Have I thanked you recently?" Clark asked.

"For what?" Sabrina leaned into Clark as the fire warmed an unusually chilly late September night in Chicago. "Burning those fake pictures? That was both of us."

"For everything," Clark said. "It hasn't been an easy three months, but you've made everything worth it."

He was speaking of the sacrifices that Sabrina had made so they could be together and work on the issues that begged to be settled before they could move on. They had spent the last few months in each other's almost constant company, digging deep into their hearts to bring out feelings of trust and forgiveness. Talking, saying things they had never spoken to each other about what they feared, hoped, and prayed about.

"So much of what we needed never left us," Sabrina said. "The love, the want, and the desire made it easy to deal with everything else."

"I was so focused on getting you back that I didn't think any of the other stuff mattered. But I have to say that I feel like I know you better now than I did during the three years we were together."

Sabrina lifted her head, looking up at him. "As much as what happened hurt us both, I think it needed to happen. I let my entire identity depend on you, and that was a recipe for disaster."

"And disaster was what we got." Clark kissed her forehead. "I let my pride get in the way of stopping at nothing to get you back. We could have saved ourselves months of misery."

"I can't believe it's only been three months since fight night," Sabrina said.

"The night that changed everything." Clark leaned back, feeling exhausted just thinking of all that had happened.

"The night you became more famous than the athletes you cover."

"I don't know about that." Clark had gained an incredible amount of national attention as the journalist who broke the story, had all of the exclusives, and was offered a minimum of five book deals. "You're the one whose life has been upended."

"I know we decided I should move back to Chicago for my safety until they made sure Tommy's crew was out of circulation, but I would have come here anyway."

"You left a great job."

"That Nick got me." Sabrina shivered, getting a chill just thinking of him. "No way. Besides, the owners weren't too happy with what you and I exposed."

"They were exonerated from any involvement."

"The damage has been done," Sabrina said. "Leaving the Acropolis was definitely the right choice."

"It's a good thing," Clark said, squeezing her tight. "I wasn't going to leave Vegas without you. I knew the second I heard that Nick and Benny were turning on Tommy in exchange for witness protection, everything would be fine."

Sabrina turned around to face him, her eyes showing her concern. "Will it?"

"The case is airtight. There's no way—"

"I mean us, Clark. We'll be just fine, won't we?"

"Do you have any doubts?" he asked.

Sabrina tilted her head to the side with a contented smile. "No doubts, but I don't want you to get the wrong idea."

"About?"

"You don't get a free pass on anything, buddy. If another woman comes to me and—"

Clark placed his index finger on her lips, silencing her. "It will never happen for as long as I live. You never have to worry about that, Sabrina. You know that, don't you?"

She nodded.

"I want to show you something." Clark stood up and reached under the pillow of a sofa, sliding something out that was hidden in his palm.

"You hiding things from me already?" Sabrina asked, getting excited.

When he opened his hand to reveal his surprise, Sabrina felt herself gasp, bringing her hand to her chest. It was a black ring box.

"You kept it!" Sabrina leaped up from the floor. "You kept the ring!"

"No." Clark opened the box, revealing a brilliantly shining two-karat oval diamond with a white gold band. "That ring was our past. We're starting a new life and that calls for a new ring. Now, there's only one thing left."

"What?" Sabrina felt her entire body shaking now. "What's left?"

"You have to say yes, silly."

"Yes!" The scream was so loud it had to be heard for blocks.

Sabrina didn't care. For her, she couldn't celebrate enough. As Clark slipped the ring on her shaking finger, all the months of pain and regret, self-doubt and loneliness were wiped away. Sabrina knew she could be strong enough to deal with whatever would come, but now she knew that Clark would never put her in a situation where she had to.

That was what it was all about. Trust. What she thought they had lost forever was now theirs in abundance and theirs forever.

Clark slipped the ring on her shaking finger. There weren't words for him to tell her how happy she was making him. But he didn't need to tell her. He planned to spend the rest of his life showing her.

ABOUT THE AUTHOR

Angela Winters is the author of several romance and romantic suspense mass-market paperback novels. Her first novel, ONLY YOU, was published in January 1997. Followed by SWEET SURRENDER, ISLAND PROMISE, SUDDEN LOVE, A FOREVER PASSION, THE BUSINESS OF LOVE, KNOW BY HEART, LOVE ON THE RUN, DANGEROUS MEMORIES, SAVING GRACE, and HIGH STAKES. Angela's first novella, NEVER SAY NEVER, appeared in a Mother's Day anthology titled MAMA DEAR in May 1997. Her second novella, COMING HOME, appeared in a holiday anthology titled SEASON OF LOVE in October 2002.

Angela's novels have received strong reviews from the *Romantic Times, Romance in Color, Affaire de Coeur, The Romance Reader,* and others.

A native of Chicago, Illinois, Angela received her bachelor's degree in journalism from the University of Illinois. She currently resides in the DC metro area. She is a member of Romance Writers of America, Washington Romance Writers, and the Organization of Black Screenwriters. You can reach Angela at her e-mail address: ajw827@yahoo.com. More information can be found at her Web site at www.tlt.com/authors/awinters.htm.